The Reset Button

Margaret Fitzgerald

Contents

Prologue

"**P**ass it!" somebody hollered from the other side of the room before we felt a ball zoom past us. We whipped our heads to its direction and saw that Jasper Dean was now spinning the basketball on his finger, chuckling at his teammate who passed it.

"I can't believe you were once friends with Jasper Dean," she snorted, forking her salad into her mouth, "He's childish in every way and you're not."

My eyes locked with him for a brief moment. Like we were silently communicating, we held each other's gaze. It was something we understood each other since childhood; no words were needed in able to reach out our thoughts.

"Savannah!" Kyla cracked me out of my trance. A teammate of Jasper swung his arm on him and that was when both of us turned away from each other.

Since we were kids, we were the best of friends. He didn't know why but we stopped talking to each other. Well, I was the one who stopped talking to him in the first place.

Chapter 1

"Didn't I tell you to never go spread dirt on the school floors?!" I yelled with my hands on my hips as I stared at the dirty hallways. I would have understood if it was because it was raining outside and the mud stuck to all their shoes but right now, I knew for sure that the immature varsity team went to play out in the school field during the lunch break.

The jocks started to scramble around, clearing the hallway as fast as they can to make sure they didn't get caught.

These idiots are the reason why I can't calm down.

"How about you let the janitor clean this up then we'll have lunch," somebody suggested, stepping beside me.

I turned to her before letting out a tired sigh. Unlike Kyla Bailey, my best friend, I'm not as easy-going and mellow as she can be.

"I'm doing my best to make sure that the adults are not troubled," I told her, walking to the cafeteria with her by my side, "They're as busy as can be."

"I still don't see why you're so determined to do," she said, stepping in the cafeteria line, "Sure you're student body president but the whole school is terrified of you."

True to her statement, every single person avoided me. Their eyes reflected hatred, fear and simple annoyance.

I selected my meal for today and paid for it, waiting for Kyla to get hers. Something I always wanted to do was to keep this school in check. It had this horrible reputation and when I was chosen as student body president, I made sure that I'll change our bad image. I had to be strict in order to do it, which ended up with most of the students getting scared of me.

Somewhere, I made the wrong turn.

"You should be acting more of the vice president," I pointed out but she only laughed. Kyla was pretty popular – someone with her beauty was bound to be known. Even with her quirky and bubbly personality, she's responsible and is capable of holding up the position assigned to her.

"You should try to relax a little bit," she retorted playfully.

Though she was smart and all, she's a little too laid back.

"Pass it!" somebody hollered from the other side of the room before we felt a ball zoom past us. We whipped our heads to its direction and saw that Jasper Dean was now spinning the basketball on his finger, chuckling at his teammate who passed it.

"I can't believe you were once friends with Jasper Dean," she snorted, forking her salad into her mouth, "He's childish in every way and you're not."

My eyes locked with him for a brief moment. Like we were silently communicating, we held each other's gaze. It was something we understood each other since childhood; no words were needed in able to reach out our thoughts.

"Savannah!" Kyla cracked me out of my trance. A teammate of Jasper swung his arm on him and that was when both of us turned away from each other.

Since we were kids, we were the best of friends. He didn't know why but we stopped talking to each other. Well, I was the one who stopped talking to him in the first place.

The reason was so obvious, he became the jock and the teachers started to praise me. He became busier with basketball practice and I started to devote my time into studying. Other than that, I hinted that he had a crush on Kyla. Back then, I liked him... a lot. It was one of your cliché having a crush on your best guy friend.

How awkward would that be?

We drifted apart, I got over my puppy dog crush on him and he stopped talking to me altogether.

"Do you have a fever?" Kyla asked, placing a hand on my forehead, "You seemed out there for a while."

I shook my head and looked at my untouched pasta, "Just thinking about my math test later," I lied through my teeth.

I sometimes think what would happen if we were still friends up until this day.

"You'll ace it for sure," she snorted, "You always do."

I only caught the sight of Jasper's back as he and his teammates retreated out of the cafeteria followed by the mass of cheerleaders.

"I have to work hard to get a scholarship into Brown Uni," I said as a matter-of-fact.

She leaned against her seat and pushed her empty bowl away, "You're loaded and smart, no need for a scholarship."

"My brother is rich," I corrected, "I'm living the comfortable middle class life."

My brother really did hit jackpot in terms of relationships. He married the richest girl in the city we lived in and now, he's traveling all over the world. He supplied us with enough money whenever we need it, but we were taught by our parents to be practical, spoiling ourselves with whatever we deserve.

When the bell rung, I grabbed my things and walked out of the cafeteria with Kyla in tow. Just like the parting of the red sea, students cleared the way for us to walk through.

Sadly, I knew for myself that I was a terror.

When I entered my English class, I took my regular seat which is to everybody's absolute surprise, is next to Jasper.

We ignored each other, doing our best to make sure we don't need to communicate. I kept to my own business and he kept his.

Ms. Hughes, our teachers, stepped in front and held a big pile of books in her arms. I was quite surprised that the boys didn't make any move to free her slim arms from the weight it was taking. Ms. Hughes was young and beautiful, attracting most of the boys in the school.

She grabbed a chalk and wrote the words Romeo and Juliet on the blackboard. She turned around and smiled at us, grabbing one of the copies of the said book from the pile that sat on her desk, "As I know that you're all tired of this tragic love story, we have no choice but to study it."

Groans erupted from the class but she simply waved it off, "Now we'll just have a simple homework since you obviously know what this book is all about."

Great, another project that I have to deal with.

"It's quite simple actually," she assured, placing the book back down on the pile, "I'll just pair you off and you would have to reenact act two, scene two which is the balcony scene."

Ah, the sweet and romantic balcony scene where Romeo shouts sweet nothings to Juliet. Girls were obviously excited for this, praying that they were paired up with a decent guy. The boys? They looked like they wanted to get out of here as soon as possible.

"It's just one scene so a week should be enough for practice," Ms. Hughes said before drawing in a bowl from under her desk, "In here are a lists of names, I would get in one girl and one boy, please don't argue with your partner, it's only one week."

I tapped my pencil mindlessly on my notebook, waiting patiently for my name to be called. I'm alright with any boy, I think I could whip them into a decent Romeo in a week.

"Savannah Everett," Ms. Hughes called out before plucking in another name from the bowl. Well, there was one boy that I refused to be paired up with. I'm just praying that Ms. Hughes doesn't his name.

"Jasper Dean."

Well, looks like Lady Luck isn't smiling over me today.

Gasps were sounded around the whole room and I slowly turned my head to the side, we stared at each other for the longest time, refusing to lose the battle of silence.

Almost everybody knew my history with him. We were seen together every day during freshman year when we both had no idea who was who.

When we still stuck together through thick and thin.

"Alright," Ms. Hughes clapped, "Please go sit next to your partner and talk about your plans while I pass along copies of the book."

The class scrambled to find their Romeo and Juliet, while Jasper and I kept silent. We were aware that most eyes of our classmates was on us, like this was more of a drama than the ones we see on tv.

"Here you go," Ms. Hughes chirped, passing us two copies of the book. We only stared at it, avoiding eye contact as much as possible. Our teacher who was as knowledgeable as ever felt the awkward air before she smiled, "Maybe you two were paired up for a reason."

She then moved along to pass the books to the other students. Maybe English will be the first subject that I will fail.

The class ended with neither one of us saying a word to the other. Jasper packed everything in his bag and as he was just about to leave, he dropped a piece of paper on my desk. When he was out of the room, I unfolded the paper and read his handwriting.

I need to pass this class. Let's just work around this and get it over with. I need your number to work a schedule, slot it inside my locker before heading home.

I crumpled the paper and shoved it inside my bag. I exited the class room and passed on with the day as usual. Dismissal came and I waited on Kyla, writing my phone number on a page of my notebook and ripped it out, folding it neatly.

"Ready?" Kyla asked, linking arms with me, dragging me to her locker. Another fun fact, Kyla's locker was right next to Jasper's.

"It's nice to finally take a break," she started to drone on, "I mean, with all these school work then with the job of being president and vice president, not to mention we have a part-time job," she continued to ramble on. While she was busy talking and shoving things in her locker, I lifted the paper and slotted it in the holes of Jasper's lock.

Kyla and I work on this café called One-Eighty Degrees Coffee, which was now owned and bought by my brother's wife. It was a homey little café and I loved working in it, but it's hard to juggle all these responsibilities.

I clutched my binders closer to my chest and as I was about to turn so I could walk to the exit, somebody bumped into me causing all the things I was holding to fall on the floor.

And here comes the demon president, "I reminded you idiots over and over again to never run in the halls!"

There were three boys and they all stiffened. They switched gazes and one of them bent down to pick up my belongings while the two scrammed.

Oh, what a pair of gentlemen.

"Idiots," I mumbled before I looked at the guy who bumped into me.

Jasper Dean.

He realized who I was and placed everything I picked up back in his arms. No words were exchanged before he ran after his friends.

"Are you alright?" Kyla asked, checking for any damage and I shook my head.

You know, sometimes I look back at the times Jasper and I used to hang out. Most of the times, I wish I could find a reset button in our friendship.

Chapter 2

Not proofread.

"Seriously, you've been spacing out a lot today," Kyla pointed out, tying the back of her apron, "Are you sure you're alright."

I've been staring at my phone the whole time, as if Jasper would suddenly call me out of the blue. I look up at her face which was a mixture of concern and annoyance. Letting out a small nod, I stuffed my phone into my bag before I slammed my locker shut.

"Just thinking about school," I said vaguely. Well, I was doing this project with him.

She shook her head before finally allowing this topic to slip. After she gave me a gentle pat on the shoulder, we head out of the locker room and into the kitchen.

Chefs were buzzing around, preparing the orders being brought to them. A line of intricately garnished food was lined up, ready to be taken to the respective costumers.

"Hi Tristan," Kyla chirred, practically skipping to one of our part-time cooks. He looked up from the plate of pastries he was preparing and he offered the both of us a smile.

"Hi girls," He greeted, finishing what he was doing before wiping his hands clean, "Ready for work?"

Tristan Hansen was a student at our school – also, he was Jasper's best friend. From what he has told us, Jasper knew that he was working as a cook but he never told where. He mentioned that he knew his best friend would react differently if he found out that it associated to me.

Honestly, Jasper and I were the best at avoiding each other. Please note that if Ms. Hughes never wanted to play matchmaker with her darling students, we would still be playing the 'let's ignore our ex-best friend' game.

"Looks tasty," Kyla commented. Tristan showed his appreciation for the compliment but I want to butt in to tell him that it wasn't the pastries that Kyla was talking about.

She's absolutely smitten by the guy, she used to talk non-stop on how wonderful it is that the two of them were working at the same café. After that, she started to ramble how fate had done this to the both of them and on off she goes as she ramble on. This was usually the part I start to ignore her.

"Maybe I'll spare you two a taste during your break," He winked and I swear, I could see Kyla melt into a puddle right there.

Looking at the clock, I decided to save my friend from making a complete fool out of herself. I tugged at her arm lightly, "Come on, we need to work."

The look in her eyes told me that she wanted to stay here and talk to him. I shook my head as I started to drag her out to the hall, "Keep on the good work," I threw at Tristan before I pushed open the swinging doors of the kitchen.

"I swear, we could have kissed if you didn't interrupt our moment," Kyla pouted, taking a pen and a notepad.

God, my best friend is delusional.

"And I swear that you could have risked every chance you have with him," I mimicked her tone as I rolled my eyes.

She stuck out her tongue at me, just like what a child would do. That's the thing about Kyla, she knows when to be mature and when to be fun and playful.

"Just go and wait on tables," I told her, pushing her slightly to one of her assigned table that was occupied by a slightly awkward couple.

Those were the worst kind of costumers.

Another waitress walked up to me with her hands gripping a tray full of cups, "Could you take table nine for me, I'm kind of full?" She asked, eyeing the said table.

Without a moment of hesitation, I nodded. We still had a little bit more time before the dinner rush arrives and I was more than bored waiting to work.

I approached the table and as I got nearer, I slowed down. There sat a boy and a girl, though the boy's back was facing me. The thing that made me stop all together was the woman seated right across from him.

Years may have gone by since I last saw her but there was no doubt it was her. She lifted her head from the menu and when she spotted me, her eyes turned into a sparkle of delight.

"Savannah," She grinned in recognition and finally, my feet obeyed my commands as they stopped right in front of their table.

True to my speculations, Macy Dean was sitting right across from her brother.

Jasper looked at anywhere but me, clearly ignoring his sister's delight.

"It's been so long since I've seen you!" She stood up from her chair as she went to hug me. I didn't know what to do, it's really awkward. It has been years since I last saw the woman and the guy that introduced the both of us to each other was no longer talking to me.

Please earth, swallow me up right now.

She pulled back and my unresponsiveness didn't seem to bother her one bit, "Oh right, you're working."

She sat back down, trying to look like a regular costumer but both of us knew it was too late for this. She was practically bouncing off of her chair as she said her order.

I nodded as I scribbled whatever she was saying before I turned to Jasper. No eye contacts, just a look of expectation in his way.

"Coffee," He finally mumbled after a long while.

"What's wrong, little brother of mine?" Macy teased, "You've suddenly became all quiet."

I wonder if she knows that her brother and I are no longer in speaking terms.

He shook his head, waving her off. This was my cue to leave, I don't want to stay in the presence of these two for more than a minute longer.

"Your order will be with you in a while," I said like the usual protocol. I turned on my heel as I tried to walk as normally as I can back into the kitchen.

Heel, toe. Heel, toe. Heel, toe. Don't trip, Savannah; they're watching you.

Pushing the kitchen door open, I felt like I was going to crash on the floor but I kept my cool and delivered the piece of paper where I had written their orders.

Tristan noticed that I was practically out of life as I slumped against the wall. He approached me with his eyebrows scrunched up in question, "What happened out there?"

I was thankful that Tristan was one of the few students in the school that wasn't afraid of me. We talked on a daily basis during work but when we're at school, we just gave a nod of acknowledgement every time we pass each other at the halls.

That's just how it goes.

"Jasper is out there," I gulped, "With his sister."

I thought that Tristan would keep his cool, tell me what I should do. Imagine my surprise when he started to pace back and forth, cussing under his breath.

"Shit," he cursed, "What if he finds out that I'm here!"

He shouldn't be the one worrying here, he was safe and hidden in the kitchen while I was given no choice but to face them with a straight face.

I poured some coffee into a mug before I settled it on a tray. Before I went out, I turned to Tristan, "Just stay in the kitchen, I'll tell you when they're gone."

He nodded gratefully before I kicked the door open and went back to the dining area once again. Taking deep breaths, I walked back to table number nine. Remember, don't trip.

Of course, this couldn't become anymore cliché. Somehow, the universe is against me.

In the midst of concentrating on how to walk, I failed to actually watch where I was going and I tripped. Just before I was near their table, causing the mug to fly up in the air and to spill its contents.

This would have gone perfectly alright if it wasn't for the fact that Jasper's hair was now soaking in black coffee.

Macy looked at her brother with shock for a moment before she started to burst into laughter.

"Your face!" She laughed, pointing at him.

She may have been enjoying the expense but I was mortified. Quickly scrambling to my feet, I claimed the tray that clattered to the ground and also the mug that had a crack on the side.

"I'm so sorry," I apologized, rushing to get some napkins, "I'm such a klutz!"

Carefully, I started to run a napkin along his hair, frowning as I stared at the mess I've made.

Why can't I do anything right when I'm with this guy?

He grabbed my wrist, stopping any future movement from me. My whole body went shut as he pushed my hand away before he stood up and headed to the bathroom.

I looked down at the napkin I was using to help him clean up before I frowned. He hates me more than ever now.

Macy saw my expression before her jolly face turned into a soft and caring smile, "Don't feel too bad, Savannah. Jasper is just a little hot headed because of the coffee," She let out a slight giggle, realizing how she sounded like before she turned serious once again, "But don't worry, he's not mad at you."

"Easy for you to say," I sighed, throwing the napkin on the table, "I'm pretty sure after everything that I've done, I wouldn't be surprised if he despises me."

Macy shook her head, "Everybody makes mistakes, and it's just that you tripped while delivering him the drink."

I want to tell her that it wasn't the only horrible thing I've done to him. I completely ignored him, I stopped talking to him up until we were now strangers. Back then, I thought it would have been the best for both of us.

We were drifting away in different social circles, the peo-ple were praising him for his athletic abilities while they scrammed away from me like I'm the devil.

I looked down on my foot and I felt a hand on my head. Macy patted me, not like a dog but like a mother reassuring her daughter, "You know that Jasper would never be mad at you. He will always be ready to forgive you in a snap. You're too important to him."

Oh Macy, if only you really knew.

"Wait outside, I'll send him out when he's done in the restroom," She smiled warmly. I eyed the mess that I've made on the floor but just before I was counter, Kyla stepped in with a mop and bucket.

"I got this," She reassured, "Now go, I've had enough of dealing with a depressed Savannah Everett."

So maybe she a little loco on the head, but Kyla was a great friend nonetheless. I never told her a thing about Jasper, she just knew that I was once friends with him because everybody used to talk about it. That's all, yet she's standing there like she understands everything.

So I did what I was told, I left the café, standing there by the glass entrance, waiting anxiously for him to come out.

I'm only going to apologize for the coffee, but that was it. It's not like I'm going bawl in front of him and just relay how that past years went. I admit, I was lonely without him; I lacked my usual form of entertainment that his silliness came with.

I do admit, I need to be in speaking terms with him again. I know we will never be able to reset everything just like that, but I want to remove this never fading tension between us.

The door next to me swung open. I didn't turn to its direction, only waiting for a certain somebody to approach me.

"What the hell Macy?!" I heard his voice complained before he was violently shoved to my eye sight.

He glared back to the inside of the café where I'm sure Macy was posed there with a victorious smirk on her face. Slowly, it turned my head to take a peak and she mouthing, "Talk."

He turned to me, staring at me briefly before looking away.

How are we even going to talk if we can't even look at each other?

Well, I was the one who started ignoring him in the first place so I should also be the one to start fixing this situation.

"Hey," I said softly.

That was the time I ever said any type of greeting to him for the past three years.

Clearly, he was taken into shock as his eyes snapped to my direction. I refused to meet his gaze, it was a big effort to even say those three letters.

After a while, I thought he was going to walk away, tell himself that I'm not worth his time. He's reminding himself that I don't want to be associated with him, he's thinking that I hate him as much as he hates me right now.

"Hi."

I don't know why, but that simple word was enough to place a gushing wave of relief to wash all over my body.

We were taking baby steps but at least we can greet each other now. This is progress!

Now why were we here again?

My eyes met his shirt that now sported a nasty stain.

Oh right, my stupidity.

"I'm sorry about the coffee," I muttered.

Gosh, this is embarrassing.

He looked down on it before he shook his head, "It's alright... I guess."

Where are we going with this? I knew it wasn't alright, I knew he was mad at me because I ruined his shirt.

"That's all," I stammered, entering the café quickly as I can. I can't face him, this can't really be happening.

Ignoring Macy's call for me, I sprinted into the kitchen then to the locker room, sinking to the floor.

Why am I so pathetic whenever I'm facing Jasper?

The familiar warning of a text message sounded in the room and light seeped through the slots of my locker. I opened it and fished my phone out of my bag.

It was an unknown number, I looked at the message.

I don't know if I should ecstatic or freaking out right now. Nonetheless, I closed my eyes and I finally allowed myself to think, maybe everything is alright.

This time, I placed the phone in my pocket, safely where the message is still displayed.

It's alright. -J

Chapter 3

"Just a thought," Kyla started, forking some of the cake Tristan gave us into her mouth, "What would the school be like if you and Jasper were still friends?"

Catastrophic? Disastrous? Weird?

"It's just wrong," I replied vaguely, drinking from my glass, "I broke off our friendship for a reason."

She sighed, completely unsatisfied with my answer. She finished off her pastry and pushed away the empty plate, tapping her finger impatiently on the table.

We were currently on our break, and what a relief it is. The costumers who stayed after my escapade with Jasper were giving me looks as I did my job. Co-workers eyed me with a bundle of emotions I don't want to even figure out.

I don't even want to think about the questions Kyla was bombarding me. I knew I kept the poor girl hanging when I refused to answer any questions about my former best friend, but when I'm comfortable with it, I'll start talking.

"Savannah," Kyla drawled out my name slowly, "What really happened?"

I was jealous that Jasper was falling for Kyla. He never admitted it but I saw the signs, it was better for me to just forget about him than see the pain of watching him look at my best gal pal with so much adoration. Back then, that was my only reason.

When our senior year came, I came to the conclusion that our school would have been so hectic if they realized that their student body president can easily succumb to their star athlete, I had to cut off all ties with him.

Now, I just watch him from afar, observing his every move and think about everything that had happened between us.

I got over my little crush on him, but the longing of having him by my side as a best friend never faded.

I miss him, that's a fact.

"It's for the better," I stated, pushing myself off of my chair.

Is it really?

Kyla shook her head but she stopped on prying for any more information. We headed back to waiting on tables and entertaining our customers.

With a cup of coffee placed on a tray, I walked to the table of a lady. I placed down her order before plastering the same old smile I was required to show.

"Enjoy," I told her, using a polite tone, just like always.

"You look down, dear," she observed, "Is a boy troubling you?"

Kind of, sort of, maybe, yeah.

"Keep your chin up," she smiled softly, "You can never move forward if you keep on looking back."

I nodded my head at her words, telling her to enjoy her drink; I spun on my heel as I retreated back into the kitchen.

"My shift is over," I said as I passed Tristan, who already changed out of his work clothes, "See you tomorrow."

When I was about to push the door of the locker room open, he called out after me, "Want to go grab dinner or something?"

I turned to the inside of the room and I saw Kyla nod vigorously. She has yet to change her clothes, but she looked like she was about to jump out of the room so she can spend some time with Tristan.

"Sure, the three of us can go when we finish changing," I told him.

The door closed behind me and Kyla erupted into a set of squeals, "Dinner? I'm eating dinner with him?"

I want to remind her that I'm also going to be there, but I rather allow my best friend to have her moment of joy.

Changing into my jeans and shirt, I closed my locker shut and adjusted my bag strap on my shoulder, "Come on, Juliet, your Romeo is waiting."

She was still in cloud nine when we met up with Tristan in the parking lot. I seriously had to walk in front of her just in case she wanted to place her name in shame. I could at least act as a barrier between these two, with the grin she was giving, she couldn't believe her luck.

Tristan was still oblivious of her crush on him. He didn't know that whenever he teased Kyla, she falling for him harder than ever.

When we reached a burger joint, Tristan instantly ducked behind us, as if the two of us could hide his huge body.

I knew why he was hiding behind two girls who was a head shorter than him – half of the basketball team was there, having the time of their lives.

He should thank the lucky stars that Jasper was hanging out with his sister right now, he wasn't there to see us. My stomach was growling but I knew I had to do the right thing.

"Join them," I told him, turning my head to look at him, "I'm pretty sure my mom already made dinner ."

Even with the sullen look, Kyla nodded her head in agreement to my encouragement. She knew what would happen if anybody saw us hanging out.

Tristan looked torn on what to do, he's a good kid and his reputation doesn't deserve to be tarnished just because he worked at the same café that I do.

"See you tomorrow at school," I turned from him, holding Kyla's hand while I dragged her along with me. Her walking was slow but I understood why, we just passed up the opportunity to dine with her crush.

Just as we were out of the door, it swung open to reveal the guy I've been bumping into much lately today.

Is it me or this had been the most interaction we had in a day for three years?

When he noticed me, we just stared up at each other. We've been doing that a lot.

Surprisingly, he nodded at me before presenting me with a simple, "Hello."

Kyla froze, my jaw dropped, Tristan paled, and the basketball team who just realized that their captain was there all stared at him like he grew a second head.

Clearing my throat, I finally allowed myself to speak and say something that wouldn't end myself up in embarrassment, "Hello."

He threw another nod before he went around us and to the booth where all his teammates was packed in to. Tristan slowly followed his steps but his eyes were trained on me, switching to Jasper then right back at me.

I was as confused as he was.

When we were outside, Kyla snatched her arm away from my grasp and stepped right in front of me, "Something did happen outside the café."

It wasn't a question, it was a statement. A very accusing statement, but she was correct.

I tried to walk around her but every step I make, she mirrors it, making sure that I didn't escape her accusing gaze. With an annoyed stomp, I sighed at her, "Kyla."

She grabbed my hand as she proceeded to march to her car, "We're going to your house, grab some food, lock ourselves in your bedroom while you tell me every single detail."

I didn't bother to argue because I knew she would end up having her way. That's Kyla Bailey for you, she'll squeeze every single detail out of your crushed soul.

Pushing the front door open, we peeked inside the kitchen to see if the food is ready. Sure enough, my mother was already transferring food into individual plates.

"We're home, mom," I greeted, approaching her. She glanced our way before smiling at us, placing down the empty pan, she wiped her hands on a dishtowel before walking up to us.

"How was work and school?" she asked brightly.

Oh, I finally talked to my ex-best friend that I haven't approached since the day I decided to end our long time friendship. Everything is just peachy.

"It was great," I smiled. Like hell would I tell her all of those things.

She raised her eye suspiciously but after a while, she decided to let it go. That's my mom for you, she understands a teenager even though she isn't one anymore.

"Are you eating with us, Kyla?" she turned to my best friend, "We have enough food for another plate."

"That would be great, Ariel," she beamed. My mom refused to let herself age, resulting that she insists to every single friend of mine to call her by her first name, "But we have a lot of work to do, mind if Savannah and I eat in her room?"

Mom shook her head, practically shoving two filled plates into our hands, "Enjoy, you two."

She probably wanted to grab this opportunity to finally have some alone-time with my dad over a nice dinner. My dad works in an office all day long and only goes home just in time for dinner. This resulted that the two of them barely get some time alone to do anything romantic, since I'm always there.

Carrying our food with us, we stepped into the living room just as my father entered through the front door.

"Good evening girls," he smiled politely though you could clearly see that he was tired.

"Hey Dad," I greeted, followed by another one from Kyla. We headed upstairs into my room where the minute my door closed, Kyla started to fire me her questions.

There wasn't much to explain. It's just the first ever exchange of words we had for a very long time, before I went bolting out. I didn't mention the text, I want to think of it as my own little special thing.

Maybe that could be my new comfort word. Alright.

"I'm sorry if I'm going to touch this topic," she started, sitting on my bed next to me, "Why did you break off your friendship?"

Should I tell her? Yes. Can I tell her? No.

I can't look at her in the eye and tell her that she was the primary reason why I stopped talking to him. If only she knew that it was because of her, I spent days of putting away every single memory I had of him. I wanted to forget him, it was extremely immature, but it was for the better. It saved me from a gruesome heartbreak.

We will never be together, I've accepted that.

"It's a long story," I replied softly.

I felt her arms went around my body, hugging me in comfort, "We have all night. You know that you have to get it out of your system at some point."

The lights from the room next door captured our attention. Another fun fact, Jasper is my next door neighbor. It was one of the main reasons why we became best friends.

For a long time, we would have conversations through the window. We were fine when our parents still refused to give us mobile phones, besides, it was more exciting to slide our windows open and have a little chat till the latest hours of the night.

"Looks like Jasper's home," Kyla concluded, she turned to me and pulled me up to my feet, "Talk to him."

Was she crazy?

I just can't open my window and just talk to him like the past three years never happened. It's not that simple.

"Kyla!" I protested as she neared my window.

We stepped, just right in front of it. She turned to me and gave me an encouraging nod, "You two will never solve your problems if you don't go past the hey's and hello's."

"Then maybe I don't want to solve our problems!" I yelled. After the words escaped my mouth, the both of us stilled in silence.

That may be the biggest lie I have ever told in my whole life.

She shook her head, slowly backing away from me, "You're a strong girl, Savannah. Just talk to him."

She got out of my room, probably just waiting outside my door like the good friend that she is. I pulled open my curtains until saw his window. It had its own blue curtains to conceal the other side.

I can't do this. Not now, not ever.

Sliding the glass open, I allowed the wind to enter my room' papers on my desk fluttered a little, but other than that, it was no difference.

How do I even make him open his window?

Kyla Bailey, I'm going to kill you for making me do this.

Just talk to him? Does she even know the shock I went through when he greeted me earlier at the burger joint?

Looking at the closed window right across from me, I knew we had to fix everything.

For the longest time, I've been living in the regret of ignoring him. He could still been by my side, making me love life. Maybe he would have defended me through the judgmental eyes of the student body.

"I'm sorry, Jasper," I whispered to the air, as if my words could reach him.

I grabbed whatever knick knack that I had laying around, knowing it's no longer of importance to me, I chucked it at the closed window, praying it rattled him that I'm here.

Please, open the window.

I can see his shadow move inside and my heart stopped beating for a quick second as he came closer to the curtain.

Closing my eyes, I didn't want to see him open the window. Maybe I could wake up any second from now and find myself next to Kyla as she continued to drone on about her crush on Tristan.

That wasn't the case right now, though.

"Savannah," short and gentle as ever, I hear him say out my name. I thought I will never hear his voice say it again.

Slowly cracking my eyes open, I saw him staring at me.

Chapter 4

He's looking at me, he's real, he's not turning away. God, help me!

My name, he said my name! It sounds so foreign to my ears, years had gone by since I last heard him voice it out.

Now what should I supposed to do now that I have him here?

"Hi."

Get pass the greetings, Savannah!

"Hey."

No, don't reply with a greeting, we're never going to pass this!

I could hear my wall clock ticking, timing my moment and reminding me of my failure. Grabbing the edge of my curtain, I closed it, shutting my view of Jasper.

I'm so pathetic.

Minutes ticked by and I just stood there, gripping the curtain with a shaking hand.

When will my pride finally allow me to apologize?

"Savannah!"

Wait a minute, was that him? Did he just call my name?

"Jasper," I called out but I'm not brave enough to face him.

Once again, I'm so pathetic.

On the plus side, I was able to get past the greetings this time. Baby steps!

"Please open the curtain," his tone wasn't exactly pleading, but it was something similar.

I'm not ready to see him face to face. Right now, I have the safety of my curtain, but if that's gone, I may faint right here.

"Please," he repeated.

Jasper Dean doesn't say please. People gives him anything he wants, he just says a word and the whole school is at his beck and call.

Taking a deep breath, I pushed the cloth aside, now staring at Jasper's brown eyes, waiting for any sign of sudden movement that will put me to my end.

Wait, what?

"Hey," I croaked out.

One more greeting from you Savannah Everett and I'm about to kick you in the shin. The whole point of this thing is that you no longer need to put so much effort in saying a simple hello!

Great, now I'm arguing with myself inside my head.

"How have you be-" he started but I suddenly cut him off.

Prepare yourself Jasper because you have to keep in synch with whatever I'm saying.

"Look, I'm sorry that I ignored you, I'm sorry that I'm freaking out right now, I'm sorry that I can't even get past the greetings, but I need you to know that I'm on the verge of fainting because this is the first time I talked to you in three years and if you think that I can act normal at a time like this then it's like you haven't been there when we were growing up!" I said all in one breath.

He stared at me like I was a lunatic, and I'm starting to believe that I am one.

"What?" he asked.

"I'm not repeating myself," I grumbled under my breath without even thinking.

"Are you sane?" he almost chuckled, observing my movements.

Nope. Hindi. Nulla. Geen. Tidak. Non. Nicht. Nie. Nah. No.

I bowed my head down and whispered, "I'm sorry."

"What did I do wrong?" he asked, fishing for an explanation why I suddenly cut off our longtime friendship.

I can never tell him. Admitting it meant that he will find out that I had this crush on him. I will never be able to live it down if that happened.

"It's just..." I trailed off, keeping my head down so I didn't have to look into his eyes.

Are we on speaking terms now?

"I'm sorry," he suddenly apologized, using the same gentle tone as I did.

He did nothing wrong, he even made the effort to rekindle our friendship when I started to avoid him. He did everything to fix what I was breaking.

It's all my fault and up until now, I'm wallowing in guilt and regret.

Kyla is an amazing friend, she was so oblivious to her involvement into this and I want it to keep it like this. Same with Jasper, he knows nothing and I want it to stay like this.

I know we can never fix everything and put it back the way it was, at least I want to tape the pieces together. You can see where the rips were but they still stick together.

"It's been a long day," I sighed tiredly, "I should probably sleep."

With the coffee, burger joint, and now this, I desperately need a good night's sleep.

He looked upset that I didn't respond to his apology but he nodded nonetheless, "I'll talk to you tomorrow."

Wait, he'll talk to me tomorrow?

"Goodnight," he finally said, waiting for me to say it back.

"Night," I mumbled, finally shutting the window and pulled the curtains so that I can no longer see him.

Well, I survived this night.

Walking to my door, I opened it and Kyla sat on the carpeted hallway, her head slightly tiled to the side as I saw her breathe slowly, indicating that she fell asleep.

Kneeling right in front of her, I smiled at my best friend, "Thank you, Kyla."

I owe her for making me do this. Step one – getting past the greetings – check.

Looks like I have to make room for two on my bed once again. Slowly shaking her, I woke her up, "Kyla, let's go to bed."

She stared at me groggily before nodding, I helped her up and I allowed her to plop on her side of the bed.

I prepped myself up for bed and just when I was about to slip under the covers, I stared at the closed window and I smiled, maybe this isn't such a lost cause after all.

The horrible morning though, I forgot to set up my alarm clock causing both Kyla and I to wake up late.

My eyes popped out of their sockets when I saw the time being showed by my clock and that's when I started to shake Kyla so she would wake up.

"First period starts in twenty minutes!" I yelled at her, causing her eyes to open wide.

Yup, we're definitely awake right now.

"You've got to be kidding me!" she groaned exasperatedly, shooting out of bed, "I'm borrowing some of your clothes."

This isn't the first time Kyla had a sleepover, in fact, her stays are so frequent that she has her own toothbrush in our bathroom. I called dibs while she dug through my drawers, looking for something that will fit her style.

We rushed downstairs and true to my speculations, both of my parents left early resulting to the expense that nobody was there to wake us up.

Each of us grabbed a granola bar from the pantry and we sprinted to Kyla's car that was parked in my driveway.

"You didn't even had a chance to tell me what happened with Jasper," she complained, pulling into the streets of the city, her hands glued to the steering wheel as we sped through the usual morning traffic.

"We talked," I replied vaguely, gripping my seatbelt as Kyla went over the speed limit, taking every single turn with precise calculations, never pausing or breaking.

"Seriously, he obviously did nothing wrong," she defended his side, "You're just being a sassy snob."

"Thanks," I snorted sarcastically, "You're such an encouraging best friend."

She started to slow down when we knew that we were close to the school, finally putting safety first.

"I mean, he looks like a kind friend," she continued on, "Tristan looks satisfied with the position of being his best friend."

"Why does every conversation we have seems to rotate back to Tristan?"

"Because he's perfect," she shrugged lightheartedly, releasing slight giggle.

The school finally came into view and Kyla made a turn to enter the students' parking lot. She drove to her usual spot, turning off the engine before pulling out her keys from ignition.

"Made it at the nick of time," I commented, swinging my bag over my shoulder as I exited her vehicle.

"So proud of my baby," she grinned, patting the roof of her car, "Now let's go."

Today, I don't want to do anything with Jasper. I'm going to try my absolute best to avoid him, the conversation last night was enough to put a wall of awkwardness between us. It's thinner than what it used to be, but it's still there.

Step two, make my brain function properly when I'm with him.

As usual, the people scampered away from me as I walked down the halls as if I had huge tiger growling at them right in front of me.

Seriously, I don't have the energy to deal with these idiots right now.

Aside from the slight bump in the hallways, which is when I found the drinking fountain extremely fascinating, I was doing a pretty good job of avoiding Jasper.

Of course, English class had to butt in.

"Sit next to your partner," Ms. Hughes smiled oh-so-sweetly, clapping her hands and gesturing for the class to do what she asked.

Still as awkward as we were yesterday.

Oh Ms. Hughes, you're a spec of lint on my flawless "Avoid Jasper Dean during the Whole Day" plan.

"Romeo first met Juliet during…" she started to drone on, discussing the famous Shakespeare tale.

A piece of paper slid in front of me, I picked it up and I turned to Jasper but his eyes were glued to the teacher talking in front of us.

Are you avoiding me?

Great, we reverted back to passing each other notes. What is this, elementary school?

I'm seriously considering that I won't reply to me but that's just an extremely obvious answer.

Clicking my pen, I scribbled down a quick and shot reply that was obviously a lie.

No.

He threw the paper back to me.

What was that little escapade in the hallway then?

Is he really bringing that up?

Earlier, I saw him in the halls just between second and third period, I went into a state of panic. I couldn't go anywhere but forward because people were literally a tsunami of students trying to get to their classes on time.

The solution my pathetic brain could think of is staring at the drinking fountain, looking at it with outmost interest.

It was so shiny, did the janitor used some special cleaner to wipe it?

Since my attention was occupied by the gorgeous drinking fountain, I failed to notice the trash can right in front of me.

Like a freaking tree that just fell at the middle of the highway, it clattered, pausing all of the rushing students' movements. Yes ladies and gentlemen, the student body president just ran into the trash can. You may now take pictures for further embarrassment.

One of my many spectator was the reason why I even ran into the damn thing.

I was too busy appreciating the beauty of the drinking fountain to see the ugly trash can in front of me.

The stupidity of how it sounded was making me cringe. Seriously brain?

Right, good luck with that. So, was the trash can not worth the attention of your gaze?

For the first time, my lips curved upwards and I cracked into a smile.

"Shut up," I mouthed at him.

He stuck out his tongue playfully and he placed his gaze back to Ms. Hughes talking in front of the classroom.

Conclusion, I did miss the times Jasper made me laugh with little effort.

We got past the greetings, I can now smile when I'm with him, what's next with our little ladder called the rebuilding of our friendship?

Chapter 5

"Savannah!" I heard Jasper call out as I walked out of the classroom.

People whipped their heads to our direction and I internally slapped my forehead. Seriously, these boy should know that he's always on top of the rumor mill.

Especially if it involves me.

I kept on walking but I slowed down my steps so he can catch up.

"What?" I asked quietly, I was pretty sure people are eavesdropping right this moment.

That's was when he blanked, as if he just called me for just the heck of it. I stared at him, waiting for him to say anything but nope, his mouth was just wide open, waiting for flies to get in.

"Right," I drawled out, stopping right in front of my locker, "Is this about the project?"

He shut his mouth before his face brightened once again, "Yeah, the project!"

Lifting a brow at him, I slapped a stapled script right on his chest, "Learn the lines, we'll practice tomorrow after school."

He looked down on the script before beaming at me, "Yes ma'am."

Alright, this boy is too cheery even in normal standards. I slammed my locker and without even a goodbye to him, I walked away, turning right to my classroom.

Once I was out of view, I released a loud sigh. Well, I survived that conversation.

The thing is, people were still staring at me. Rolling my eyes at them, I went to my desk, took a seat and glared at every person who dared to look my way.

The chair next to me was soon occupied by Kyla and she grinned at me, "What's this I've been hearing about you and Jasper."

Seriously, it hasn't even been five minutes and even my best friend got the news already. That's high school gossip for you.

"Kyla," I groaned but she kept staring at me with those twinkling eyes.

"This is great," she squealed, leaning over to give me a side hug, "I knew that talk last night would do some good."

One problem, Kyla has one big mouth. Just the mention of a 'talk last night' was enough to turn heads. Sending a dark look at my best friend, she retreated her hand and slowly straightened on her seat.

"Sorry," she coughed out before returning to her jolly mood, "But come on, you two talking is a big deal around the school. I mean, the last time you two were even seen speaking to each other was the first week of sophomore year, the last days of your friendship."

During the end of my freshman year, I spent the whole summer away from home, in a camp that Kyla invited me to. It gave me a good excuse to be away from Jasper, our first summer apart. It then I made a decision, it can never be the same again.

Monday, the first day of classes, I still spent my lunch with him and Kyla. Tuesday, he was invited by his seniors from the basketball club to eat with him. Wednesday, he was seen with a senior cheerleader, making his popularity rise. Thursday, our last ever lunch together. Friday, I finally gave my one last silent goodbye to him when I gave him a sad smile when I passed him in basketball practice while on my way home.

The week after, I avoided him at all cost. He kept approaching but I stood my ground, I never once looked at him. A month later, he got what I was silently doing and the string called our friendship finally broke.

He never seemed affected by it, in fact, he looked so happy whenever he was with his teammates. He was much happier with them compared to the times we hung out.

The day seemed to drone on really slowly. Mainly because I've been the topic of many conversations as I passed down the halls. I wasn't even in the mood to chastise the students, all I wanted was to leave the school quickly.

"Finally glad this day is over," I muttered, sliding into the passenger seat of Kyla's car. Kyla snickered as she threw her bag to the backseat before starting up the car.

"You're just being a sourpuss," she laughed, driving to One-Eighty Degrees, "Cheer up a little, at least you're in speaking terms with Jasper right now."

We arrived at the café and we got in through the back door. We slipped inside the locker room and we started to change into our uniforms.

Yes, I'm jumping for joy that I can now talk to Jasper. The down side is, we can never be normal. Every single person is going to look at us the minute we talk, how much more attention will we grab if we started to hang out.

Pushing the door opened, I was once greeted by the usual sight of the bustling kitchen. Tristan zoomed right past, probably running late as it is.

"Tristan looks like he's in a hurry," Kyla pointed out. The said person disappeared into the boy's locker room, getting ready for work.

"He's running late," I shrugged, tying my hair up into a ponytail, "Now come on, we have some tables to wait."

We entered the dining hall where it was almost empty, aside from the four occupied tables.

"Savannah!" I heard Macy sang as she pushed the glass doors of the café open, "I knew you would be here."

Oh gosh, dealing with her is still going to be awkward.

"At least I have you around," she breathed out in relief, "I'm only going to be here for a week and my little brother is ignoring me to go with his lackeys."

I cracked a smile at her term. It was kind of true, because of his high popularity, Jasper had a bunch of people following him around, ready to become his servant. The only people

I knew he was sincerely friends with are Tristan and some boys from the basketball team.

"Are you busy, you want to catch up?" she questioned, looking around at the half-empty café.

Looks like there's no way out of this.

"Sure," I faked a pleased smile and she grinned at me.

"Great," she clapped, "I'll go get a table. You get us two mugs of coffee, my treat."

Before I could even say a word, she was already heading to one of the booths near the wall. I groaned before trudging to the kitchen, my steps heavy with frustration.

"And this one is the banana cake, a family recipe," Tristan said to my besotted best friend, her attention fully on him.

I was pretty sure she wasn't even listening to him as she forked some of his cake into her mouth.

"Kyla," I called over, but nope, she's stuck on Tristan Land.

Stomping right to her, I tugged on her ponytail to grab her attention. She jumped on her seat before turning around to give me a dry look, "What?"

"Macy Dean is right outside and I have no idea what to do," I breathed out, pulling out a stool so I can sit next to her.

Tristan chuckled at me before pushing my own slice of his banana cake, "So I heard you and Jasper are buddies now."

Great, even he is interested on that topic.

"He said a total of six words to me the whole day," I muttered. Yes, I counted.

Still, nothing can beat yesterday. It came in so fast, with Ms. Hughes' English project, our run in the Burger Joint then the talk we head through our windows, just like what we used to when we were kids.

It was like a whole day broke something that has been happening for three years. One day, that was how long it took.

"Jasper has been a lot more cheerful this day," he commented, "I'm pretty sure it has something to do with you."

I resisted a smile that was coming up my lips. At least I'm not the only one who's affected by this.

"I'm a lot more concerned by the fact Savannah actually counted the number of words he said to her," Kyla giggled.

I'm never going to live this down.

Turing back to Tristan, I asked him, "What did he say about me?"

Tristan's amused smile turned into a full on grin. I don't know if I should fear this or be excited.

"Well first, he grinned at me before saying that you're finally talking to him," he laughed, "And then he practically bragged to the whole team that the student body president is his friend again."

Kyla started to burst nto a fit of giggles and I slapped my hand on forehead, dragging it down to my whole face.

Tristan sobered up, turning to me, "This is actually the happiest I've seen him since we became friend," he told me honestly, "It's like he has this side which only you can trigger."

I snorted at his statement, thinking back to the times we spent together. He was in fact a really jolly soul, the both of us used to team up to play pranks of his sister back when we were kids.

Wait a minute, his sister.

"Macy's still waiting outside," I suddenly remembered, shooting up from my seat as I hurriedly prepared two mugs of coffee, burning myself in the process.

I heard Tristan and Kyla's laughter as I pushed open the doors with a tray in my hands. I approached to where Macy is as she was occupied with her phone.

"Alright Jasper, we'll see you later," she said a sweet good-bye to her brother before placing down her phone. She smiled at me before her eyes landed on the coffee.

"How long does the coffee need to be prepared?" she questioned as I took my seat.

"Sorry," I apologized under my breath.

She shook her head in amusement, reaching for one of the mugs, "I hope you're free tonight."

Please don't tell me it has something to do with her phone call with Jasper earlier.

"You're joining Jasper and I to dinner," she announced as if it was the most wonderful thing on earth.

Wrong.

Kyla was passing by after she just served the woman in the booth behind us. I quickly grabbed her arm and pulled her to me, "Sorry but I need to help my best friend here with her project."

Macy's face fell as Kyla looked at me dumbly, hoping that I'll explain the situation to her.

"Oh," Macy frowned, "I just thought it would be kind of fun because I missed hanging out with you and Jasper."

With the mere mention of my ex-best friend's name, Kyla's eyes started to sparkle as she twisted her arm out of my grasp.

"That would be no problem," she grinned sweetly, her eyes twinkling with mischievousness, "I'm sure my project can wait."

Oh Kyla, you're so dead to me.

"Isn't it due tomorrow?" I gritted out, giving her a warning look.

But nope, the fact I was struggling with my lie only made this more enjoyable for her.

"I could always get an extension," she winked, "I'm one of my teacher's favorite student."

"Kyla, I insist," I tried to sugarcoat my tone but my self-control was winding down.

"And I insist that you go join Jasper and his lovely sister here for dinner," she used the same tone as me, only hers was mocking.

Macy watched our discussion before tilting her head to the side, "So is that a yes or a not to the dinner?"

I said, "No," at the same time Kyla muttered, "Yes."

Macy's eyebrows scrunched up in confusion and that was when Kyla grabbed my arm, pulling me up to stand, "We're just going to have a little talk."

Macy slowly nodded, still confused, as Kyla started to drag me back to the kitchen.

"Thanks a lot, bestie," I sarcastically muttered, snatching my arm from her grasp.

"Look, I thought you were in good terms with Jasper now."

"I am," I told her, "But it's not like we're back to normal."

"You're so stubborn," she groaned, stomping her foot on the ground.

I knew that, she didn't really have to point out the obvious.

"We're not friends just yet," I informed her, "Acquaintances, maybe, but not yet friends."

"He thinks that you two are," Tristan suddenly cut in.

"It's like you two suddenly pressed the reset button on your friendship yesterday," Kyla said.

"It's just one night," Tristan urged, "How bad can it be?"

Extremely. You're not going to be sitting in a public restaurant in such an awkward position.

My eyes switched from Tristan to Kyla, their expressions telling me to do it. They really are meant to be, they're both extremely persuasive.

"Fine," I finally muttered in defeat, "But only one night."

Turning on my heel, I trudged back to where Macy is sitting. This is going to be one hell of a dinner.

Chapter 6

"Stupid dinner," I grumbled under my breath, placing on my shoes.

Macy specifically told me to dress fancy. The minute I came home and told my mom about the dinner invitation, her eyes brightened as if she finally had something to do with a daughter.

She pushed me into my room, basically shoving every single dress I owned into my face. She treated me like a life-size Barbie, curling my hair and applying my makeup. I swear, she's more excited about this than what I'm supposed to be.

Deep breaths, Savannah, you've ate with the Dean siblings long before.

That was before you suddenly cut off your friendship with Jasper.

Oh shut it, little voice in my head. I'm seriously starting to go crazy now.

The curtains of my window was closed, preventing Jasper to have any view of my bedroom. He wouldn't exactly want to see the mess my mom and I created. Various articles of clothing and shoes were thrown around carelessly.

This is going to be a bitch to clean up when I get home.

Happy thoughts. Pretend you're in a My Little Pony tea party instead of a dinner with those two.

Wait, what?

Somebody really needs to check me into a mental hospital.

The doorbell rang and I almost fainted. My mother passed my open door while she was walking to get the door.

"Good luck, honey," she encouraged sweetly before scampering to answer the door.

I'm going to need more than luck to survive this thing.

Remember, don't act stupid. Nod when you agree, shake your head if you don't. The less you talk, the less damage you'll be able to make.

Just for props, my mother called for me, "Savannah!"

She knew that I was aware that it was the Dean's right outside our front door. She was buying me extra time to calm myself down.

Looking at myself in the mirror, I nodded at myself, throwing a little look of encouragement at my reflection. Spinning around, I grabbed my purse as I started to walk out of my room, going downstairs to where everybody was waiting.

"Ariel!" I heard Macy squeal, they came into view when I was at the top of the stairs. She threw her arms around my mother, using her as another victim of her unbreathable bear hug, "It's so good to see you again."

Mom laughed, calmly hugging Macy back, "You too, how's it going with the job?"

She finally found the thought to release her, but she still smiling from ear to ear, "It's tough but nothing this girl can't handle."

I started to slowly walk down, gripping the railing of the stairs to keep myself stable. Breathe, Savannah, this is only one night.

Jasper was the first one to catch sight of me while he leaned against the wall with the most bored expression on his face. He brightened up like somebody pressed a switch in him and he smiled right at me.

The same smile that got me falling for him years ago. It never lost its magic but too bad I'm no longer in the same mental state as before.

"Hi," he greeted once my foot was safely pressed on the floor.

"Hey," I nodded, offering him a polite smile.

Macy turned to us, greeting me with the same grin she showed my mother, "You look amazing, Savannah."

"Thanks," I mumbled quietly.

Macy said a goodbye to my mother, grabbing her brother's hand and dragging him with her outside. I walked up to my mother, taking in a deep breath.

"You'll be fine," she assured, tilting my chin up, "Just remember, those two are the same old kids that you used to play with when you were little."

"But I haven't talked to them in years," I grumbled.

"You're a strong girl, Savannah," she encouraged, "Just talk to them."

It was the same words Kyla said to me while convincing me to talk to Jasper last night. I was starting to think that I'm not really strong as what everybody makes me think.

She started to pushing me to the door, "Now go out there and be the daughter I took the time to raise," with one final goodbye, she shoved me outside and slammed the door right in front of my face.

Thanks mom.

"Told you she was coming out."

I turned around and saw the two siblings sitting at the hood of Jasper's car. They were smiling up at me, showing that they held no grudge.

A pang of guilt hit me as I thought that I made them wait. I was so scared of this event that I wanted to avoid them when they have been nothing but kind to me.

"You guys mad?" I asked, dreading for their answer.

The truth, I have nothing to be scared of. These two are so nice when I've been nothing but rude.

"Of course not," Macy replied sweetly, "Now come on or we'll be late for our reservations."

Jasper rounded the car and slid into the driver's seat. Macy took my hand and dragged me to the passenger seat where she basically shoved me in there before I can mutter a protest.

"Macy!"

"What?" she questioned innocently, "I'm pretty sure that I'll be third-wheeling the whole night."

"Macy!" I yelled, a little more flustered than before. Could this get any more embarrassing?

Jasper merely chuckled beside me, pulling out of my drive-way.

They tried to engage me into a conversation but just like I reminded myself earlier, I nodded if I agree and I shook my head if I disagreed.

We immediately got seated in the restaurant and I might say, it was kind of classy in a good way.

I tried to distract myself by staring at the menu. I pretended to choose a meal but all the words were a fuzzy picture.

I wonder what they're thinking right now. Are they regretting that they invited me?

I can't even utter a single coherent thought, I'm that pathetic.

"Savannah?" Macy's voice cut my train of thoughts. I blinked a few times before my eyes focused on my surroundings.

A waiter was standing in front of table, patiently waiting for my order.

Jasper tilted his head to the side, asking me a thousand questions with his eyes. Besides, that was how we used to converse during the duration I stopped talking to him.

"She'll take the steak, medium well with the side of steamed vegetables," Jasper recited to the waiter.

The boy nodded, repeated all of our orders before retreating to place our orders.

How did Jasper know what I wanted?

"You alright?" he mouthed at me while Macy started to talk about her work in New York.

I stiffly nodded at him before placing my gaze on Macy.

"Enough about me," Macy said, "Talk about yourself, Savannah."

No, that's not part of the plan. The trick was to just nod and shake my head. Talking was not inside my to-do list inside my head.

I opened my mouth before shutting it again, looking like a goldfish.

Macy and Jasper exchanged some looks, questioning my sanity.

Gosh, I really am pathetic.

"I'm going to the restroom," I suddenly told them, shooting up from my chair.

Before they can ever say a word, I was already walking away from our table. I pushed open the restroom door and I went inside a cubicle. I closed the toilet before sitting on it, burying my face in my hands.

I'm just wrecking this dinner for the both of them, I think that it's best if I left.

Why did I even agree to this dinner in the first place?

It would be just too rude if I suddenly left right now. Truthfully, I'm the only one who thinks this is extremely awkward.

Macy who obviously had no idea what happened was still treating me like what she usually does and Jasper is pretending like the past three years never happened.

Me? I was being a stubborn little girl.

Just survive this night and it will all be over. Taking a big inhale, I held it in before releasing my breath, ridding myself of my frustrations. Slowly standing up, I unlocked the cubicle door. I passed by the sinks and slowly whisked a few sprinkles of water on my face. It was enough to refresh me but it wasn't too much to destroy my makeup.

Gripping the door, I pulled it open. When I stepped out, I was shocked to find myself face to face with Jasper.

"Thank God," he let out, relief present in his voice, "I thought you got into trouble or something."

He's not mad that I basically abandoned them?

He reached out and grabbed my hand, "Come on, our food arrived," he pulled me with him, returning to our table.

Macy kept tapping her manicured fingers on the table. Her fingers only stopped when she caught sight of me, and she quickly stood up, engulfing me in her arms.

"You're so stupid," she stated, worry flooding in her tone, "Don't make us worry like that ever again."

They're really not mad.

My hand was still in Jasper's and I was still Macy's arms.

They care.

When the all three of us were seated again on our chairs, we begun to eat. This time, I actually spoke to them.

"I still can't forget that time I brought my first boyfriend home and you two caught him in a net," Macy reminisced, causing the both of us to laugh.

I allowed myself to let go. My mother was right, they're still the same kids that I grew up with.

They don't hold a grudge and for once in my life, I should stop over thinking things.

"Walk Savannah to her door, I'm taking the car home," Macy said to her brother, stopping right in front of my house.

"Yes ma'am," Jasper muttered, making Macy shoot him a dirty look. The quivering of their lips clearly showed that both of them were fighting a smile.

"Well, that was nice," I told him, my voice sounding confident the whole night.

With these two, I found myself a few years back again.

"I'm glad," he smiled, finally stopping right in front of my door, "But is there a reason why you took so long inside the restroom?"

"It's just..." I trailed off, finding the right words to explain it, "It's been three years."

That simple phrase made Jasper understand why I was so hazy the whole night. He stood up straighter, staring me right into my eyes.

What is he going to do?

"You know the good old days when we were joined at the hip?" he asked.

I mentally snorted, as if I could forget. I've spent years craving for all of it to happen again.

"How about we just reset everything?"

A smile was slowly creeping its way over my lips. I just looked at him as he continued on.

"Forget everything that happened and just remember that we're Jasper and Savannah," he stated, "The two reckless kids that every babysitter refused to take care of."

I laughed at his statement, remembering the trouble our parents went through when nobody was there to look after us while they had fun of their own.

We have been inseparable since that faithful day in the school playground where he was the only kid to approach me when I was all alone.

"Alright," I finally said, saying yes to his suggestion.

Out of the blue, he pulled me into his arms, wrapping me up in a hug. My eyes widened in shock as I was frozen into place.

Jasper Dean was hugging me.

"I missed you," he whispered as if a weight that has been hurting him was finally lifted.

Slowly but surely lifting my arms, I returned the gesture, hugging him with all my might. He's here, I wasn't avoiding him and he wasn't running away.

We're Jasper and Savannah, the two reckless kids that was inseparable.

"I missed you too."

Chapter 7

"**I** told you it will be alright," Kyla practically boasted as we entered the school. She was practically bouncing since I picked her up this morning, begging me to tell her details of what happened last night.

When I mentioned his little speech, she squealed like we weren't in a closed vehicle. I was deaf by the time we pulled into the school parking lot. It was a good thing I didn't even bother to mention the hug or else she would never leave me alone about it.

Now she's walking up with so much pride, claiming that if she and Tristan weren't there, Jasper and I would never become friends again.

I'm giving her a day before I burst her happy bubble.

"Good morning, girls!" Tristan suddenly greeted, causing us to jump in surprise.

Wait a minute, is he really talking to us in school?

He swung his arm on our shoulders as he continued to walk with us through the busy hallway, "Nice day we're having, right?"

People were staring. Every single person we passed looked like they were about to faint in shock and disbelief.

Trust me, I was mirroring the same expression.

Kyla looked up at him and questioned, "What are you doing here?"

"I go to school here," he replied, pointing out the most obvious thing in the world.

"You know what I mean," she said.

"I don't see anything wrong with it," he shrugged as if it was no big deal.

I thought we had a strict rule that we're not going to converse in school. All talk will be done during work, when we're all on our break.

The students started to point at us, their jaws dropping as we passed them. Something in me snapped and I commanded, "Go to your classrooms!"

Somebody from the mass of teenagers even had the guts to say, "The bell hasn't even rung yet."

Do they really want to anger me at such an early hour in the morning?

"To class!" I screamed at the top of my lungs, using the most furious tone I can manage. Kyla flinched beside me, Tristan retreated his arms from our shoulders, and every single students started to scamper out of the hallway.

You could practically hear a pin drop after a few seconds since I yelled.

"So that is how it happens," Tristan muttered from behind me. I looked over my shoulder to place my gaze on him as he looked at the empty halls that was filled with students a minute ago.

Congratulations Tristan, you have now experienced the president that students fear. You even had front row seats to that amazing show!

"That was kind of harsh," Kyla commented, looking at the few lockers that the students accidentally left open the haze.

I bowed my head in shame, I seriously have temper issues. I slammed one of the lockers shut, biting my lip as I held back my thoughts.

"Savannah?" Tristan slowly approached me as if I was time bomb ready to explode with one touch.

The thing is, I am one.

Why do I always have to explode like that in front of everybody? The little things people do was enough to get into my nerves.

I don't even know why I was elected to be student body president. I flunk the part completely.

"What happened here?" Jasper walked up to us, looking around the empty halls, "Am I late already?"

Tristan and Kyla kept silent but they pointed they looks at me. I sighed, shrugging right at him, telling him it was no big deal.

"Tristan, can you walk Kyla to her first period?" he asked his best friend, staring at my sullen expression.

Tristan nodded in understanding, he gave Jasper a pat on his shoulder and he nodded at my direction. Kyla walked up to me and tried to give me a warm smile.

"See you later," she said, giving me a side hug, she leaned in and whispered into my ear, "Don't make a big deal of this, alright?"

The two of them walked away from us and my eyes were trained on their retreating figures.

"You ready?" Jasper questioned, taking his place beside me.

I snapped my head to his direction and quirked my eyebrows in confusion, "Ready for what?"

He only gave me a small smile, grabbing my hand and pulling me to the exit.

"Jasper, class will be starting soon!"

"So?" he inquired as if it was no big deal.

Let me tell you, it's a freaking big deal! If they found out, I'm going to be in so much trouble.

He dragged me to his car and opened the passenger seat for me. I just stared at him in disbelief as he smirked right at me, waiting for me to enter the vehicle.

He must be crazy if he thinks that I'm doing this.

Jasper quirked his head to the side before slamming the door shut. Maybe he finally got the idea that I'm not going to miss class for whatever he has planned for me.

He reached out for my wrist as he pulled me to his side, slowly walking to the school gate, "If you prefer walking, that's alright with me."

Somebody please knock some sense into this boy.

I planted my foot firmly on the ground, refusing to go along with him. He lifted a brow, clearly amused at my attempts to stop him as he smirked right at me.

Oh shoot, I know that mischievous look anywhere.

He picked me up and threw me over his shoulder before he started to skip happily out of the school area.

There's a thing called kidnapping!

"Jasper let me go!" I screeched, hitting his back repetitively.

With my upper body upside down like this, I know I'm going to hurl any time soon.

He ignored me as he continued to stride to our destination as if there was no teenage girl clearly hanging for her life on his shoulder.

Now I'm wondering whatever he did to make me agree to become best friends with him years ago.

Somewhere along the walk, he slowly pulled me down and I leaned against a light post, clutching my head.

"I'm going to kill you," I scowled, praying that this headache will be gone.

He looked at our surrounding before nodding in approval, "We still have a little more to go but we're far enough from the school to know you're not running back any time soon."

Damn. Where are we going?

"By the way," he started to walk once again, looking at me over his shoulder, "You might want to go easy with the pastries, you're so heavy."

I stomped my foot childishly on the side walk, shooting him the nastiest glare I can manage with my head still pulsing in pain, "Jasper Dean, you're so dead to me!"

His laughter echoed through the empty streets, waiting for me to catch up with him. Groaning in response, I pushed myself forward and slowly marched my way to him.

I'm just waiting for the right moment to launch my super ninja skills right at him.

As we moved forward, our surroundings slowly became familiar. We stopped right in front of a metal fence, at the other side showed the playground connected to a school.

The same playground where Jasper and I used to sneak in, even during class hours just to play and talk.

"Remember?" he questioned, gripping the fence, staring the thing in front of us, "When you're having your drama filled days, we usually skip class."

The same thing that we used to do in elementary school was happening right now.

Ever so carefully, Jasper slowly climbed up the fence and I gaped right at him. He stopped right at the top of it, looking at me expectantly.

He really is crazy, but the thing is, he was my crazy best friend.

"You do know that I'm not really skilled in the art of breaking and entering."

Jasper rolled his eyes and reached out a hand for me to take, "Come on, I'll help you."

Looking at the playground at the other side of the fence, I sighed. I'm really going to regret this later.

I placed my foot up and allowed it to rest on the fence. I gripped the metal with so much force that it started to dig into my skin.

Jasper helped me when I was finally in his reach. We settled at the top, looking down on the drop to the ground. With a wink at my way, Jasper slowly climbed down, jumping halfway through.

Alright, all I have to do is to go down. Don't think of the fall that may soon end into your own death.

Jasper chuckled at me, "Jump, I'll catch you!"

I find it hard to believe that he can do it. I bit my lip, staring into his comforting brown eyes. He was assuring me, the minute I let go of the fence, I'll find myself in his arms.

Thinking back, he has never let me down on purpose. I just hope he doesn't break that streak today.

Taking a deep breath, my hands that were clamped on the metal fence slowly lost their grip. I closed my eyes, waiting for the impact on the ground.

I felt Jasper catch me but the minute he did so, we fell back into a heap into the ground.

Jasper groaned underneath me after he used his body as a cushion for my fall. Even with the pained look on his face, he still managed to smile smugly at me, "Told you that I will catch you," he grinned, "But just like what I said before, stop pigging into those pastries."

I glared at him, hitting his stomach before I got up. He grumbled under his breath, slowly getting up to his feet, dusting off the dirt on his clothes.

The place still looked the same as what it did when we were children studying in this school. They replaced a few sets with new ones, but other than that, the format of the rides were still the same.

"Why did you bring me here?" I asked, my fingers feeling the smooth plastic of the slide, marveling at the sight.

It was the same slide we used to play on.

"I know you, Savannah," he said, sitting on one of the swings on the set, "Well enough to know when you're feeling down."

I've been feeling down since I learned you like Kyla. Why haven't you noticed that?

"So you thought a little trip to our childhood playground will lift up my mood?"

He nodded, slowly swinging back and forth. The metal frame protested at the heavy weight of his body, creaking with every swing he made.

We settled into silence as I stared at everything around me. It was like everything was coming back after years of being ignored.

Jasper was here with me, he dragged me to this playground as we ditched school, and as always, we were both lost into our own thoughts.

This is nice.

"What did I do wrong?"

I snapped my attention to him as his eyes were trained on his shoe as it made patterns on the ground beneath it.

"Why did you ignore to me?"

That was one question that I desperately wanted to avoid. He deserves an explanation but the reason was just so stupid. He did nothing wrong, I was the one who was always causing him trouble, even when we were kids.

My stupid crush back then got in the way of our friendship. Add up his growing popularity due to basketball, it was a recipe for total doom.

When I wasn't answering him, he sighed rather loudly in defeat, "You're not going to tell me, are you?"

Correct, my friend.

Maybe somewhere in the future, I'll step out of this pathetic position that I am in. We just started our friendship again, I don't want to risk it because of a stupid explanation.

"I'll save that for another day," I promised him, sitting on the swing next to him, "How about we just enjoy right now?"

He shook his head, a smile coming to his lips, "You haven't changed a bit, Savannah."

But he has. I never predicted that he will be the king of the school; I knew that he would be in the varsity team but I never guessed back then that he will be practically ruling over the students. He was on the top of the popularity chain, everybody knew and respected him.

While everybody feared me.

Maybe all this time we were friends, I was holding him back. His activities skyrocketed when I left him, it was like the minute I was gone, he finally broke free.

He's was just kind enough to hang out with me.

His hand settled on my head, ruffling my hair, "And you still have that same look when you overthink things."

"You're much better without me," the words left my mouth before I can even stop them.

He froze, looking at me with confusion, "What do you mean?"

Before I can tell him to wave it off, the bell of the school rang. We looked at each other with troubled expressions, we knew well that it was time for their recess.

"Come on," he rushed out, grabbing my hand and pulling me up to my feet.

"What do you suggest?" I asked, looking at the fence. We both knew it was going to be difficult to climb it up again, and if anybody saw us, they may report us to the police.

"The direct way," he said simply, tugging me to the door of the school.

Oh please don't tell me.

He sprinted through the halls of the school that was starting to get filled with children. Jasper quickened his pace, remembering every single turn through this school.

We stuck out like a sore thumb, we were a foot taller than every student in this school. A teacher spotted us and she yelled, "Stop, you two there!"

"Run!" Jasper told me as I tried to keep up with his pace. I wanted to remind him that I'm not well inverse into sports as he is.

We spotted our destination, the exit of the school building. He practically dived to it, avoiding the students as he left. I huffed out, trying to catch my breath when we stopped once we were finally outside.

"That teacher might be still chasing us," he let out, peeking inside through the door, "We better keep on going."

"Jasper!" I screeched, "I'm going to die if we have to run another round."

We spotted the teacher, trying maneuver herself through the throng of little children. She yelled at us, telling us to stay where we are or else she will call the police.

"We're already damned anyways," Jasper chuckled, pulling me to him as he started to sprint once again. He bounced down the steps, and I hurriedly went down.

When we were safely away from the school, I collapsed on the sidewalk. I can barely care about the temperature of the cement, I was tired from all the running.

"You better watch out tonight, I'm killing you while you're in your sleep," I scowled, wiping the sweat from my forehead.

Out of nowhere, he started to laugh. Not the usual chuckle, but a full knee slapping, hand clapping, tear jerking laugh.

Did I say something wrong?

"That was amazing!" he cheered, looking at the path we just took.

He has lost it.

"Did you see that teacher?" his eyes twinkled in joy, "I can't believe we just escaped her."

He fell onto the ground next to me, letting out a breath of happiness, "Haven't had this much fun in a long time!"

Haven't freaked out this much in one morning before. Nevertheless, that's what Jasper Dean is for you, the one guy that is annoying and reckless but can make anybody smile with such fun.

What was I thinking when I let him go?

He was right, even with the fiasco and everything, he made me forget the expense this morning. Other than that, he proved that our friendship and memories still stood.

Just like that playground, there were new rides but a few bits and pieces stayed. Everything looked the same, but it was clear as day that they changed a few things to make sure the place will last longer.

To make everything better, you'll keep a few things but you also have to replace some with newer and better ones.

I looked at my wristwatch, sighing at the time, "But now, we need to head back to our own school."

Looking at the long way we have to walk I groaned, I should have gotten into Jasper's car from the start.

"We can take our sweet time, when we come back we'll be just in time for lunch," he told me, getting up to his feet. He offered a hand and I took it as he pulled me up.

"I'm going to be in so much trouble when they find out that I skipped," I groaned, expecting the worst.

Jasper chuckled, falling into step beside me as we carefully walked away from the past, known as that playground, as we started our journey back to our high school – the present.

Chapter 8

Now, I've clearly accepted the social difference between Jasper and I. I know that he hangs out with the rest of the varsity team along with the cheerleaders, while I spend my days with Kyla. I'm completely fine with that, we won't change the daily routines of our lives just because we became friend again.

Guess I was completely and utterly wrong.

"You've got to be kidding me!" I groaned, eyeing the jam packed table filled with the jocks and cheerleaders. They pressed up about three tables together just to make enough room for all of them.

Kyla crossed her arms over her chest, lifting a brow at both Jasper and Tristan, "We're not going there."

They thought that I was perfectly fine for the two of us just suddenly sit with the biggest clique in the school. They were all laughing and playing with each other, acting like they were a bunch of celebrities.

Please, give me a break.

"They won't hurt you," Tristan chuckled, finding this all too amusing.

Oh I know that they won't hurt me. One wrong move, and I'll be the one who will be doing the beating.

What I'm afraid of is that the two of us will completely fall out of place. I could practically see rainbows and sparkles emitting from their table, it was sickening.

Looping my arm with Kyla's I gave the boys a dry look, "We're perfectly fine by our own," we started to walk around them, keeping our heads held high.

"I'm never going to get used to this," Kyla told me as we sat down on an empty table, "What are we going to do, Savannah?"

First things first, we need to get some food because I'm starving.

Scanning around the cafeteria, I made sure Jasper and Tristan was nowhere around. It's going to be a quick sprint to the lunch counter then back to this very table.

Just as I was about to drag Kyla with me, four trays was set down on the table. Kyla and I shared a look as the two boys sat down right across from us, grinning as if this was a completely normal scene.

"Roast beef sandwich for Savannah, your favorite," Jasper said, pushing the tray with the said sandwich next to a juice bottle.

"And a tuna sandwich for Kyla," Tristan pushed the tray of her meal right in front of her.

We looked down at the trays of food the boys got us before shifting our gaze to the two of them.

Looking around the room was the biggest mistake.

Every single student's jaw was currently hanging wide open, waiting for flies to get in. When my eyes casted over to the jocks' table, their groupies was staring at our table with outmost disbelief. I swear, some of the cheerleaders were glaring at us.

What the hell is happening?

"Don't worry about them," Tristan assured, snapping our attention to them. He gave the both of us a comforting smile, telling us not to be bothered by everybody.

"I'm glad that you got along with them just fine," Jasper told his best friend, "I thought you were going to freak out just like the rest of the team."

Tristan shot us a wink, emphasizing the fact that his job was a secret from his best friend, "I don't see what's wrong with these two, I like them already."

I still don't get why he still have to hide his work from us. It would no longer be weird or awkward for Jasper to find out Tristan, Kyla and I were working at the same place. We're all back to the normal kind of friendship already.

It's his choice anyways.

These two started to look like our bodyguards, they were practically with us everywhere we go. They walked us to class, they strolled down the school halls with us, and they were practically our shadow. Even though, anywhere we go, we couldn't miss the shock the students displayed.

I wonder how long it would take until people would finally stop gaping.

The bright side, the compromising feel during English class was no longer present. Since Ms. Hughes allotted the class for practice, it was basically a free period.

Jasper propped up his feet on top of his desk as he scanned the script that I made. He made noises of approval as he flipped each page, but when he reached the end, he looked at me, "Where's the kiss Romeo and Juliet always have?"

"In the real piece that Shakespeare wrote, there was no kiss. It only appeared in some adaptations," I informed him, highlighting my lines.

Why is he even mentioning that when it had no importance?

I didn't have work today and Jasper said that he could excuse himself from basketball training, placing an opportunity for the both of us to practice.

It was going to be a breeze, taking an hour at the most.

We decided to rehearse inside my house. When I got inside, I hollered out if anybody was home. When no reply came, I assumed that both of my parents were gone. I lead Jasper to the living room as if he's visiting for the first time.

He has been here multiple times, as much as I visited his home. We considered each other's houses as our second home when we were younger. Our parents were close friends so they welcomed the other couple's child with open arms.

I made sure the script was short and simple, the faster we got off the front of that classroom, the better.

He recited his line swiftly, as if those words were natural to him. His eyes were trained on the paper, mouthing the words as he tried to memorize the phrases.

When it was my turn, I took a deep breath and read the lines printed on the paper, "Romeo, Romeo, Wherefore art thou Romeo?"

I admit, my acting was stiff. I could hear Jasper trying to hold off his laughter and I kept my eyes on the paper, refusing to look up at him. This is embarrassing enough.

"Deny thy father and refuse thy name or, if thou wilt not be, but sworn my love, and I'll no longer be a Capulet," I continued, trying to soften up my words. I sounded like I was a zombie, my tone completely monotone.

"Shall I hear more, or shall I speak at this?" he recited, as if he was really listening to his lover, contemplating if he should listen more or interrupt her little monologue.

How can I make this as natural as he can?

He spoke the last line and that was when we finally looked at each other. Even if he was pouring some emotions into his speech, I knew for sure that he was smiling amusedly at me the whole time were rehearsing.

"That was great," he clapped mockingly, "But next time, talk like a human more than a robot."

I grabbed the throw pillow from the couch and chucked it to his direction. He caught it swiftly, using the years of basketball to help with his agility.

"Nice try," he chuckled, throwing it right at me, hitting me square on the face. I glared him, dropping the pillow back on the couch.

"Let's do this one more time," I huffed.

Slowly but surely, my words started to became smoother, I no longer sounded like I was a child petrified on her first day of kindergarten.

"I think we got this in the bag," I stated a little too confidently. He rolled his eyes playfully and flick my forehead.

"That's only what you think."

Dropping on the couch, I let out a sigh, leaning my head against the back of it. So far, this day started out horrible and then Jasper managed to cheer me up, but then came the escapade during lunch.

I wonder how long he will keep this up before he finally gives up and realizes that we're in two different social circles. I'm grateful that he's my friend again, but it doesn't mean we'll change the things we've been doing throughout our high school years.

He rested his feet on my lap, I tried to pry it away but his legs were practically heavier than half of my body.

"Haven't been to this house in so long," he said, leaning back, "Even though it's about five steps from my house."

Our houses were right beside the other, we see each other during school, our parents are great friend, yet we seem to be so far apart.

"I'm sorry," I finally let out.

He never looked like he missed me as much as I missed him, but nonetheless, I owe him a nice and official apology.

I was the one who was so stubborn and allowed something as petty as my crush for him get in the way of our valuable friendship.

"What for?" he questioned, sitting up but the weight of his feet remained on my lap.

Shrugging lightly, I let out a deep breath, "For everything."

The times that I ignored you, the times I intentionally avoided you, the way I always tore my gaze away from yours when you try to reach me, or for simply being a bad friend.

The thing was, I may be furious with the whole student body but even if Jasper messes up, I couldn't bring it in myself to get mad at him. He made multiple pranks with his friends around the school, but not once did I scold him.

I'm pretty sure everybody noticed that Jasper Dean has this immunity against me.

It was simple, if he showed that little innocent smile of his, I find myself instantly forgiving him.

"It's alright," Jasper reassured, using the same words when I apologized for the coffee incident.

Makes me question myself, was it really alright?

"Yes, it's really alright," he chuckled, making me notice that I said that out loud.

He removed his feet from my lap and ruffled my hair, "Come on, smile."

I stared at him as he looked at me, smiling with the same old expression that showed nothing but kindness. That's how he charmed me to become his best friend, and that is also how he charmed me into gaining a crush on him.

The corners of my lips started to twitch upward, giving him the thing he requested for. He looked please, patting my messy hair, "Don't stress about it."

"But I mean it," I told him lightly, "I really am sorry."

"I told you, everything's alright," he stated, "I'm just glad I have my Savannah back."

His Savannah.

Well, he's my Jasper.

The front door swung open to reveal my mother, she spot the two of us lounging on the couch and she grinned. She knew everything that had happened, she was as observant as ever. She realized that when Jasper's visit became infrequent, something was up.

She tried to comfort me, asking me what was wrong but I kept my mouth shut. She eventually allowed it to slip, but I knew that she was already foretelling that we were soon going to become friends again.

Is she psychic or something?

"Jasper," she grinned, taking off her coat, "How are you?"

"I'm fine, Ariel," he greeted my mother. Just like everybody, my mom made Jasper call her by her first name.

"Are you staying for dinner?" she asked, balancing the paper bag of groceries in her arms, "I'll make some extra."

We shared a look and I nodded, telling him to say yes to her. He turned back to mom and smiled, "That would be nice."

She clapped her hands, clearly pleased with his answer as she strolled into the kitchen, "I'll make up something nice and hot," she started to say, "It's been getting cold lately."

"Well, winter is almost coming," Jasper pointed out, looking at the window where the autumn leaves were swishing around.

I groaned, just thinking of that season. Second to prom, a dance that the school held in exaggerated celebration was the winter formal.

Don't get me wrong, it's nice to have fun and dance the night away, but the superstition behind it was too much. Rumors say that the first and last person you dance with on the night of the winter formal will be the person you'll stay and love forever.

As if that's possible. How can one little dance affect your whole relationship with another person? What do you expect, because you're dancing with somebody, you'll suddenly have an epiphany that after all these time, you'll find out that you like that person you're swaying with.

How about no.

What's worst it, I'll be managing the preparations as head of the student body.

"I'll help, Ariel," Jasper said, standing up. He looked at me expectantly and I smiled softly, standing up also.

"Now that's the smile wanted to see."

Chapter 9

"So what's happening with you two?" Tristan asked, propping his elbows on the table in front of us.

I rolled my eyes at him, waving his statement off as I wiped the table with a piece of cloth. Kyla giggled next to me, helping take down the chairs from the top of the tables, prepping up for our opening.

"Nothing," I replied bluntly, when his smirk grew, I lifted my eyebrows before spraying him with the cleaner on the face. He flinched backwards and I smirked in victory, moving to wipe the other tables clean.

Kyla grinned to my direction, giving me a forewarning that I'm going to go through a long interrogation later on.

My friends pestering me on a Saturday morning was not part of my schedule.

"Moving off topic," I coughed out awkwardly in an attempt to avert the conversation from me, "What's up with keeping your job as a secret?"

Tristan sighed, helping take down the chairs from the tables, "It's nothing."

I lifted a brow, that answer did not satisfy my curiosity even a bit.

Kyla eyed Tristan suspiciously, helping me with the tables, "I thought we're already fine to talk to each other in school."

Tristan frowned at Kyla's statement, looking at my best friend with an apologetic look. A blush instantly crept up her cheeks, letting out a theory that he wasn't supposed to hear her statement. She quickly looked down on the table, wiping it with a new vigor.

She's literally a school girl with a crush.

"What I still don't get is why you're even working," Tristan said, "Your brother practically owns this place, you're rich!"

"He's rich," I tried to emphasize, I'm tired of explaining this over and over again, "I'm living comfortable middle class life."

"No," he wagged his finger, "We're living the comfortable middle class life, and you just want something to keep you busy."

Rolling my eyes at him, I threw the cloth that I was using to wipe the tables. It hit him square on the face, and he reached out to peel it off, his face scrunching in disgust.

"Hansen!" the main chef yelled from the kitchen, calling Tristan over. He sighed, disliking the guy more and more by the day.

"My duty awaits," he groaned out, trudging to the kitchen.

"Did you see that?" Kyla suddenly skipped to my side, bouncing with happiness, "He got sad when I mentioned my disappointment."

If Tristan is here, she's meek and shy, when he's not, she's a bubbly overexcited chick.

But we just love her anyways.

"Come on, we're about to open," taking one more look at the polished table, I smiled in accomplishment as the two of us retreated back into the kitchen.

"When will our manager come back?" she sighed, looking around for our boss. I shrugged, it's better if we just left the woman to her own. Her best friend was getting married overseas, thus, she's away from work right now.

As if this place needed her, the staff were organized enough to handle without a manager. They cooperated with each other, and they're nice even to the part-timers like us.

"So how's little Romeo?" Kyla teased, poking my side making me jump into the air. I stepped away from her as she grinned at me.

"Shut up," I cut off which only made her laugh harder.

The oldest of the waiters, whom our manager placed in charge, herded all the staff in the kitchen. She examined each and every one of us, taking in the attendance of the workers. She clapped her hands and breathed out, "Ready to open?"

We nodded, more than prepared to take on a day of service. She smiled before she went outside to unlock the front doors of the café to open it to the world.

"It's going to be another slow day," I sighed, sitting on one of the stools, "I can't wait to get out of work later."

"We just opened," Kyla pointed out, hopping on the stool next to me, "But I agree, work on a Saturday is horrible."

Tristan chuckled, sneaking two slices of chocolate cake for us, "Turn those frown upside down," he pushed the plates, "It isn't too bad."

I scoffed at his statement but I dived into the cake anyways. I praise the chefs in this place for making the best pastries out there.

Tristan pulled out his phone from his pocket, tapping on the screen. His face morphed into worry, looking troubled at whatever it was on the screen.

Kyla and I shared a look before turning to him, "What's wrong?"

He placed the device on the counter, a text message from Jasper was displayed on the screen.

180 degrees coffee later at lunch. My treat.

Not good.

"Tell him you have work."

He shook his head, snatching his phone back, "He knows I get off on lunch during Saturdays."

Taking a deep breath, I slammed my palm on the table and stared him right in the eyes, "Tell him."

He gaped at me as if I was telling him to do a suicide mission. For him, it might as well be, "I can't."

We just can't see why. We're friends again, Jasper knows that we're on friendly terms, there's nothing to hide anymore.

Or maybe I'm just overlooking something.

He shot a quick reply which we knew that he's going to end up in one of the tables outside with his best friend right across from him. Hey, I'm not the one to interrupt with their perfect guy time.

He's just digging his own grave.

A minute after he sent the message, my phone started to vibrate. I fished it out of my pocket to see Jasper's name flashing on the screen. The three of us shared a look and I answered it, placing him on speaker so all of us knew the conversation.

"Savannah, you working today?"

Tristan stilled, waiting for Jasper's words. I let out a statement of confirmation and he hummed from the other line.

"Are you getting off during lunch?"

And that did it, we knew where this is going.

"Yes," I trailed off, keeping my attention to Tristan's reactions.

"Great, Tristan and I are heading there for lunch, come and join us, bring Kyla too."

This is just brilliant.

I told him that I will be there and we said our goodbyes. The minute the call ended, Tristan groaned and buried his face in his hands.

"Just change out of your work clothes," Kyla suggested, "If this goes smoothly, your secret will still be safe."

This is going to end in failure, I could feel it.

Pushing myself off of the stool, I grabbed a pen and paper before I went out to the dining hall. I'll let those two plan whatever they need to do.

The time went by fast, and soon enough, it was noon. The three of us called out for permission that we were going on our break and Tristan sprinted to the locker room to change out of his uniform.

"Game time!" Kyla cheered, taking off her apron and throwing it inside her locker. The both of us went out of the kitchen and we spotted Jasper seating in one of the booths.

Ladies and gentlemen, hold on to yours seats as you munch on your popcorns because this going to be a show you would not want to miss.

We approached him and he was tapping on his phone, he smiled right up at us, gesturing to the spot across the table from him.

"Where's Tristan?" Kyla tried to sound nonchalantly, but it came out forced. She sent me a wink and I internally slapped my forehead.

The bell by the entrance dinged, signaling that somebody came into the café. By that someone, it meant that it was Tristan.

He was puffing out for air right behind Jasper's chair. He looked at us and we nodded subtly at him, he fixed his hair and straightened up his posture, before he strode casually to the front of our table.

"Sorry I'm late," he chirped, a little more enthusiastic than what he usually sounds like.

He turned to us in surprise, gasping for extra effects. Oh dear Lord, this is not going to end well.

"I didn't know you guys are here!"

"Tristan!" Kyla squealed, shooting up from her spot, "It's so good to see you again."

In Jasper's perspective, they just saw each other yesterday. This is partially stupid.

Then they hugged, as if they haven't seen each other for years.

Jasper eyed them, raising a brow. He turned to me and pointed at the pair, giving me a questioning look; I merely shrugged, deciding to keep my lips shut as this plays out.

Our waiter came, a co-worker that Kyla sternly briefed about the plan.

"Can I get your order?" she asked stiffly, her hands shaking as she held a pen and paper.

"Menu!" Kyla not-so-quietly whispered to her. She was a junior at another schoo , and she gasped at her mistake.

"I'm so sorry," she apologized hastily, running to grab four menus. She raced to us with the menus in her hands, when she finally came in front of us, she scrambled to hand them to us but it slipped right out of her hands.

Kyla glared at the poor girl which made her fidget more under her gaze.

Well, I've had enough of this.

Standing up, I took the menus from her hands after she picked them up and turned to my friends, "Welcome to One-Eighty Degrees Coffee, here are our menus and we hope that you enjoy your stay," I relayed to them the recommendations at the waitress shrunk at her spot behind me.

Jasper grinned at me as I answered questions about the menu. I knew that he memorized everything in it, but I also knew that he wanted me to play the waitress part for him.

Kyla and Tristan looked at me and I gave them a dry look. Their eyes were apologetic as they told me their orders. I wrote down my own meal on the notepad, before I grabbed their menus back and handed them back to our waitress.

"Don't be nervous," I whispered to her, "I'm leaving everything up to you."

She looked up at me, her eyes twinkling with gratitude and admiration as she meekly nodded and retreated to the kitchen.

Turning to my best friend, I plastered a fake smile that was obviously forced, "Kyla, why don't you show Jasper that thing we saw in the parking lot earlier."

"What thing?" she questioned and when I looked at her, telling her to go along with whatever I was saying, her mouth formed into an 'o' shape.

She stood up and gestured to Jasper, "Let's go."

They went out and I stared at Tristan, shaking my head at him, "You need to tell him."

He looked down and nodded, "I know."

Smiling encouragingly at him, I gave his shoulder a friendly pat, "I have no idea why you're hiding this," I told him, "But Jasper's one of the most understanding person out there, trust me, I know."

The corners of his lips started to lift up as he allowed my words to sink, "I really am glad that you and Jasper are friends again."

"Me too," I let out softly.

With those words, I gave him a small push to the direction of the kitchen, "Tell the little lass that everything is off," I said, referring to our young waitress.

I decided that I'll do my job as the waitress. I grabbed my apron as he prepared our orders, telling the chefs in the kitchen that this meal was something special. He placed everything out on the tray, nodding right at me.

We knew that Kyla and Jasper were back on our table, probably wondering where we are.

Pushing the doors of the kitchen with the tray in my hand, I walked to the table the four of us were previously occupying.

"Oh you went back to work," Jasper pointed out when I started to lay down the plates and glasses on the table, "Where's Trist?"

I didn't answer him, I handed the tray to one of the waiters walking by before I sat down on my chair. Kyla quirked her brow, asking me the silent question where her crush is.

I smile at her, telling her to just eat her food.

Jasper forked in a portion of his food inside him mouth and hummed in approval.

"Good?" I asked and he automatically nodded.

"The best," he let out, stuffing his mouth.

"Would you want to meet our cook?"

Kyla squeezed my hand, finally getting what I'm doing. She looked worriedly at me but I smiled at her.

People, we have a new plan.

Jasper looked taken back at my question but he agreed anyways, "Okay?"

I stood up, retreating back to the kitchen where Tristan was pacing back and forth nervously. The staff in the kitchen caught up quickly that something was up and allowed their youngest cook to worry.

"Ready?" I asked, he nodded nervously.

Taking a deep breath, he looked at me, "Ready."

Before we were out of the door, I turned to him, "Just so you know, I'm glad Jasper chose you to become his best friend when I left him, instead of a douche."

He smiled at my words, following me out of the door.

One day, he's going to explain to me the reason for keeping this a secret, but until them, I'll trust him on it.

The shock was visible on Jasper's face when we approached our table again. Kyla gripped the edges of the chair, he nails digging to the wood.

Everything happened in slow motion, Jasper stood up and left the café without a single word. Tristan froze next to me, Kyla followed with her the direction where Jasper disappeared, and I only shook my head in disappointment.

"Follow him," I pushed, he looked at me in disbelief but I only nodded to the direction of the door.

He sprinted off quickly, swinging the glass door of the café open as he chased after his best friend.

"That could have gotten worse," Kyla sighed, standing next to me, "I mean, a fight could have happened."

Impossible, those two loved each other as friends so much that nothing can break them. This was just a small scuffle.

We slowly walked to the door, opening it and even from the door, we could hear their conversation. We only picked up bits of it, but it was clear that they were yelling.

"Years!" we heard Jasper yell, "You knew about it!"

Tristan knew about what?

"... acted like... doesn't want to," was Tristan faint reply.

Acted like what?

I know it's wrong to eavesdrop but this getting more interesting by the second.

"Ever thought about me, bud?"

"You thought it was easy for me to face you knowing I was hiding something?"

They're talking about the reason why Tristan kept it a secret.

I wanted to hear more, slowly approaching where their voices were coming from, Kyla took a hold of my hands. I looked back at her and she only shook her head.

This was a conversation between them, we had no right to be associated about it.

"Let's go back," she mouthed, pulling me back to the inside of the café.

Chapter 10

The school quickly noticed that the two captains of the basketball team weren't talking to each other. What's worse, they're occupying different tables at the opposite side of the cafeteria.

Kyla only observed from the door as half of the student population was staring at Jasper, while the other half was staring at Tristan. None of them dared to go near them, valuing their lives as they eyed the two guys from a safe distance.

Silence.

Jasper and Tristan were always side by side, they acted more like brothers than anything. Now, it looks like they don't even know each other.

"You go to Tristan, I get Jasper," I whispered to Kyla, switching my gaze from the two boys.

She nodded before she said, "Good luck."

We gave each other an encouraging look as we split apart to each of the boys. I pulled the chair in front of Jasper and I sat down on it, staring at him.

His eyes were blank, staring at the sandwich on his tray as if he never even noticed me.

Clearing my throat rather loudly, still no reaction. Reaching out, I slapped his shoulder and he jumped up in surprise.

He blinked before his eyes focused on me. He smiled, one that didn't reach his eyes as he turned to greet me, "Hey Savannah."

Frowning, I told him to drop the act, "I was your best friend, Jasper, for so many years, I know you're not happy."

His lips pressed into a tight line, pushing the tray of his lunch away from him. Sighing, he sunk down on his seat, tapping the table with frustration.

"Did you guys intentionally made me look like an idiot?" he asked, staring into my eyes.

Frowning, I shook my head to deny any such thing, "Tristan wanted to keep it from you, we just went along with it."

Slamming his fist on the table, he grumbled under his breath, "And you never once thought to say anything from me, I thought we were friends again, Savannah!"

"We are," I stated, standing up and looking down at him, "Tristan is my friend too, he had his reasons and I was in no place to meddle."

He pushed himself up from his seat, yelling at me with such anger in his tone, "So now he's your best friend while I'm just pushed to the side all these years?!"

I froze, biting my lips as I just stared at him, shaking my head. I know that I hurt him with the fact that I ignored him, but I thought we pushed that all behind us now. He's just reminding me how terrible I was, just how big my mistake.

"For three years you ignored me, and then I find out you were buddies with my best friend. You know, Savannah, you're the worst friend I can have."

He was the one who told me to let it all go, and I did, but right now, he's just reminding us about this big barrier in between us.

Trying to blink the tears that were threatening to spill, I slowly backed away from him. So all these time, this is what he really felt about me?

This is what I was afraid of, Jasper has too big of an effect on me.

His eyes softened as he reached out to hold me, "Savannah," he muttered comfortingly, "I'm sorry."

"It's not her fault!" somebody yelled and we snapped our gaze to the other side of the cafeteria.

Tristan stood up from his spot, looking directly at the two of us. The cafeteria was just watching the exchange between these fighting best friends, thinking it was some television show or something.

Jasper glared at Tristan, stomping right out of the room. I just stared at him, not finding the strength to go after his retreating figure.

Kyla and Tristan quickly ran from their spot from the other side of the cafeteria. Kyla quickly engulfed me in a hug, "He didn't mean it."

"He's just angry," Tristan tried to soothe, rubbing comforting circles on my back.

"He doesn't want me as a friend," I let out, but my voice cracked the minute I spoke.

Great, now the whole school is watching me cry because of Jasper. This is one of the reasons why I broke our friendship, he was my ultimate weakness.

Kyla practically became my body guard, glaring at every possible human being that came close to our proximity. The student body was quite shocked, the vice president that was usually full of rainbows and the person that kept me from killing them, was actually the one who was emitting such a dark aura.

Let's just say that I'm lucky to have her as my best friend.

One thing though, she wasn't there to protect me against Jasper during English period.

The classroom was filled with tension as Jasper and I sat next to each other. His eyes were pleading me, apologizing with a language with spoke through our looks. Right now, I'm doing my best to avoid his gaze.

Even Ms. Hughes noticed how bad the situation was. She gave out the period for practice, with a quick reminder that we were to present our scene tomorrow.

How can I do it with Jasper?

The minute Ms. Hughes announced that our time was free, Jasper jumped out of his seat and kneeled in front of my desk.

"Savannah," he whispered softly, his eyes looking so lost on what to do, "I'm really sorry."

How funny is this scene? His big figure kneeling in front of me, pleading for forgiveness.

Reaching out for my hands, he gripped them in his as he stared at me like a lost puppy. Now, I would be completely heartless if I don't melt with that look.

Darn you, Jasper Dean, do you have any idea what's your effect on me?

"Forgive me?"

Right then and there, I melted into a puddle.

Nodding slowly, a smile broke into his face as he stood up, rounding my desk as he sat on it when he was finally in front of me, "You're the best."

"Did you mean any of it?"

"Never," he told me, nothing but sincerity in his tone.

Now I just need to find out a way to patch things up with him and Tristan. It must be a pretty big deal for Tristan to keep it a secret, and a bigger of a deal to cause this big of a riff on their friendship.

Apparently, it's something that has been going on for years, that's what I picked up from their conversation last Saturday. Also, somebody acted like he or she didn't want something to happen.

This is so confusing!

"What are you thinking about now?" he asked, flicking my forehead to gain my attention.

I shook my head and sighed, I just hope Kyla is doing much better progress than I am with Tristan's side.

So when school ended, the two of us drove to my house and the both of us were perched up on my bed to summarize whatever we found out today.

For me, I found nothing.

Kyla on the other hand, fished out something interesting, "Tristan claimed that Jasper had no problem with his career choice, he's just bothered by the place."

"One-Eighty?" I questioned, leaning against my headboard.

She nodded, tapping her chain to formulate a conclusion, "Nothing seems to be wrong with the café, any thoughts about it?"

Shaking my head, I hugged a pillow to my chest, thinking, "He doesn't appear to have a problem about it. We used to spend time there even when we were best friends back then."

Even if we cut off our friendship, I could still spot Jasper visit the café a little now and then. It was surely seldom, but it still happened. Those were the times I avoided being assigned to his table, but he looked completely normal during those times.

My dear Jasper and Tristan, what are you two hiding from us?

"Why don't you talk to him?" Kyla suggested, motioning to my closed window, "Maybe get more clues?"

"The last time I tried to get something out of him, he practically yelled to my face that he hated being my friend," I scoffed, "I don't think I want to repeat that."

Rolling her eyes, she pulled me up to my feet and pushed me to the front of the window.

"If you really want to ask him, why don't you do it?" I inquired, pushing the curtains open. Jasper's window was opened and you can see him tapping mindlessly on his notebook as a pair of headphones was pressed up on his ears.

"Because he always listens to you," she pointed out, slowly retreating to my door, "I'll be back once you're finished talking."

Staring at him, I let out another sigh. Now how do I get his attention?

Grabbing a comb, I aimed before throwing it through his open window. By the end of the year, my bedroom will be empty because I practically threw everything at him.

The comb didn't land anywhere near him, but it did hit the glass on his dresser, which consequently shattered. He flinched at the sound, and stared at the thing.

Okay, I owe him a new one.

Taking off his headphones, he examined the thing before he raised his gaze to me. I waved awkwardly, praying he wasn't mad.

To my surprise, he grinned, stepping around the shattered glass on the floor of his room and went near to his window, "Hey."

"Sorry," I mumbled, lifting a finger to point on the glass, "I'll buy you a new one."

"Don't worry about it," he shrugged, leaning against the windowsill, "So what does the amazing Savannah Everett need from me?"

"Why are you and Tristan fighting?" I suddenly managed to say. Like a band aid, I just fired the question right at him.

Just like that, the playful look he had on slipped away. His face pressed into a tight frown, the cheeriness in his eyes disappeared and turned into an unexplainable look.

Now I'm curious.

"Savannah," he drawled out my name, giving me a silent warning, "Don't trouble yourself with this."

Other than the fact it was controversial that the two best friends are fighting, it was clear as day that Jasper was as depressed about this as Tristan. This affected him to at a high degree, it was pretty obvious. I won't be able to settle down unless I can see that joyous smile of his.

"Please," I pouted, widening my eyes to make it look like a puppy begging for food. I clasped my hands together and placed them in front of my chest, giving him my best pleading look.

He stilled for a moment, biting his lip as he stared at me.

Nothing can beat the puppy dog pout.

"Stop being so cute!" he blurted out, closing his curtain leaving me there.

Tilting my head to the side, I stared at his blue curtains. Well, that was a different result than what I was bargaining for.

Chapter 11

Placing down my tray on the table, I pulled out the chair on sat on it, smiling at Tristan who eyed me suspiciously from across the table.

"Hey?" he questioned, observing me as I uncapped my bottled water.

"Hi," I greeted, trying to sound casual.

Of course, feeling like a bird in a middle of a rhino stampede is completely casual.

Since fishing any information from Jasper is out of the question, Kyla and I agreed to switch places. So here I am with Tristan, and at the other side of cafeteria, Kyla is probably giving Jasper a hefty interview.

Maybe she can find out why Jasper just suddenly left me hanging last night.

Stop being so cute.

What did he mean by that?

Setting my chin on the back of my hand, I quirked my head to the side, "Mind explaining to me why you and Jasper are currently in a silent war?"

His lips pursed into a tight line, shaking his head, he pushed away the tray of his lunch, losing his appetite because of my simple question.

Oh my darling Jasper and Tristan, why can't this be like first grade? Just a simple mud pie and you're all back to being playmates.

"It's complicated, Savannah."

Their friendship is complicated? No, what's complicated is when Jasper and I were so close then I suddenly got jealous because he started to like Kyla. I ignored him and broke our friendship, but miraculously, because of one simple coffee accident, we're back to being friends once again.

Now that's complicated.

Seriously, I just accidently poured coffee on him and here we are. Take that as an advice, ladies.

"Just a hint," I urged.

Sighing, he ran a hand through his hair, "First Kyla, now you."

Well, we are trying to solve a mystery. For what I know, we're working at the same place that caused a rift in your friendship.

"Let's elaborate this," he finally gave in, setting his palm on the table and tapped his fingers on it, "When did I start working at that café?"

Leaning back against my chair, I muttered my answer, "Junior year."

That was easy, I remember back then when we were all so surprised to learn Tristan Hansen was going to work at out little café. Even as a junior, his popularity was slowly rising. I had a reputation as a studious student, but the student body wasn't terrified of me back then.

It was one of the reasons why I befriended Tristan easily without him hesitating. All he knew was that I had a past friendship with his best buddy.

He nodded in confirmation before he continued on, "When did you end your friendship with Jasper?"

"Sophomore year," I replied easily, "And that was when you became his best friend."

He hummed, notifying me that my answer was correct, "Connect the dots, there's this someone in that café."

Tristan started to wiggle his eyebrows, clearly implying something.

Wait, there's someone in One-Eighty?

The only people Jasper knew who was working there are Kyla, Tristan, and I. Why would he be so upset because the three of us were working at that café?

Unless he was jealous of Tristan. Then that means...

"I finally got it!" I slammed my palms on the table as realization flashed across my face.

Of course, how could have I been so blind?

"You do?" he asked in surprised before smirking, "I knew that you were smart."

The bell rang signaling the end of lunch. I swung my backpack over my shoulder as I looked at him, "Thank you, Tristan, I finally know why."

"Glad that you stopped being so dense."

Nodding, the students started to file out of the cafeteria, in that sea of people, Kyla and Jasper were in there.

"Jasper still likes Kyla," I voiced out my theory.

The grin that was on Tristan's face fell quickly. He gaped at me as I started to head out.

"Savannah wait, what did you say?"

I knew he heard me clearly, plus I was being carried away by the crowd, "I'll see you later at work!" I managed to call out before he was finally out of my eyeshot.

The thought of the whole ordeal made something in my heart swell – and it's not in the good way. Jasper still likes Kyla, after all these years.

I shouldn't be sad, mainly because I no longer had any feelings for him.

Right?

Besides, our friendship is so fragile at this moment, that if I grow my old feelings, it will break and shatter.

I should be happy for them, but the sad thing, Kyla likes Tristan. Great, now we have a love triangle going on.

Do I support Jasper's feelings for Kyla or should I support Kyla's endeavor to be Tristan's girlfriend?

Right now, the latter seemed much more appealing to me.

Jasper Dean, why do you have to make things more complicated?

Not only that, I have to face him later as we do our little balcony scene re-enactment for English class.

Oh the joys of school.

Half of the dyads apparently formed a some sort of relationship during the week they were partnered, and let me tell you, watching them make out in front of the whole class was hell of awkward.

"Jasper, Savannah, you're up," Ms. Hughes told us, gesturing for the both of us to go to the front of the classroom.

Jasper and I shared a look as we got up and went into our positions. He gave me an innocent smile and I couldn't help but return it with my own.

I gave the signal and we started to act whatever we have rehearsed. Our moves were flawless, and I got the hang of putting some emotions into my lines.

If I didn't know any better, we were acting like true lovers with the way we talked.

When we were finished, I was about to turn back to the class and take a bow like the usual protocol.

To my complete and utter surprise, Jasper gripped my shoulders, locking me into place. He leaned down and ever so softly, he pressed his lips on the tip of my nose.

It was so light that if my focus weren't solely on Jasper, I would have never felt it.

But I did, and it was enough to make a blush creep to my cheeks.

What the... Did he... I thought...

As quickly as it began, he pulled back, did a fast bow to the students who were gaping as much as I was and, and trudged back to his seat.

When my brain was trying to process everything, Ms. Hughes cleared her throat loudly. My gaze switched to her and she had the biggest grin I had ever seen on a teacher.

I scrambled back to my chair, my face practically red from everything that just happened. From the corner of my eye, I looked at Jasper who wasn't even taking a glance at my direction. He was staring at whatever pair was currently presenting.

That wasn't in the script!

He likes Kyla, he can't just kiss me. Even if it was just on the nose, that's a big no-no. You don't do that to your crush's best friend.

Without a care in the world, I dropped my head on my desk, a sound erupting from the contact. I flinched, but that was the least of my worries.

Now I know why my stomach lurched when I found out why Jasper and Tristan were fighting. No matter how hard I try, there's this little part in my heart that tells me have that I have this microscopic crush on Jasper.

But it's so small, all I need is to push it far away.

Calm yourself, Savannah.

One problem, if Jasper keeps acting like this, the reason why I broke our friendship may just come back.

After all of that, Jasper was the one who started to ignore me. When the bell rang, he practically sprinted out of the classroom.

That went on throughout the day. Of course, the student body quickly discovered the happenings inside that little classroom, Kyla tried to pester me with it but I told her that

I would gladly answer to all of her questions if I wasn't so confused myself.

"Hello there, our little ball of sunshine," Tristan muttered sarcastically as I lazily marched out of the locker room.

I glared at him, dropping on the stool right in front of the counter he was working at.

"I'm confused," I mumbled truthfully, dropping my head in my arms.

I felt him pat my head, chuckling at me, "You should be."

"Not helping!" was my muffled reply.

"Little piece of advice," he told me, "Don't just go jumping into assumptions."

"And what does that mean?" I grumbled, lifting my head.

He shook his head as he continued on with the pastry he was working on. Kyla erupted from the locker rooms and went to the both of us.

"So how's the growing romance between you and Jasper?" she asked for the umpteenth time this day.

Tristan tried to hold back his laugh but failed inevitably. I gave him a dry look and he tried to pass out that laugh for a cough.

Kyla giggled at the scene before turning her attention to me. Oh the irony of this whole thing.

Here's the girl who was part of the reason why everything that's happening is confusing as of right now. I have a mental checklist of things I need to get done.

First, mend Jasper and Tristan's broken friendship, have Jasper to start acting normally, have myself acting normally, do whatever it takes to make sure Kyla and Tristan gets together.

Wait, what was the last one?!

Chapter 12

"Just saying," Tristan said, leaning against his chair, "For a girl who people claim to be smart, you're so clueless."

"It would be great if you will tell me why I'm clueless," I huffed, picking up a fry before dropping it back down on my plate, not finding it in myself to eat.

He and Kyla shared a look before grinning, clearly a gesture that meant they were hiding something from me. This is so frustrating.

Jasper was still avoiding me and so here I am, sitting at the cafeteria with Kyla and Tristan. We still grabbed a bit of attention, but nothing too major. People are starting to get used to the fact that we're all friends now, to the point that nothing seems to be shocking anymore.

The tables have turned and I have no idea why.

From the looks of Tristan and Kyla, I'm seriously missing something in this equation.

Resting my chin on the palm of my hand, I released a sigh. Somebody please clear this up before I go mad.

I tried to get something out of Jasper but all I received was a grunt. I gave him a soft smile and he nodded in acknowledgement to my direction as he sat down on his chair next to me.

That's when I felt it. My stomach lurched as I gripped the edge of my desk, taking deep breaths as I tried to calm myself. Our project was done, we have presented our scene in front of the class, and now, we're back to normal.

The bad kind of normal.

Ms. Hughes was droning on in front of the class, further discussing a literary masterpiece but I just blanked out. My hand was gripping my pen as it hover on the page of my notebook, but my mind was nowhere inside this room.

Damn it, Jasper, you're doing this to me.

Kyla met up with me so we can go to our next class together. She noticed the huge distance between Jasper and I as we walked out of the classroom. She frowned as she subtly pointed at him, I shook my head in response to her silent inquiry.

When I noticed a boy dropped a crumpled piece of paper on the hallway. I bent down and picked it up, staring at the retreating figure. I don't know what made me so mad, but this little piece was enough of to fuel me up.

"No littering!" I yelled, taking a few steps forward before chucking the paper to the student who dropped it.

The boy flinched as the contact, turning to look at me. I pointed at the paper that fell to the ground and I glared at him.

I was back to being a bitch.

Jasper was one of my many spectators and I stared at him. He was standing in the midst of the crowd, looking like he was ready to sprint to my side. The problem was, he didn't.

I kept walking to my next class with Kyla trailing right behind me.

"Savannah," she called out, pulling me into the nearest restroom. She locked the door, preventing anybody from bothering us, "You alright?"

Jasper used to assure me that everything was alright. Did he felt this way when I suddenly broke our friendship or he simply didn't care?

"Kyla, why is Jasper avoiding me?" I asked softly, sitting on the rim of one of the sinks.

"I'm as confused as you are," she replied, standing in front of me, "But if you two solved this before, you can definitely do it again."

"Can't you see?" I stomped, "The fact this is happening again is clearly a sign."

"Oh my gosh!" she groaned, covering her face with her hands, "You're so freaking stubborn."

Please just tell me what the hell are you and Tristan are hiding see we can go to a peaceful land where unicorn exist.

She ran a hand through her hair, letting out a frustrated sigh. She leaned against of the wall, closing her eyes as she let herself think for a moment.

"I love you, you're my best friend, but you're so blind some-times," she mumbled, "I bet you a hundred bucks that before the end of the week, you and Japer will be acting like nothing happened."

My lips pressed into a tight line as she took my hand and pulled me to a starding position, "Now come on, we're already late for class."

She turned around and unlocked the door, swinging it open. She gasped and I scrunched my eyebrows in confusion, walking up to her so I can see what got her so surprised.

Jasper was leaning against the lockers, tapping his foot as he tried occupy himself. When he caught a glance of the opened restroom door, he pushed himself off the lockers and gave us a forced smile.

Kyla glanced at me and mouthed, "I told you so."

Ignoring her, I shook my head at Jasper, "Dean, you're late for class."

The coldness in my voice was enough for him to take a step back. He looked at Kyla and my best friend merely shrugged, deciding to keep herself out of this predicament.

"I'm sorry, Savannah," he let out.

Just a few days ago, he called me out for being a bad friend, I allowed it to slide. Now, he deliberately avoided me and now he's apologizing for it so casually without a bit of explanation why he did it in the first place.

He was mad the last time so I understood him, now, I'm kept in the dark.

"Go to your class, Dean, before I report you for cutting," I told him with authority.

Yes, we were being a hypocrite but I'm annoyed right now. Mood swings is practically my companion right now with how I've been acting.

"Can you leave us alone?" he turned to Kyla, pleading her with his eyes.

Now why would he make her leave when I'm pretty sure he wants nothing but to spend time with her?

I grabbed her hand and I pulled her with me, "To class, Dean!"

While we were heading down the hall, I could hear Kyla mumble under her breath, "So stubborn."

We headed to my house, thankful for a day without work. She was sprawled on my bed as she chewed on her pencil, trying to solve the math problems scrawled on her notebook. I was sitting at my window, the one overlooking our street, finishing the book that I was assigned to do a report on.

My eyes darted out to the sidewalk outside as I saw Macy marching up to our house. I groaned, not really prepared to see her right now.

The doorbell rang and a few second later, my mother was already yelling for me to come down.

"Macy," I said to Kyla, putting on my slippers as I headed downstairs.

She looked like she was ready to leave any time soon. She had business suit on with a big bright smile across her face.

"Hi," I greeted awkwardly.

"Goodbye, Savannah," she told me, stepping to give me a hug, "I'll be back for Christmas."

"You're leaving already?" I asked and I felt her nod. She pulled back, her smile still present on her features.

"People needs somebody to help them with their weddings," she laughed lightheartedly, though I can see it in her eyes that she didn't want to go just yet. Macy was a high profile wedding planner, and she's one of the best out there.

The thing was, she barely had time for a break. She was constantly on demand, people admiring the amount of nuptials she had put together.

"We'll see you soon, Macy," my mother spoke.

"I hope by the time I get back, Savannah will finally forgive my dear brother," she teased, looping an arm around my shoulder, "He's really feeling so down next door."

I bowed my head in shame, how embarrassing is it to be told by his sister? My mother on the other hand, found this situation all too amusing.

"Hopefully," she breathed out, "But my daughter has too thick of a skull to do that."

"Mom!" I yelled in exasperation.

"What?" she blinked innocently, "Don't try to deny it, dear."

I slapped my forehead as Macy and mom shared a laugh. Macy finally stepped away from me and headed back out of the door, "Well, I just wanted to see you all before I left, tell James I said goodbye."

She nodded as she waved for me to lead Macy out. She said her final goodbye to her as I escorted her to the front door.

"Jasper may be all that to everybody else," she said as she was out on my porch, "But he's a total puppy to you."

My face fell as I scrunched my eyebrows. She tucked my hair behind my air as she looked at me with a sisterly fondness, "Take care of Jasper for me, besides, all of us approve of you."

Now, I was more confused than ever. She waved goodbye at me as she walked away from my house, trudging back to her home next door.

Closing the door, I turned to my mother, "What did Macy mean?"

She smirked as she shrugged playfully, "Now where's the fun if I just told you why?"

I returned back to Kyla and it appeared that she was already done with her homework, she stuffed everything back into her back as she fell on my bed, "I think I get it now."

"Huh?"

She pushed herself up as she shot me a wink, "You're only viscous when you and Jasper aren't speaking to each other."

Thinking back, she was good if she managed to observe that. In the duration of the week when Jasper and I started to talk, I managed to cool down. I wasn't threatening every single student death with just a brush of my shoulder. But earlier, when the thought that he was ignoring me settled in, just a simple crumpled piece of paper was enough to tick me off.

How sick does that sound?

"Now let's analyze this," she said, crossing her legs like she was about to solve a big mystery, "He's probably mopping around next door because he has this mentality that you hate him."

I suddenly remembered Macy's words when she said that Jasper was feeling down back at their house. Does that mean he's as upset as I am?

"Now isn't this interesting," she smirked, "You have the mighty Jasper Dean eating at the palm of your hand and he has the devil student body president wrapped around his little finger."

Registering her words, I blushed at her accusations before I grabbed a pillow and threw it at her direction.

That's not it, it's never going be it.

Jasper may have a big effect on me but I'm certainly sure that I affect him that much. Sure, we used to be best friends, but that's impossible.

She laughed as she easily avoided the pillow before she went to stand. She skipped happily to my window and my eyes widened as I realized what she's going to do.

She's going to call Jasper.

She slid the glass open, ready to yell at Jasper. We could clearly see that his window was open and just a simple call was enough for him to hear us.

Before she could even open her mouth, I tackled her to her the ground before covering her mouth with my hand.

"Shush!" I whispered harshly.

She struggled under me, trying to push me off her. I dug my nails at her arm in an attempt to make her stop fighting, because even with her petite body, she was strong.

"Idiot!" we heard somebody. We shared a look before she successfully threw me off of her.

She peeked through my window and I followed the suit, staring at Jasper who was pacing back and forth in his room.

"What?" Kyla asked quietly as we watched him run his hands through his hair multiple times.

"Such a fucking idiot!" he continued to yell.

From the looks of things, he was alone inside his room. The pillow on the floor was signal that before we noticed his self-loathing, he was using that thing to vent out his frustration.

I grew slightly concerned as he dropped to his carpeted floor, burying his face in his hands.

Then I started to have a mental debate if I should ask him or should I just allow him to be dramatic on his own.

He started to lift his head up and I pulled Kyla with me as we ducked down to make sure we weren't caught eavesdropping.

When we were sure he wasn't looking anymore, we continued to watch as we lifted our head to watch him once again.

"Do you have to fucking mess up all the time?" he asked himself.

He looked so annoyed, and all those words were directed to himself. As I watched him pull his hair and pace around the room, my heart clenched with worry.

What has gotten into Jasper?

Chapter 13

When the first snowfall hit the ground of our precious city, every single student in our high school started to buzz about one single topic.

The winter formal.

As much of an excitement it is for everybody, it's not actually a big yahoo to the student council. We pushed this thing until the last minute and now we're running around trying to get everything stamped, signed and ordered.

I even asked my manager at One-Eighty to move my work schedule just to fit enough time to do both jobs.

Jasper and I were still not talking to each other, but Kyla kept me updated on him. They still conversed regularly and even though I'm half of the reason why we're ignoring each other, I still felt something at the pit of my stomach.

Alright, I'll admit it, I'm jealous.

"Pre-order thirty silver balloons and the same quantity for the blue ones," I tapped my pen as I stood at the head of the table.

The long wooden table held the officers of the student body, jotting down notes as we tried to go through with this dance.

Kyla cleared her throat from my right side and I stared down at her, "Yes?"

"We already went ahead with the balloons," she informed, though with the smirk she was showing me, I was worrying that she was implying something else.

I'll worry about that later, we still have to plan everything else.

Papers were rotating around the table, each member inspecting the print, stamping it before signing and then passing it to the next person.

"We'll start drafting the floor plan tomorrow," I told them, tucking in the stack of paperwork into an envelope, "If you don't have any questions, you may leave."

"Wait!" Kyla halted, shooting up from her seat.

All heads turned to her and I asked, "Any questions?"

"Why don't we head to the gym right now?"

Groans erupted from the people inside the room and I quite agreed with them, we were all exhausted.

"It's been a busy day, I'm sure we could do that tomorrow," I told her, picking up my bag, "Meeting adjourned."

The screeching of chairs sounded across the room as people started to pack up and leave, throwing goodbyes at each other in the process.

Kyla pouted as we were the final two to exit the room, locking the door before we started to head down the hallway. Of course, my best friend still remained persistent.

"It would have been better if we went to the gym," she grumbled under her breath.

She was clearly up to something, I just have no idea what it is.

The next day, I had no choice but to break my promise to Kyla, especially after I had received a call from my manager.

I was parked outside Kyla's house, pressing on my horn to alert her that I was already here to pick her up. My ringtone started blaring and I picked it up with a tired sigh.

"Hello?"

"I know you asked for a reschedule, but can at least one of you two come to work, we're really short on staff?"

I tapped the steering wheel and closed my eyes contemplating on my answer. With everything, I had no time to spare for things like this. Aside from the preparation for the dance, I still have enough drama to go deal with.

It's been only a few week or so and I've been missing Jasper like crazy. We ignored each other during English class even though we're only a meter apart.

Not only that, it seems that he's still mad at Tristan. The latter kept reassuring me that Jasper will cool off soon enough, but from the looks of everything, we're not really moving forward with anything.

Wait a minute, maybe Tristan can help me.

"Will Tristan be there?" I asked, looking out to the front door of Kyla's house, making sure she wasn't out yet.

I heard some ruffling from the other line, the manager was probably looking at our schedules to check about my question, "Yes, he's scheduled to work later this afternoon."

"Great, I'll be there," I stated and then I saw Kyla head out of her house, waving goodbye at her mother who was standing at their porch.

Giving her a goodbye, I hung up and threw my phone into my bag. I rolled down my window and waved at my best friend's mother.

"So are we prepping up the gym later?" Kyla questioned enthusiastically as she slid into the vehicle, strapping on her seatbelt as she threw her bag to the back.

Shaking my head, I pulled out of her driveway, turning to drive to the main street, "Can't, our boss asked if I could work later."

Her face fell and from the chirpy look she had on, her expression morphed into something of frustration, "I'll take the damn shift for you!"

We can't do that, Kyla, I'm up to something with our resident chef.

"You were the one assigned to organizing the table arrangement, you're much more needed than I am," I told her, stopping at a red light, "It's just one day, and you can manage without me, just call me if you have any troubles."

She crossed her arms over her chest as she looked absolutely aggravated with my statement.

Calm down, girl, it's just one day, and it's not like I'm stealing Tristan away from you.

The thing is, Jasper threw me a weird look when I breezed past him during English. He was wearing the same expression Kyla had when we dismissed yesterday after the meeting. It was a look I knew all too well, he wanted to ask me something.

Ask away, Jasper, I'll answer. I'm ready to call quits if you're going to talk to me.

Just as what I predicted, he kept his lips shut as the rest of the class rolled on and I sighed rather loudly when he stood up after the bell rang.

Kyla was no help either, she kept insisting that I should help with the floor plan for the gym. I had my trust on her that she was perfectly capable of doing this job without me.

I had to wait until she wasn't looking before I could sprint away from her. She had me under the radar the whole day because she was so against me working.

I'm sorry, Kyla, but it's time for me to stop being a moron and finally attempt to mend my friendship with Jasper.

"Tristan!" I called, running up to him after I had changed into my uniform.

He looked up from the batter that he was mixing and gave me a smile, "Glad to finally see you in the café again, where's Kyla?"

"Don't even mention her," I groaned, pulling out a stool. I had enough with her, the only thing she hadn't done to stop from leaving was gluing me to her side.

He gave me a curious look but with the face I was sporting, he shrugged it off, doing the wiser decision of letting the topic go, "So what does our wonderful president need from me?"

They did say that the best way to a man's heart is through his stomach. Well, Jasper had placed up a huge wall, it's going to take me a buffet to even penetrate him. So let's do this in a lighter way, a cake.

"Help me bake something for Jasper."

The grin that made its way on his face was priceless. His eyes twinkled as he instantly abandoned the batter he was mixing and gave it to another chef that was walking at our direction.

Weird.

"Let's start!" he chirped, breezing past me as he walked through the shelves, cabinets, doors and other places in the kitchen, grabbing ingredients and tools for our little cake.

We ended up whipping a chocolate cake. While it was baking in the oven, Tristan was helping me mix up the icing.

"Why are you so nice," I hummed mindlessly, "I mean, you're fighting with Jasper and yet you're here helping me make something for him."

He clicked his tongue, pushing the bowl to my side of the counter, "Because I know the reason why we're fighting," he said, "And instead of feeling upset, I'm actually happy for the bloke that I call my best friend."

Now can you please tell me why you two are arguing?

He pulled the cake out of the oven and as he started to put the icing, I filled up a piping bag before practicing on a piece of parchment paper.

I turned out to be crap at doing this so I allowed Tristan to do the job of scribbling my simple message on the cake.

Sorry.

It was one word and I hoped it was enough to get my message across. He boxed up the thing and taught me how to put a fancy ribbon or it.

"Now I need to find a way to bring it tomorrow," I sighed.

Kyla would suspect something if she saw me carrying out tomorrow. As much as I wanted this fight to be over, I don't want her babbling about it too much.

"I'll do it," Tristan volunteered, grabbing the bowls we used and dumping it into the sink, "I'll ask the lunch lady to store it in the cafeteria fridge, just ask her for it any time you're ready to give to Jasper."

I squealed and give him the biggest hug, "I owe you big time, anything you want, just tell me!"

Something changed in his expression and as I pulled away, he tapped his chin, "Anything?"

Alright, now I'm scared. Looking at the cake I made, I nodded at him. It couldn't be too bad, right?

Besides, Jasper's forgiveness is worth it.

"Help me with Kyla," he finally admitted, shooting me a pleading look.

My mouth gaped open before I closed it again. I kept repeating it, looking like a goldfish as I stared at him.

Tristan likes Kyla.

The smile on my face couldn't express how happy I am for these two. Now just a little push and we have an award winning couple in our hands.

"Sure."

Kyla was positively glaring at me when she picked me up this morning. As if the dirty look wasn't enough, she stated that I was her slave because I ran away from her yesterday.

Remember, Savannah, Jasper's forgiveness is worth it.

"Let's head to the gym," Kyla said, grabbing my arm after the last period bell rung.

I shook away her grasp on me as I turned my gaze to the cafeteria doors, "I have to do something first, I'll be right there."

"You're not running away again!" she demanded, ready to pull me with her.

"Look, I'll buy you that freaking sweater you wanted," I groaned, stepping away from her, "Just let me do something before I do there."

She eyed me carefully, considering my bribery. Trust me, you're going to be so thankful for me on the day you and Tristan get together.

"You have fifteen minutes," she grumbled, turning on her heel to head to the gym.

I exhaled through my nose as I ran to the cafeteria, requesting my cake from the lunch lady. She smiled warmly at me as she handed me the box.

"He's a lucky guy," she stated softly, looking at the cake in my hands.

I'm not sure about that. I'm stubborn, a bitch, a freaking weirdo, yet he's still here with me.

"Thank you," I said to her instead as a polite gesture.

I couldn't find Jasper anywhere. I scouted the whole school and I had no such luck. I called Tristan to see if he knew his best friend's whereabouts but he resentfully told me that he was already on his way to the café so he knew nothing about Jasper.

It didn't help that Kyla started calling me, demanding that I go to the gym this instant.

"It's been fifteen minutes!" was her final words to me before she hung up.

Ah my dear best friend!

My finger was hovering Jasper's name on my contact list, contemplating if I should call him or not. But if I do that, it will ruin the surprise of this whole thing.

Kyla shot me another text and I groaned, might as well shut her up. Going down the steps, I kept my eyes peeled as if Jasper would suddenly jump out.

I'm seriously hoping for that.

Unfortunately, I found myself outside of the gym doors with the box still in my hands. Well, here goes nothing.

It was like going inside the gym is a raising of a white flag, admitting defeat after my search for that freaking basketball player that has been messing with my mind for the longest time.

Maybe he went home already.

Frowning, I pushed the doors open, my head down as I did so.

I didn't want to lift my gaze. I'm now inside, but the real surrender was looking at what has gotten Kyla so worked up.

"Savannah!" I heard the voice I had been searching for all day.

I snapped my head up and I all but gaped at the sight in front of me.

When Kyla said that they went ahead with the balloons, she wasn't kidding.

You know those letter balloons? Well, seven of those things were lined up, blue and silver alternated as it spelled out a message. Jasper was standing at the center, his arms crossed over his chest. With his stance, it looked like he was confident about everything but one look in his eyes, I knew that he was nervous.

What the hell was he nervous about? That I won't like this?

Apparently, that was the case.

Looking at the balloons, I just stared at awe.

I M S O R R Y

People inside the gym started clapping, but Jasper was frozen. His face completely mortified when I didn't move from my spot.

I looked down at my cake and I felt slightly embarrassed. He went out on his way to do something this big, while I on the other hand, just baked him a flimsy cake. Actually, Tristan was the one who made it, I just attempted and failed at every step.

"Please say something," he begged, staring right at me.

My eyes roamed around the room until it landed on Kyla. Out of everybody, she looked the most curious. It was as if she was predicting my moves, what will happen, but at the same time, she was afraid that her assumptions was wrong.

Now I know why she was so insistent on going to the gym. I then pictured Jasper setting this up two days ago, and then doing the same yesterday, but every time he did it, Kyla would go inside and tell him the bad news that I wasn't coming.

"Can you please leave us alone?" I requested softly, yet my voice still held authority. Kyla herded everybody outside, but not without a wink directed at us before she finally closed the doors of the gym.

It's only Jasper and me.

Walking up to him, I noticed that he stiffened. Stopping in front of him, I thrust the box to him. He looked down on it before lifting his hands to grab it.

"It's not as grand as yours," I mumbled. He pulled on the ribbon and opened the lid. He stared at the thing for a full minute, processing everything.

I was scared on how he will react. Will he laugh at my failed attempt? Be disappointed because compared to his, it was a very small gesture?

He reached out and ran his finger through the icing, placing it to his lips to taste the chocolate goodness.

He gingerly put down the box on one the tables already set up. He bent down and wrapped his arms around my waist, hugging me as he lifted me off the ground.

"Jasper!" I squealed, grabbing onto his shoulders.

"You're amazing, you know that?" he grinned.

I'm amazing? He's the one who did this balloon thing.

"Am I forgiven?" I asked when put me down, wringing my hands as I waited for his answer.

"Am I forgiven?" he fired back my question.

We stared at each other before bursting in laughter. Here we are, scared that we have offended the other one, but in fact we were just running in circles.

He held my hand in his and I melted at his touch. He ran circles with his thumb and I softly smiled.

"If we ever argue again, I'm going to beat myself up for being such a fucking idiot," he grunted.

"Nope, I'm going to beat myself up for being so stubborn," I quipped back, finally feeling relieved.

He chuckled, wrapping an arm around my shoulder as he turned me back to the balloons, "Those are my second order, I accidentally popped the first ones when Kyla said you weren't coming the first day."

I pictured Jasper running around the gym, being frantic that I wasn't coming and I don't know why, but it actually made me happy. He cared enough to do that.

Reaching out, I squeezed his hand and turned to the box on the table, "How about we feast on that thing and forget everything."

"Agreed," he nodded, leading me to where it sat, "Let's never fight again."

I laughed as I shook my head, "Impossible," I stated with a smile, "Because we're Jasper and Savannah."

Chapter 14

"Now tell me again why you and Jasper were fighting?" Kyla asked as she stepped out of the dressing room, twirling in front of me the dress that she had tried on.

I paused for a moment, wracking my brain for a reason. You know what? I don't even know anymore.

Shrugging I examined the dress before giving her a shake of my head, "The important thing is that we've made up."

She nodded before turning back to the dressing room to try on a new dress, "I guess that's better than you two fighting," she sighed as I heard her unzipping the article of clothing, "You're seriously another person when you're not in speaking terms with him."

I sighed as I crashed down on one of the chairs, playing with the paper bag that held the dress that I bought for the winter formal.

Trust me, Kyla, I know that I'm different without him.

"Has anyone asked you to the dance yet?" I inquired, lifting my head to meet the closed curtain that concealed her body.

Tristan has still been asking for my help in order to get together with Kyla. As much that he has confidence in everything else, he turns out to be nothing but shy when it comes to asking out a girl he truly likes, and in this case, we have the smitten Kyla Bailey.

"Nope," she replied instantly, opening the curtain as she stepped out, waiting for my verdict.

Seriously, I've already given Tristan instructions on what she likes or some options on how to ask her, all he has to do is to act.

"Nice," I nodded in approval at her dress. She grinned before walking back to take it off and change back into her own clothes.

"Do you think Tristan will ask me?" she sighed wistfully as I heard shuffling from her side of the curtain.

If he grows a pair, yes, he will ask you.

"Do you think Jasper will ask you?" she then asked, opening the curtain, clutching all of the clothes she had tried on, dumping them to a saleslady as she took the one that she chose to the counter.

I froze at her statement before frowning. Do I want Jasper to ask me to the dance? Yes, a thousand yes. Do I think Jasper will ask me to the dance? No.

Shaking my head as an answer to her question, she merely smirked as she handed the cashier the dress before fishing for her wallet in her purse.

The way she just smirked actually makes me fear for my sanity.

"I bet you that Jasper will ask you to the dance," she proposed, handing the cashier her payment, "If he doesn't, I'll buy you anything that you want."

With her tone of voice, I could almost picture her in a white outfit stroking her cat as she looks at me mischievously.

That made me instinctively take a step away from her. She looked at me before bursting into a fit of giggles as she took the paper bag and receipt of her dress.

"Trust me, he will ask you," she winked, thanking the cashier before walking out of the store.

The mall was particularly busy, which was no surprise considering it was the weekend. We were a week away from the winter formal, and thank the heavens, we only had to put a few minor finishing touches on the decorations for the gym and we were good to go.

How can she be so sure when it's pretty obvious that all Jasper wants to be is friends?

I, for one, don't even know what I want us to be.

More than friends? Possibly.

"Speak of the devil," Kyla mumbled, pointing at a direction.

I followed her finger and my lips pressed into a tight line as I saw Jasper roaming the mall with his friends.

A few from the basketball team as with a few girls from the cheer team.

My ego is then wounded when I saw a girl wrap her fingers around his wrist as she tugged him to look at something from a shop window.

"Want to go eat lunch?" I asked hastily, praying that Jasper doesn't see us.

"Huh?" that was the only that was able to leave her mouth when I suddenly grabbed her hand and pulled her to the escalator.

We shuffled through the crowds as I kept my eye on Jasper, making sure he doesn't look at our way. Why am I even hiding in the first place?

He let out a hearty laugh from what one of his friends said and that made something in heart sink. He never laughed that way when he was with me.

Ouch, just plain ouch.

My grasp of Kyla's hand loosened just as we were about to step on the elevator and I looked down, biting my lip.

"Go to him," Kyla muttered next to me, giving me an encouraging look, "He'll be happy to see you."

He's already happy, can't you see that?

"Come," she tugged on my arm as we started to slowly walk to their small group. One of the boys caught sight of me and tapped on Jasper's shoulder to turn his attention away from the chatting girl.

He lit up like a Christmas tree and that made me smile a little bit.

He excused himself as ran up to me, meeting us halfway, "Hey."

"Hi," I mumbled, looking at his friends. No emotion was present on their faces as they waited patiently for the famous Jasper Dean.

"What are you doing here?" he asked, before his eyes landed on the shopping bags we had clutched in our hands, "You're shopping."

Nodding, Kyla wrapped an arm around my shoulder and grinned at Jasper, "We were dress shopping for the winter formal."

Jasper smiled, nodding at the piece of information as he continued to stare at us. Kyla groaned as she did it in a more obvious tone.

"Savannah here got a beautiful dress," she started to urge, "It would be amazing under the lights of the dance floor."

Nope, still nothing from him.

I wanted to facepalm so hard because of her, if she was trying to make Jasper ask me to the dance, she could have at least done it in a more subtle way – this just looks like I was desperate.

"You know dancing," she continued, I was one more second away from forcing her mouth shut, "With a partner, a boy," she looked at him hopefully.

Jasper, you're an amazing guy and as much as I want Kyla to shut up, get the damn hint – even if the possibility is an absolute zero.

Maybe he actually gets it, but just doesn't want to ask me.

"With a date!" she practically yelled to his face.

"A date?" he suddenly gasped in surprise, a bit of anger flashed quickly in his eyes, "You got a date?"

I opened my mouth to deny his accusations but he grabbed my shoulder and forced me to look into his eyes, "Who is he?"

Down boy, there's no date.

"Calm down," I told him, reaching out to release his hold of me, but he shook me lightly, his eyebrows scrunching with sadness.

"Who is he?"

I didn't want to see that look on his face. If he's going to play the overprotective best friend card, now's not the time.

I reached out and massaged his forehead, trying to get rid of that emotion taking over his face, "No date."

"No date," he repeated, closing his eyes as he released me, relaxing under my touch.

I like it when we're acting like this.

Kyla shot Jasper a disappointed look as she shook her head in defeat. At least she tried, Jasper is just dense like that.

"Jasper, we're going to lunch!" one of his friends hollered at him.

Jasper looked down on me then back to his friends and I balled my hands into a fist, allowing my nails to dig into my palm.

To my complete surprise, he waved at them goodbye, "I'll see you guys next time."

They all looked at me and I suddenly felt so small under their gaze. The heck, I've been terrorizing the school since the start of the year and a few of his friends looking at me like that got me all tiny and insecure.

When I turned to Kyla, I could practically see her beaming in mischief as she fished for her phone inside her purse and faked a gasp.

Seriously girl, take some acting lessons.

"My mom just texted," she announced loud enough to steal Jasper's attention from saying goodbye to his friends, "I need to go."

Bullshit, this is just another one of your plans.

"But you drove me here," I pouted, attempting to convince her not to leave.

I don't think I can handle it.

"I'll drive you home," Jasper instantly volunteered, he then look at me with those pleading eyes, asking me not to go.

Now who in the world who has a heart of stone that can reject that?

"Great," she grinned, pulling me into a side hug, "I'll call you later."

When she said those words, it meant that she wanted a full report on how this day had gone. She smiled as she started to walk away, swaying the paper bag in her hand.

"Shall we?" Jasper asked, taking my shopping bag from my hands as he took out a hand for me to take.

Turning to where Kyla had disappeared then to the spot where his friends previously stood, I took a deep breath as I settled my hand on top of his, "We shall."

The grin he showed me was the best thing in the world, it looked like he had won the lottery.

Wrapping his fingers around my hand, he started to tug me to start walking.

"Lunch?"

And that was how I ended up on a table inside one of the restaurants located inside the mall as I clutched the menu in my hand, scanning over the names of the dishes listed off.

I looked up at Jasper and he still had that silly grin on his face, "What's funny?"

"Nothing," he said, covering his face with a menu, "This almost looks like a date."

A blush crept up to my cheeks as I started to focus my eyes on the menu, trying to make it a distraction.

How can he just say that out of the blue?

"Wouldn't this be better if Kyla hadn't left?" I mumbled unconsciously.

"Kyla?" he suddenly dropped the menu and looked at me with a questioning look, "Why?"

Because you like her, duh.

"Don't you want to date her?" I muttered rather bitterly.

The only reason why I'm not so depressed was because I knew Tristan was going to get Kyla, well, if he ever makes a move.

Might as well have this conversation with Jasper, but I'm not just going to blurt out that it was the reason why I broke our friendship years ago.

"Kyla?" he repeated with the same tone, "You thought I wanted to date her?"

Doesn't he want to date her? Am I right or am I missing something?

"Am I wrong?" I quirked a brow.

"Wrong!" he practically yelled which made me lean back on my chair. He saw my reaction as he settled himself back on his chair, "Sorry."

"Wrong," I said in audible whisper.

He didn't like Kyla?

Hell, I broke our friendship for no good reason. I might as well slap myself.

He doesn't like Kyla, the look on his face said nothing but absolute sincerity, and I had no other choice but to believe.

Another emotion was present on it, he looked almost worried.

"You alright?"

He fisted the table cloth as he shook his head, "How long have you thought that I liked her?"

"Freshman year," I replied quietly. And there goes another masterpiece on Savannah Everett's wall of shame, "Isn't that the reason why you and Tristan are fighting?"

"Wrong!" he repeated and my mouth clamped shut.

Tristan Hansen, you have a lot of explaining to do because I'm thoroughly confused.

"Damn it, Savannah, all this time you thought I liked Kyla?" he asked though it was pretty obvious what my answer was.

He buried his head in hands as he pulled on his brown lock, muttering curses under his breath.

Seriously, Savannah, why are you such an idiot?

Remember what's our new plan? Make up for being such a moron to him.

So instead on dwelling on this, I looked around the restaurant and sighed, we gathered up the attention of the people near our table.

Again, I'm an idiot.

I reached out and held his wrist, slightly pulling it away so he'll release his hair and lift his head to look at me.

"How about we just enjoy lunch?" I suggested, also let's forget my stupidity.

He nodded, calling for the waiter to take our orders. Just like the previous meals I had with him, I didn't even need to open my mouth, he already knew what I wanted to eat.

He eyed the paper bag on the floor then looked at me, "Is really beautiful?"

"The dress?"

He nodded and waited for my answer, looking at me with outmost interest, though I'm pretty sure the topic of what my dress looks like actually bores him to death.

Though I'm quite swelling with pride because of the one I chose, "Yeah."

"Will it really be amazing at the dance floor?" he asked, referring to Kyla's statement from earlier.

I want to just tell him that it was her plot to lure him into asking me out. It was really simple, not sequins, no father, no glitter, just something plain, but I admit, the simplicity is what makes it beautiful.

Shrugging, I gave him a truthful answer, "I don't really know."

"What color is it?"

"Why are you suddenly so interested with my dress," I laughed and he stilled, staring at me.

I covered my mouth with my hand, was my laugh embarrassing or something?

"I like it when you're happy," he grinned.

Ah my dear Jasper, if this continues, I'll start liking you much more than how I used to back then.

"Can I drive you to the dance?" he asked, "You know, to save gas?"

I lifted a brow at him as he tugged on the sleeve of the sweater he was wearing, waiting for my answer.

That came out of the blue and with the matter he was sweating, I don't know how to take it.

"Sure."

It might not be the date like Kyla bargained for, but as I know it, this is as close as its going to get.

Chapter 15

Pinning my hair up, I laughed along with Tristan as he tried to wheeze out a sentence from the other line, "Again, he's taking you to the dance to save gas?"

Tristan called me just so because he was asking if I could get Kyla to dance with him, or if it was too much if he suddenly drove to her house and ask her to the dance on the spot.

I think we all know how that would end up in.

Somewhere along the conversation, I told him about how Jasper, being such an eco-friendly guy, asked if we could drive together to the dance to save gas. The prices must be hitting him really hard if that's happening, but even I'm not stupid enough to realize he wants to go to the event together.

Just the thought of it makes me all happy inside. It might not be a date, but hey, I'll take what I can get.

"Yeah," I couldn't help but giggle, remembering the way Jasper conveyed it.

When going to a dance, I'm pretty sure the environment is the last thing in a guy's mind.

"I can't believe him," I heard him say as I placed another bobby pin to clip away my fringe, "He really has to man up."

"Says that guy who chickened out on asking Kyla to the dance," I couldn't help but bring up.

"Don't remind me," he groaned in frustration, "Are you sure pink is the right color."

I couldn't help but roll my eyes at my phone, as if it was Tristan himself. He goes and asks me for the color of her dress and now he's complaining because it was pink.

"Of course," I said with exaggeration, "Plus, pink is such a manly color."

"Don't even start!"

"That's actually your fault for not asking her out earlier," I told him, reaching for my earrings, "Or even a day before."

Who in the world asks a girl to the dance on the same day of the event? The answer, Tristan Hansen.

"At least I didn't make up a stupid excuse of being so concerned with the consumption of gas," he defended himself.

He and Jasper should really become friends again, these two are practically the same. I mean, they are both pretty lame when it comes to asking girls in dances like these.

"Well I have to finish getting ready, I'll talk to you later tonight," I spoke, standing up as I went to scout for my shoes, "And hopefully you'll have a date by then."

I heard him chuckle and I smiled, "Right, save a dance for me."

He hung up and I took my phone, locking it before I slotted it inside my clutch. Well, now for my shoes.

Tristan is a great guy and Kyla is a great girl, put them together and we'll have an extremely adorable couple. Just saying, I've called dibs on being the maid of honor.

Walking to my window, I slightly opened the curtain to take peek of Jasper's room. He was facing the mirror and I couldn't help but laugh at the coincidence.

He was wearing a blue tie, the same color and shade of my dress.

It's either he found out and matched purposely with me, or he just found the color blue appealing.

He was on the phone with someone, rubbing his temples in anxiousness and I couldn't help but wonder who he is talking to.

Shaking my head, I closed the curtain. Here we go, tonight's the first dance that I'll have with Jasper – if he asks me to anyways.

Walking down the stairs I almost turned back into my room when I saw my mom clutching a camera with the biggest grin on her face. I turned to dad and gave him a pleading look and he only shrugged, telling me to just go with whatever my mom wants.

"I couldn't wait until that boy gets here," she almost squealed. This is my mom everybody, the teenager of this household, "Finally, I thought he will never ask my daughter out."

"It's not a date, mom," I denied, crossing my arms over my chest, "We're just carpooling."

"Hush up," she chided, "You two are so cute together."

I resisted to slap my forehead as I turned my attention to dad, "What do you have to say about this."

Another shrug, leaning against the wall, "As long as he doesn't hurt my princess, I'll keep him alive."

I gaped at the two of them, who has parents like this?

Oh yeah, me!

The doorbell rang and my mom let out an excited squeak. I swear, she's more enthusiastic than me.

"Mom!" I complained as I turned to get the door.

I could see his figure from here, fixing his tie as he held something red in his arms. When I opened the door, I realized that it was a fresh bouquet of roses, arranged to its beauty.

"Hi," I greeted with a smile.

I wasn't able to get a good view of him earlier through the window, but he looked absolutely dashing in his suit. You could see the blue vest and blue tie underneath the black coat he had on, looking down at me with his eyes twinkling with the foyer lights.

Now how am I going to enter the gym with this good looking of a person next to me? This will feel so downgrading.

With my greeting, the only thing I got for return was a, "Wow."

Is there something wrong with my dress? Are my heels too short or too high? Am I wearing too much makeup?

He cleared his throat to stop myself from my internal panic as he slowly passed the roses into my arms, I looked up at him then down to the roses.

Alright then, he got me roses, get me something to hold on because I might faint.

He saw my reaction and he looked down nervously on the floor, "My mom told me to get you roses, because it's the dance and all."

"So these are from your mom?" I quirked a brow and his head shot up, waving his hands up in the air.

"No, it's not that, they are from me, I got them for you, are they too much? Should have I ordered the smaller bouquet or did you want something bigger?" he started to ramble, "Because I can get you something bigger, I mean, I may not be able to give them to you tonight, but you know what I mean," he paused for a moment, collecting his thoughts before opening his mouth once again, "Wait, I'm probably not making any sense, but I swear, if you don't like roses, I can get you carnations, lilies, or whatever you like."

"Jasper," I attempted to stop him.

"It's too much isn't it?" he groaned, it would be great if I can get a word out, "I'm sorry, I'll get you something small, I knew you were a simple type of girl. I'm so stupid, why did I have to order big one?"

I reached out for his hand and squeezed it, calling for his attention. He halted for a moment and went to look at me.

"I love them, thank you," I smiled and thanked sincerely.

His mouth clamped shut and he breathed out through his nose in relief, "Thank God!"

My mom popped her head in the foyer and grinned at the both of us.

"Sorry for my mom in advance," I whispered to him, closing the door when he was safely inside.

Please have mercy.

"Ariel, calm down," my father told her, before he finally allowed her to take pictures of us.

When I meant that she wanted to take some pictures, I meant a lot. She was pressing the button so many times that with the frame by frame pictures that she has, you can make some sort of animation.

"Mom, I think that's enough," I said in a quiet plea for her to stop.

"This is a mother's joy so smile," she told me in a scolding manner. Her logic is absolutely amazing!

Jasper chuckled at my mother's antics and I couldn't help but blush in embarrassment. Dad finally placed a hand on mom's shoulder, telling her to finally stop.

You could clearly see who the sane one in their relationship is.

"Have fun, kids," dad said, escorting us to the door. He turned to Jasper and clapped a hand on his back, "You know my rules, and I expect you to follow them."

"Yes sir," he nodded, opening the door and allowed me to step outside, "I'll keep her safe."

Dad said his goodbyes before shutting the door, finally leaving us alone.

One of the advantages of having Jasper live next door to you and being best friends with him for a long time is that my parents already trusts him, he already knows how to get to their good side.

It was freezing cold so we hurried to the car as fast as we can. Looking outside, I couldn't help but marvel at the few snow that was sprinkled by Mother Nature all over the pavement. It was like the perfect finishing touch to the decoration prepared for this night.

The school came into view and I took a deep breath, clasping my hands around my clutch, I turned to smile at Jasper, "Thanks for the roses and the ride."

"It's normal to do this for your date," he shrugged casually and I froze. It took a full minute of staring at my reaction before he finally realized what he just said. He looked mortified as he gripped on the steering wheel, his mouth gaping wide.

Nodding, I waved his mistake off, opening the door so I can step out.

"Close that!" he frantically said making yelp in surprise, automatically slamming the car door. I turned to him, my eyebrows scrunching in confusion. He held up a finger, silently telling me to wait, as he stepped out of the vehicle.

What is he doing?

He rounded the car until he was at my side, fixing his tie before he opened the door for me. He give me a small smile, offering a hand for me, "Ma'am."

I laughed at this as I took his hand and carefully went out of the car, "Why thank you, kind sir."

When Jasper Dean is being a gentleman to you, all you want to do is be by his side.

Sadly, once we entered the gym, he was instantly crowded and dragged away by his friends, demanding for group shots or a dance.

And that meant it was my cue to step away from him and allow him to bask in his social spotlight.

Maybe I can spot Kyla or Tristan somewhere so I won't look like a total loner.

As I was walking by, people commended the formal and I couldn't help but feel proud of my work. Looking around, it really was a success. Some people even suggested to hang mistletoes at some places, catching people whenever they walk under it.

It was quite entertaining if you ask me.

"There you are!" I heard my best friend's voice before I was suddenly tugged away from admiring the decorations.

She looked absolutely radiant and Tristan was right behind her, talking to one of his teammates. She looped an arm around mine and she grinned right at me, "He freaking asked me!"

I looked past her and caught Tristan's eyes, he sent me a wink and I let out a laugh, turning back to Kyla, "That's great!"

I could almost imagine the look of her face when Tristan suddenly popped to her house, asking her to go to the dance together. I knew from the start that it was an automatic yes from her, I wouldn't be surprised if she fainted on the spot.

"Where's Jasper?" she asked, looking around the perimeter, "Aren't you his date?"

Shaking my head, I denied the idea completely, "He just asked me to carpool."

Rolling her eyes at my statement, I heard her scoff, "You and I both know he wanted a date."

Looking down at my feet, I let out a small sigh of defeat, "That was what I wanted to think."

Sensing my mood shift, she frowned, "What happened?"

Scanning the room, my eyes finally landed on him and I gestured him to Kyla. She turned her attention to him and clicked her tongue when she saw that he was perfectly having the time of his life with his friend.

"Idiot," she mumbled, with her tone, it meant that she didn't want me to hear

Tristan finally finished talking to his teammate and made his way over to us, I saw him wrap an arm around Kyla's waist which made her turn into a love struck mess.

"You look amazing, Savannah," he complimented and I gave him my word of appreciation as I tried to hold back my laughter.

As good looking he was, he can't rock the color. He looked silly with the baby pink dress shirt with his neck tie having a tinge of fuchsia.

The first slow dance of the night started to play after the long playlist of party music. Tristan instantly dragged a blushing Kyla to the dance floor and I waved them, mouthing good luck to the both of them.

I swear, they're going to be a couple before the night ends.

Claiming a chair I sighed, resting my chin on my palm, looking around the room. All I want is to see this dance as a success, a clear indication that the student council's effort was not put into waste. Looking around, I knew we have done our goal.

But why am I feeling so down?

"Hey, you alright?" Jasper popped up, walking up to me.

Nodding softly, "Yeah."

He frowned at my short answer, something that was clearly a lie. Before he can even interrogate me, another one his cheerleader friends wrapped am arm around him and pulled him into the dance floor.

I want him to ask me to dance, just one song and I'll be happy for the night.

God, I sound so pathetic!

Tristan returned with Kyla and he basically pulled me with him to dance. I hesitated but I remembered that he requested for a dance, so I just went with it.

"Kyla told me," he said, his gaze making his way to Jasper who was dancing with the sixth girl since the slow dance started, "He's an idiot."

Yup, these two are really meant to be.

"I don't blame him actually," I told him, "It was just me getting too excited."

"You need a Jasper and Jasper needs a Savannah," he stated.

"Thanks Tristan," I smiled softly, "But I don't think so, he only sees me as a friend."

"Now what made you think that?"

I bit my lip, shaking my head, "Not once did he ask me to dance."

"The night is young," he chuckled.

Turns out, Jasper had no intention of dancing with me. The roses were cute, the ride was nice, but it all came down to having fun on the dance floor. I didn't acquire what I was hoping for.

So now, standing by the school doors, waiting for him to say goodbye to his friends, I pushed by the sadness that was making its way through my system.

Kyla and Tristan said their goodbyes to me before they both headed their way, having the night that they deserve.

Well, at least my two best friends are happy.

"Ready?" Jasper asked merrily, stepping beside me as he tried to spot his car.

Without a word, I climbed the down the steps and made my way to his vehicle, tapping my foot impatiently on the ground as I waited for him to unlock the car.

I practically ripped the door open when he did so, sliding into the passenger seat.

"Did I do something wrong?" he questioned, pure curiosity and uncertainness in his voice.

No, you didn't do anything wrong, I just expected too much. I really am an idiot.

"No," came another short reply out of me as I stared out of the window, watching everything pass by, keeping my mouth shut.

When we stopped in front of my house, I was just glad this night was over. I want nothing more than to take off this dress, wash my makeup off and get to bed.

"Savannah," he said softly when I went to get the roses he got me, "Wait."

I waited the whole night for you to ask me, now, I had enough.

It was clear, I was just a friend to him.

"I clearly did something wrong," he mumbled.

Nope, I'm just a bitch, sorry about that.

"No you didn't," I denied.

Staring at me intently, he ran a hand through his hair as he let out a sigh, "Can we dance?"

Is he serious right now?

"Are you asking me to dance?" this is ridiculous, "The formal is over, Jasper."

I swear, my tone was getting colder than the temperature outside.

"I've wanted to ask you all night, and there's always an interruption," he groaned, "I just want to dance with you."

The frustration in his voice was growing with every word he uttered, "Please."

"B-but it's cold," I sound so pathetic.

He took off his suit ccat and draped it over my shoulders, giving me a pleading look, "Please."

I don't know what made me do it, was it Jasper's defeated look? The way he looked at me so intently? The way he gave me his coat? The idea cf finally dancing with him? I have no idea why, but I nodded.

The next thing I knew, he was escorting me out of the car, making me stand on the sidewalk of my driveway as he connected his earphones to his phone, handing me one of the pieces as he plugged one into his ear.

Due to the fact my legs were still exposed, it was freezing, but when he pulled me closer to him, I found myself being warmed up by his body.

"Just relax," he chuckled when he realized how stiff I was. He tucked his phone into his pocket, holding one of my hand in his as his other one held onto my waist.

A blush crept into my cheeks as I bit my lip, allowing myself to listen to his song choice.

I love it when you just don't care

He tried to guide me but we both knew that I was horrible at this. He took a step forward and instructed me to take one back.

I love it when you don't take no

This practically useless, I stepped on his foot and he yelped, I shot him an apologizing look as I tried to concentrate on dancing.

I love it when you do what you want cause you just said so

"Chill," he laughed, "Take off your shoes."

"Are you kidding me?!" I yelled at him, "The ground is freezing."

"Trust me," he simply said.

You know what's the damn problem with me? I trusted him.

So I did, I kicked my heels off and flinched when the soles of my feet touched the cold sidewalk. He wounded an arm around my waist and lifted me up, placing my feet on top of his shoes, "Better?"

We were closer than ever and I don't even know what to do anymore.

Together we can just let go, pretend like there's no one else here that we know

"Sorry," he mumbled, making my head shot up to look at him.

Big mistake.

His face was just inches from mine and my breath hitched as I tried to concentrate on what he was saying.

"I always tried to ask you to dance, but somehow there's always somebody in the way," he said, "I should have just ignored them and went with you."

Resting my head on his shoulder, I shook my head. I'm probably doing this just because my face was beet red, and I'm pretty sure that I cannot manage to make out an intelligible sentence right now.

"You're famous, Jasper," I tried to tell him, "I'm infamous."

We don't care what them people say

I couldn't help but laugh at this song, did he purposely pick this one out or was it just pure coincidence?

"It's alright," I told him after this apology.

"Not it's not," I felt him shake his head.

Same old Jasper Dean.

"It's alright," I repeated, my voice urging him.

Finally, he let out a sigh of defeat, "Alright."

'Cause we don't have the time to be sorry

"Lift your head up," he requested and I did so, staring right at me.

He leaned down and pressed a kiss onto my forehead, making me close my eyes as I savored the feel of his lips on my skin.

Something so simple and chaste, but sweet and adorable.

Just like Jasper.

"We're so weird," I couldn't help but giggle, "We're dancing right outside my house."

He give me a full-on grin, "That's because we're Jasper and Savannah."

So baby be the life of the party

And they said that your last dance will be the person who you'll be together with.

A little part of me was praying that it was true. No, a big part of me was praying that it was true.

Chapter 16

"**S**avannah, wake up," somebody shook me and I groaned, turning away from whoever wants to disturb my time of solitude and sleep.

In other words, don't wake me up when I'm asleep or else I'll murder you.

"Savannah," another attempt.

I cracked on of my eyes open to meet with those green ones that were the same shade as mine, the ones I inherited from my father. I groaned as I pulled the blanket over me, "No."

He chuckled at this, trying to pry away the sheets from my hands. I'm perfectly comfy, thank you very much.

"Go away, Drew," I mumbled.

Hold up, Drew!

My eyes shot open as I stared at my brother. He sat on my bed, his hair was an obvious mess, and he still had his coat on, a clear indication that he just came home.

The bags under his eyes were a sign that he was exhausted but the grin he was showing was really something else. I flung my blanket off as I jumped into his arms, hugging the life out of him. Unlike most sibling relationships, my brother and I actually got along really well.

"You're here," I voiced out, finally pulling away, "Why didn't you tell me you're arriving today."

He shrugged as he got off my bed, straightening the clothes I messed up, "Surprise."

"Where's Celeste?" I asked, jumping to my feet, referring to his wife. He chuckled at my enthusiasm as he pointed out of my door.

"Downstairs, go greet her while I go wake up mom and dad," he said and I didn't need to be told twice. I grabbed the nearest pair of slippers as I raced out of my room, practically tripping on the heels I carelessly thrown on the floor when I got home last night.

Skipping two steps at a time, I ran down the stairs and turned to get into the living room when I saw my dear sister-in-law talking on the phone. She caught sight of me and she gave me a small smile, turning back to the person on the other line.

"Alright, I'll get back to you with those reports, happy holidays," she finally bid farewell, placing down the device and turning to me.

Her belly was definitely growing, it wasn't bulging yet that it made her appear that she was going to pop anytime soon, but it was big enough to indicate that she was indeed pregnant.

"Hi," she greeted, opening her arms to invite me into an embrace which I gladly took.

I would never forget how much she took care of me, even as somebody who was just Drew's friend, she was already considered as part of the family. You can just imagine our joy when we heard the news that they were getting married, and now, they're expecting.

"Celeste Everett!" we heard my mom yell as we heard her thundering footsteps, she had the biggest grin on when she practically shoved me away just to give her a hug.

"Nice to see you too, Ariel," Celeste laughed, returning the gesture, she mustered up a small wave to my father who just entered the room with my brother.

Seeing my family complete is the best Christmas present that I can have.

"Traveling with a pregnant lady is definitely hard," Drew sighed dramatically which earned a death glare from his wife. He raised his hands in surrender before placing a kiss on the top of her head.

Rolling my eyes at their display of affection, I scoffed jokingly, "You two are making me sick."

"Says the girl who danced with a certain boy last night outside the house," mom teased, plopping on the couch next to Celeste.

My mouth hanged open as I stared at her bring out her phone to show us a wonderful shot of me and Jasper swaying on the sidewalk last night.

How in the world?

"Is that Jasper?" Drew squinted at the picture and I gulped audibly, "The boy you used to always hang out with?"

"You two are friends again?" Celeste inquired.

"More than friends," Ariel giggled and I looked at her, my brain trying to process everything.

She saw us dancing last night and even caught it on camera.

The doorbell rang and I was praying to the heavens that it wasn't Jasper. If he suddenly entered right now, I have no idea what's going to happen to him.

Drew went to get the door and I almost pulled him back, but he was quick and when he opened the damn thing, it was the devil himself.

He looked shock at the sight of my brother, but I for one, am shock at the two bouquet of roses in his arms. On his right was bigger than the one he brought to me last night and the other was smaller.

Who knew he would actually get me more roses?

"Drew!" he looked absolutely mortified, "You're home."

My brother eyed the roses before his gaze switched to him then he settled them on me. I guess it wouldn't take too long to connect the dots.

To my absolute surprise, he slammed the door right in front of Jasper's face before turning to me and dusting off his hands, "Now where were we?" and he started to walk back into the living room as if the boy standing right outside of our house never came.

I scrambled around to open the door once again, even though I can hear Drew's protests in the background, I stepped outside and gave Jasper an apologetic look, "Sorry about him."

"He's here?" he asked the obvious and I nodded.

Now why in the world is he acting like this?

"Don't worry about Drew," I tried to comfort before pointing out the two bouquets in his arms, "But please explain this."

He looked down on them before giving me a sheepish grin, "I thought you still weren't satisfied with the one I gave you last night, so I bought you two more options."

This guy is really the sweetest.

He gave them to me, and I gave him an appreciative smile, "Thank you, but you didn't have to get me these."

He shrugged as he jammed his hands into his pockets, "But I wanted to."

Even though he was saying these words to me, his eyes were still glued to the open door behind me, as if a monster was going to appear.

No monster came, but Celeste did pop out her head, "Jasper."

The said boy straightened up in attention as he gave an awkward wave to my sister-in-law, "H-hi."

"Why don't you come in?" she offered, "Ariel just started to prep up some hot chocolate and her famous cookies."

Without a moment of hesitation, he shook his head, "No thank you."

Frowning at him, I gripped the roses harder as I saw Celeste pout at his answer, before retreating back into the house. I stared at him and scrunched up my eyebrows in confusion.

He's suddenly acting so uncomfortably.

We parted ways, but as I got back inside my house, I turned to my brother and gave him a questioning look, "What happened to him?"

Drew merely shrugged, eyeing the roses before a smirk overcame his lips, "Does my baby sister have a boyfriend."

My cheeks flamed up as I turned away so he won't see my face. Well, this is embarrassing.

"Just saying, if he's going to date you, he has to go through me first," suddenly turning all overprotective big brother mode.

Celeste laughed at this, shaking her head, "You know he's been wanting to say that for a long time now."

"In my defense, Savannah has never shown an interest in a guy before," he sighed, "But I hope he's serious with you."

"He's just my friend!" I emphasized, groaning when I saw their knowing looks.

They think they have this all planned out, but nope, whatever they assuming is just completely wrong.

Jasper and I are just friends, no matter how much you look at it, we're not a couple.

But I think we all know this tiny part of me is wish that we were.

Dad came inside the room and lifted an eyebrow at the bouquets in my arms, "He brought you more, I thought the one last night was enough."

"I vote that Jasper comes over to have dinner with us," Celeste clapped, "Wouldn't that be amazing?"

No, absolutely no.

I could almost picture it – Jasper sitting awkwardly as Drew fired question after question at him, my mom and Celeste will be giggling all night, my dad will just stare at us like this was a football game, and I would just be mortified on my spot.

"He can't do that," I rejected the idea, Celeste turned to me and quirked her head to the side in question.

"And why not?"

Alright, Savannah, think of an amazing and brilliant excuse. We're taking too long to answer, open your mouth now before you they suspect something.

I expect an answer to come out of your mouth in three seconds, it must intelligible and believable.

Three, two, one, "Jasper and I already have plans tonight."

My eyes widened when I blurted out those words, I instantly slapped a hand on my mouth.

Thank you, brain, you've been such a good help.

Mom popped her head from the kitchen, a clear indication that she was eavesdropping as every single member of my family stared at me, their faces blank for a moment.

Stop being so stupid, Savannah.

"You have a date," they all accused simultaneously.

"We don't have a date," I denied, waving my hands up in the air, attempting to lessen the damage.

Though knowing me, I will just make things worse.

"So he's joining us for dinner?" Celeste added, and I turned to also reject that idea.

"No!" I yelled all too quickly.

She raised a brow and I'm currently begging the earth to open up and swallow me. Please, I won't mind if that happened right now.

"But you said that you don't have a date with him tonight."

Somebody please explain that a night out with a boy does not equate to a date. If I opened my big mouth, I'm pretty sure that this conversation will last more than it's supposed to and the end result will not go in my favor.

"We're going out as friends," I urged.

Wait a minute, I don't really have plans with Jasper tonight and I'm doing my best to defend something that's not real.

"Alright then," mom drawled out, carefully easing back to her baking with a cheshire grin.

Great, that's how I ended up with my open window as I waited until Jasper got back into his room so I could ask him about tonight. Now I plainly look like a stalker.

If he says no, then I'll just beg him to go through with my excuse.

I saw the door to his bedroom open he got inside. When he saw me sitting here, he grinned, waving to me before stepping to his window, opening it to allow the cold winter air to enter his room.

"Hi," he greeted, looking absolutely elated.

At least he's no longer a nervous wreck.

"Do you have plans tonight?" I asked casually, leaning against my chair.

He looked surprise by my question, but answered it any-ways, "Well, some guys invited me to go bowling with them."

I frowned at this, well, it looks like I have to endure the torture known as my family tonight by myself, plus, they'll drill me after they find out that my pathetic excuse was just a lie.

"Alright then," I sighed, pushing myself up to my feet, "I just thought maybe we could go out later."

I was about to say goodbye and close my window, because it was starting to get cold, but he raised a hand to stop me. His eyes showed panic as he yelled a lot louder than he was supposed to, "Stop!"

I jumped up in surprise as I stared at him, my hand gripping my windowsill, "Yes?"

"Let's go tonight!"

"But you're going bowling," I pointed out.

"I can cancel, you're asking me right now," he instantly replied, "Where do you want to go? A movie? A fancy restaurant?"

He looked like a child getting asked to go the candy store, he was practically radiating with excitement and joy.

"I vote the mall, so we could do some Christmas shopping while we're at it," I shrugged and without a moment of hesitation, he nodded at my request.

I gave him a small smile before saying my goodbye, closing my curtain. Just in time, my phone started ringing from my bed.

Walking up to it, I saw Tristan's name flashed across the screen, answering it, I plopped down on my bed, grabbing a pillow to hug.

"What do you think Kyla will like as a gift?" was the first words that came from the other line.

"Well, hello to you too," I muttered sarcastically as I heard the background noise from the other line, "Where in the world are you?"

"At the mall," he yelled through the mindless chatters, "Help me!"

"Jasper and I are going there," I told him, "I can convince him to leave now so we can meet up."

"I think you're quite forgetting that my best friend is expressing some sort of dislike towards me at this moment," he joked.

Rolling my eyes at his statement, I rolled on my stomach before an idea popped into my head.

"You working tomorrow?" I questioned, lazily hitting on the pillow.

He hummed in confirmation as a plan stirred inside my head. Excellent, my idea will go flawlessly.

Unless, you know, the universe is against me like it always is.

A few hours later, I'm standing outside my house as I watched Jasper approach me, waving his keys to indicate me that we're taking his car.

I hugged my coat tighter around my body as I approached him, "Mind if we have lunch together tomorrow?"

Jasper may no longer want to be my friend after tomorrow, but it was worth a shot. Besides, this could already be his Christmas present to me. I just want this stupid argument to be over, even though I have no idea what's the cause of it.

"Like a date?" he asked as he escorted me to his vehicle.

My throat dried as I opened my mouth to answer him, "Whatever you want to call it."

Even though I tried to make it sound casual, I was mentally freaking out in the inside.

This is not a date, Savannah, this is not a date.

Jasper wrapped an arm around my shoulder, it was loose as if he was testing if I would shrug it off. Good for him, I didn't.

The problem was, I bowed my head down so he couldn't see my cheeks turning red like a tomato.

Oh Jasper, stop this if you really value our friendship, because if this continues, I'm going to fall for you harder than how I used to.

Chapter 17

Observing myself in the mirror, I placed on the beanie, contemplating if I should keep it or if it looks too much. Well, there's one way to be sure.

Picking up my phone, I searched my contacts for one specific girl who has nothing but a guardian angel when it comes to that quirky girl next door.

"What?" was Kyla's immediate greeting when she picked up the phone.

Sighing, I removed the beanie before throwing it to my desk, "Beanie or no beanie?"

"Damn it, Jasper, we've been planning about this thing since last night," she groaned. Looks like I've caught her in a bad mood, "She wouldn't care if you have a freaking piece of wool on your head or not."

Frowning at my phone, I let out a frustrated sigh, "You know how long I've been wanting to do this."

"I know," she mumbled from the other line, "Just be yourself, that's what Savannah truly wants."

I find it hard to believe. If 've been truly myself from the start, then she wouldn't have broken our friendship in the first place.

I still couldn't forget that horrible day, I ran up to her but she only glared at me. I tried to talk to her, to start up a conversation, but in return, she shook her head and walked away.

I wished I could have known what I have done to do that, I almost beat myself up for that. I let her slip out of my fingers and I was too much of a coward to do anything.

Looking at the open window, I couldn't help but stare at awe at the girl known as Savannah Everett. As usual, she looked as casual as she can, but she was still mesmerizing.

She was talking on the phone and the grin she was showing was really something else. She was beautiful in every single way you put it.

"Earth to Jasper Dean," I heard Kyla call from the other line, "Are you looking at Savannah from the window again? Stop staring, you'll look like a stalker."

Shaking my head at her, I couldn't help but agree to her statement. Ever since Savannah showed traces of rebuilding our friendship, I didn't want to fuck up again. So to be safe, I contacted the one girl who kept an eye at her throughout those years we weren't talking.

So far, Kyla Bailey has been a big help, but I could still feel the slap on my cheek after she scolded me when I didn't dance with Savannah during the winter formal.

Don't worry, I've been cursing myself ever since that happened.

But she forgave me, thank God she did. I have no idea what I'll do if I lose her again.

She caught sight of me from the other side and gave me one of those amazing smiles, rendering me senseless when she did.

Jasper, my boy, you have it bad.

"Good luck," she said, "Don't embarrass yourself."

Nodding, I hung up as I stretched myself. Alright, we can do this.

My first date with Savannah Everett.

I wanted to give her roses but Macy somehow convinced me that it would be too much since I already gave her three bouquets.

Nothing's too good for her.

"Hold up!" Macy stopped me before I stepped outside. She approached me, fixing my collar before smiling.

"My baby brother is growing up," she sniffed dramatically.

Rolling my eyes at my sister, I couldn't help but laugh. She was really something.

"Savannah's really special, isn't she?"

"Of course," I replied with no hesitation.

She's the best girl you can ever meet.

"Are you sure I shouldn't get her more roses?"

Macy reached up and slapped me upside the head, "If you get her one more bouquet, I'll stuff your head in it."

Laughing at my sister, I straightened myself up, I let her examine my outfit one more time. She gave a nod of approval before opening the door and practically shoving me out of the house.

Alright, clothes done. Now for the second challenge, walking up next door where her brother and his powerful wife are staying.

Don't get me wrong, Drew and Celeste are kind people, but they're a bit intimidating if you ask me. The Everett's home is as normal as it can be on a regular day, but when those two comes home, it's like the place becomes a high security mansion.

Clearing my throat, I reached up and rang the doorbell, checking my shoes to see if they're completely shined.

The door swung open to reveal Savannah, looking as adorable as ever.

"You're looking spiff," she laughed, stepping out of her house.

"First thing I saw when I opened my closet," I casually said.

That was a lie. If only she knew how long did I take trying on outfit after outfit, calling Kyla then asking for Macy's opinion. But she doesn't need to find out, I might look desperate.

I opened the door for her, and before she slid in, she looked at me teasingly before saying, "No roses?"

I knew I should have gotten the roses.

"I'll order one right now, we can pick it up on the way?" I started to babble. This is starting to become a habit of mine when I'm with her, "What size do you want? I think I have enough money for the large one," seriously, why did you have to mention the money, "Never mind, I'll get whatever you want."

She shook her head, smiling at my stupidity before entering the vehicle.

Was that a yes or no?

Getting inside the driver's side, I turned to her, "So where do you want to go?"

I actually have no idea if she wanted to head to some place specific, so I called up a reservation to most of the restaurants I know she enjoys eating at. If she wants to head to the mall, my credit card is ready in case she wants to go shopping. If she wants to go to the park, I brought an extra pair of gloves and scarves so we're prepared if we get cold, if those are not enough, I brought a blanket that's now sitting on the backseat.

Let's just say I've come prepared.

Without pausing a moment to think, she let out, "One-Eighty Degrees please."

That was not part of the plan! I did not prepare for that! Houston, we have a problem.

"Are you sure you don't want to go somewhere else?" I suggested. Like, you know, a place that I'm prepared for.

"I want One-Eighty," she pouted.

Damn that pout, it's the only thing that can make me fall for whatever she wants.

So without much of a choice, I pressed down on that gas before driving to the café she requested.

I don't get why she would come here for a date. She works here and is practically here all the time.

A waitress showed us to a table for two and handed us some menus, I almost laughed when I recognized the junior that served during that faithful day when I learned about my alleged best friend's job.

Tristan, I felt a pinch of betrayal when I found out. He knew about it, he knew about everything and yet, he never said a word about it.

Switching my gaze at Savannah, I couldn't help but internally chuckle at the scene. This almost looked like the day when I asked her to the winter formal. She looked at me weirdly when I asked if we could drive to the dance, I chickened out and made an excuse about gas consumption.

Just saying, I was one smooth jaguar when I said that gas part. Jasper and Savannah, saving the environment together!

She placed down her menu and smiled at me, standing up from her seat, "I have to go to the restroom."

Nodding, I watched her as she retreated away. Sinking down on my seat, I took out my phone and dialed Kyla's phone.

I hope she won't be so cranky right now.

"So how are you two lovebirds?" she joked from the other line.

"She wanted to go to One-Eighty!" I groaned, resting my elbow on the table, "It's not what I planned."

"Wait, you're both at One-Eighty?" she asked the obvious and I hummed in confirmation, "What day is it?"

Holding my phone away from my ear for a short while, I looked at the date before replying to her question, "Saturday, why?"

"I'm so stupid," was the last thing she muttered before hanging up.

I stared at the phone in wonder before I felt a figure sit across from me. I smiled and looked up, expecting Savannah to be there.

That happiness quickly slipped away when I saw Tristan Hansen occupying the chair right across from mine.

How come I didn't see this coming?

Straightening up, my eyes turned into slits as I looked up at him, "What are you doing here?"

"Trust me, I have no intention of ruining your date with Savannah," he sighed.

"Well, you weren't exactly a helping hand in the first place," I started to say stubbornly.

"Again, I was in no place to meddle, if Savannah didn't want to talk to you then she doesn't want to talk to you, I'm not going to force her to," he scoffed, even though, he kept his calm composure.

It was always like this between the both of us, he was the composed one while I was the one who usually goes into a state of panic.

"You knew I've liked her since middle school," I grunted, "And you also knew how much I wanted to talk to her ever since sophomore year, when she completely erased my existence in her mind."

His eyes started to become sympathetic, staring at me, "I know, you wouldn't shut up about it."

That was the reason why I was so mad at him. He knew about my crush on her, and he knew how distraught I was when Savannah started to ignore me, yet to find out that he was friends with her all this time, it was really saddening.

"You like her, don't you?" I accused.

Where did that come from?

His eyes widened at my sudden statement, "What?"

"That's the reason why you didn't tell me," I continued, "You wanted her for yourself."

He eyed me as if I just accused him of killing his own mother. He shook his head, silently chuckling to himself as I told him the most amusing thing in the world, "Oh Jasper, you couldn't get any wrong."

"I'm not stupid," I crossed my arms over my chest.

Are you really, Jasper?

"I like Kyla," he admitted without a moment of hesitation, "She's my girl, not Savannah."

My mouth gaped open. How come I never knew about my own best friend's crush?

Now I feel completely selfish.

"Not Savannah?" I asked dumbly.

"She's a good friend," he shrugged, "But she's not my type."

We looked at each other for a moment, blinking as we both allowed everything to sink in. Then, to make us look like complete idiots, we started to laugh.

Sometimes, the stupidity and idiocy of everything will just amuse you.

We heard slowly clapping and we turned to see the beauty herself walk up to us, smiling at the achievement she has done.

"Glad you two are finally done with your stupid feud."

The chime that usually signals a new costumer sounded around the café. We turned to the door and saw Kyla running up inside, slipping on the wet entrance, caused by the people getting in after stepping on the snow.

She crashed on the floor, groaning as she did so.

Savannah quickly ran up to help her best friend, the two of them laughed it off as she tried to pull up Kyla to her feet.

"They're a keeper," Tristan muttered, eyeing the two girls and I couldn't agree more.

Savannah Everett and Kyla Bailey are two special girls, Tristan and I are really lucky.

I was quite disappointed after I found out that this wasn't a date, it was just a plot by Savannah to regain Tristan's friendship, but at the end of the day, the four of us had a good lunch at the café.

"That was fun," Savannah let out her cute little giggle, dusting off the few snow from her hair.

It still lacked the date factor if you ask me, way to get my hopes up. I puffed my cheeks out like a child as I started to drive back to our homes.

"Now where are we going?" Savannah asked, looking out of the window.

"Home," I mumbled bitterly.

She reached out and wrapped a cold hand around my wrist, "I thought we were going to the park."

"What?"

Rolling her eyes, she pointed to the blanket on the back-seat, "I know you brought that for a reason."

Pursing my lips into a straight line, I drove to the side, turning to her, "But I thought you just wanted to go with your plan."

She looked away from me, staring out the window as she hid behind her hair, "I still want to spend some time with you though," when those words escaped her mouth, she lifted her hand to cover her lips.

Point one for Jasper Dean!

Grinning at her, I made a turn and drove us to the park.

Walking along the path, we stayed in comfortable silence. It's always like this, we don't need nonsense chatter to fill the air, we just need each other's company.

She wore my scarf and gloves. The gloves that was intended for me looked gigantic on her small hands, but that was what it made it look precious.

We found the driest bench we can scout and sat on it, wrapping the blanket over our bodies as we watched the peaceful scene in front of us.

Closing my eyes, I prayed to the heavens that we can stay like this. Jasper, just don't fuck up.

Switching my gaze to Savannah, I couldn't help but just smile at the sight of her. She has no idea how much she affects me.

Chapter 18

"The yearly countdown for Christmas," my mom smiled as she handed us mugs of hot chocolate as we sat down in the living room, staring at the clock located right above the fireplace, waiting for it to tick to midnight.

"One last happy birthday, Drew," I smiled to my brother who sat on the couch with Celeste. He gave me a thumb up, signaling his appreciation.

Funny thing about drew is that he was born on Christmas Eve, so every year, it was a double celebration for the family. Though with the look in his eyes, we could all conclude that he treasured the times we're together than actually thinking of his birthday.

Looking at Celeste's growing belly, I couldn't help but sigh, in just a few months, another bundle of joy will be added to crazy and rowdy family.

"Six minutes," dad muttered, settling down on his favorite chair, "You ready, kids?"

The doorbell rang and we all switched our gazes to each other, wondering who was at the door.

Well, who in the world would be visiting us at this late hour?

I volunteered to get it and imagine my shock when I saw Jasper standing there when I opened the door.

"Hey," he greeted with a soft smile.

"Hi," I said slowly, "What are you doing here?"

"Well, my family was next door talking and..." he trailed off, looking unsure of what to do.

Macy popped out from behind him and clicked her tongue at her brother, "It's not hard, you know."

"What's not hard?" I questioned, looking intently at Jasper.

She shook her head, but presented me with a wrapped box, "Merry Christmas, Savannah."

Jasper's eyes widened when he saw it, and it looked like he wanted to rip the present off of her grasp and bury it six feet under.

I thanked her as I took it from her hands. The way she was grinning at me was a clear indication that something was up.

"Open it," she requested, shifting on her feet as Jasper continued to avert his gaze away from me.

Slowly untying the ribbon, I carefully took off the lid. Macy's grin was still prominent when my eyes scanned the green thing inside the box.

Oh fuck no.

I reached down for it until my fingers found the string. Jasper stared at it, his eyes boring through the mistletoe I held out.

"Well, you know what to do," she grinned mischievously, taking it from the hands. She hanged it on the hook that was conveniently located on my doorway so it now hung right above us, "Mistletoe, now you have to kiss."

Jasper cleared his throat loudly and sent a dry look towards Macy. She smiled sheepishly as she slowly retreated back, saying something about giving us the privacy we needed.

"Actually, Macy pushed me here because she wanted me to accompany her as she gave you her gift," he explained, scratching the back of his head, "But I never thought this was it."

Nodding in understanding, I looked up and shook my head, eyeing the treacherous thing known as Macy's wonderful present, "She's probably watching us right now."

"And she's not going to let me leave unless we do something."

My cheeks heated up as my brain started conjuring up the following scenarios. As much as I wanted this, our friendship is too precious to break it for something like this. I don't even know how he feels, and now, we're being forced into something we're both so unsure about.

"Let's just get this over with," he mumbled, staring right into my eyes.

I stood frozen on my spot as I contemplate on what to do. Where's Kyla and Tristan when you need them? I need to do some sort of distraction or whisper advice into me right now.

But when I glanced at Jasper, he was waiting patiently for me, like he was prepared to turn back and walk away if I say the word no.

"One minute!" I heard my dad announce from the inside of my house. I'm pretty sure my family knew what was going on, and they decided to just let me be as I tackled this situation.

Mistletoe, now we have to kiss.

Licking my lips, I took a step forward with my heart beating rapidly inside my chest, "Alright."

Calm yourself, Savannah.

He carefully placed his hands on my waist, and I'm certain that he could feel how nervous I was. When he slowly leaned down, he took a deep breath as he paused on the spot, as if he was silently telling me it was up to me if I should continue with this.

And that was when I heard my family slowly count down until zero.

"Ten, nine, eight," they stared to say, excitement lacing in their voice.

Eight more seconds, Savannah, we can do this.

"Seven, six, five."

I stared to lean forward and his eyes fluttered shut, knowing how this would end up in.

"Four, three, two."

Oh for heaven's sake, this is not some New Year's kiss that everybody wants to have.

And they cheered as they said, "One."

That was when I realized that I couldn't do it. Not right now.

So I shifted my face so I pressed my lips on his cheek, before dropping my head on his shoulder.

I'm a coward, a complete coward, but this is the right thing to do.

Ever since I started to have a crush on him a few years back, I've always imagined how our first kiss would be like. Sure, Christmas under a mistletoe is a romantic setting, but the way this was been set up isn't.

I have this hunch that my mom is back with her camera, ready to capture the moment, and even where I'm standing, I could see a silhouette of Macy's body a few meters from us, clearly enjoying the show.

This is not how I wanted it. If Jasper does feel the same way like I'm always hoping for, I don't want our first kiss to be done out of pressure, it supposed to be spontaneous, like how my mother used to dramatically describe hers with my father, or how Celeste used to tell me how confused she was when Drew kissed her for the first time, but she admitted that from that night on when they shared it, she thought of nobody else except him.

And that's how I wanted it to be, when it happens, it's going to seal everything between us.

I felt his grip on my waist tightened and I could almost feel his emotions radiating from his body.

He was disappointed, it was clear as day.

"I'm sorry," I whispered, "I just can't."

"I know," he replied quietly.

I stepped away from his hold of me, but I reached out and took his hand in mine, "My family is watching us, your sister planned everything, and I don't think I'm really comfortable with our situation right now."

He nodded, and I released him, "Merry Christmas, Jasper."

A small smile crept up on his face, but it looked forced more than ever, "Merry Christmas, Savannah."

And as I watched him walk away with Macy back into their house, I felt my heart sank. Well, looks like it's not going to be a very merry Christmas this year.

Closing the door, I yelled to my family that I was going to bed. Luckily for me, they didn't bother with asking me anymore questions and just allowed me to be alone.

When I woke up the next morning, the first thing that came into my mind was to open my curtains to peek into Jasper's room.

Just in time, he was about to close his curtains. He caught a sight of me, and I suddenly felt ashamed of what I was wearing. Here I was in my red pajamas with my hair resembling a tumbleweed, and he on the other hand looks as attractive as ever, looking like he was ready to head out.

He shot me a small smile, but it was the same as last night before he left. He gave me a wave before he finally closed his curtains, removing my view of him.

That's it, if we're going to continue being like this, then a very awkward air will follow us everywhere.

So that thought made me pick up my phone, dialing the person who I know will help me get through this.

"Hello?" came Tristan's voice, still heavy with remains of sleep.

"I kind of have a code red with Jasper right now," I frowned to myself as I searched my closet for a change of clothes, "I need your help."

"Considering you're the reason why Kyla and I are smooth sailing, I'll help you with this one," he teased as I heard shuffling from the other side, "So what happened between you and my best friend?"

"Long story short, we found ourselves under the mistletoe and instead of kissing him like everybody would expect, I went for his cheek," I explained, grabbing a pair of jeans from one of the hangers, "And now I have no idea what he's thinking, but whatever it is, I'm sure it's not good."

"Oh young and dumb Savannah," he clicked his tongue, "You and Jasper are a pair of fools in love."

I rolled my eyes at his statement before I threw my clothes onto my bed, "I did not call you in order for you to insult my intelligence and common sense."

"Calm down," he chuckled, "But as I see it, Jasper sees this as a form of rejection from you."

"I think I've figured that out," I scoffed.

"I just don't see why you went for the cheek."

"Because," I paused for a moment, looking for the right words, "It wasn't a good time for the both of us to have our first kiss together."

"I'll give you a little secret," he said and my interest grew, "Jasper Dean, star athlete, is a very insecure little boy when it comes to one girl."

"And who's that girl?" I questioned, dreading for the answer.

"You!" he exclaimed, as if he wasn't obvious enough.

If you haven't noticed, my brain works slower when it comes to things related to Jasper.

"Do you think he likes me," I asked, my voice becoming small as if I desperately wanted to know the answer, yet at the same time, I don't want him to reply.

"I think that's for you to find out," he said from the other line, but his voice was encouraging nonetheless, "Go talk to him."

"You sure?"

"I'm sure," he affirmed, "Merry Christmas."

"Merry Christmas, Tristan," I smiled at my phone. With that as a goodbye, I placed down my phone and looked at my clothes. Well, he told me that I should talk to him.

Changing out of my pajamas, I ran a brush through my hair before I pulled it into a ponytail to make sure it was out of my face. Taking one look at the mirror, I nodded at myself, trying to make myself determined.

"We can do this," I told my reflection, before I walked downstairs.

"Merry Christmas, Savannah," Celeste greeted, "Are you alright?"

"Just peachy," I muttered, grabbing a piece of toast, "I have something to do this morning, so is it alright if I could go out?"

My mom looked at me skeptically, but she caught on quickly, she nodded as she gestured to the door, "Just be back before lunch."

And with her permission, I grabbed my coat and I ran out of my house and walked to the house next door. Attempting to fix my disheveled look, I pat down my hair before ringing the doorbell.

The sight of Jasper greeted me quickly, and the welcoming smile he was supposed to put on dropped instantly when he saw me.

Awkward feel, welcome!

"Hey," I mumbled.

"Hi," he said slowly, "What are you doing here?"

It was like last night, only the tables have turned.

Looking out to the snow covered road, I muttered to him, "Can we talk?"

With I sigh, I watched him as he stepped out of his house and quietly closed the door behind him, "What's the problem?"

"I think you know what's the problem," I scoffed, leaning against the wall, "Plus, I really hate seeing you down, especially because of me."

He took a deep breath, crossing his arms in an attempt to warm himself up, "Just answer this one question."

"Shoot."

"On a scale of one to ten, how much do you believe that two friends of the opposite gender can fall for each other?"

And that was it, something I thought I would never hear. He never said it directly, but the idea was there.

He likes me, the idea was farfetched, but I think that he really does like me.

I rested my head on his shoulder as I stared the both of us stood in comfortable silence before I finally gave him my answer, "Eleven."

Awkward feel, goodbye!

"Good," he smiled.

He made no other move other than, but we both got the message. Thinking about it now, this may be the best Christmas gift I have ever received this year. We're going to take this slow, and besides, we haven't even gotten our first kiss yet.

But hey, we're moving slowly but surely.

Chapter 19

After that day, something between Jasper and I changed. I don't know if it's for the better or not, but our bond was stronger than ever before.

As tradition calls, my family went on a long road trip to my grandparents' house to celebrate the New Year's. This is the first time I actually cared about being separated with him for a long time, and it was excruciating to hear his voice from the other line of the phone.

"You still there?" I could hear him yelling, trying to talk over the muffled music.

He told me himself that he was at a New Year's Party that his teammate was throwing, but instead of counting down the minutes with the other guests, he locked himself inside the most isolated bathroom that he could find and called me.

"Yeah," I whispered, leaned against the headboard of the bed, "I'm still here."

Even though we couldn't see each other, I can practically see him smiling, and that was the only comfort I needed.

My family was downstairs, having a feast of their own, while I excused myself to talk to Jasper, waiting for it to strike twelve in order to say goodbye to one of the most productive year we have ever experienced.

When it was only a few ticks away, I could hear yells from Jasper's side, screaming out the number of seconds left, and the more it approached one, the louder it became, but at the same time, Jasper's breathing became heavier.

I was hoping that he was wanting the same thing I was wishing for right now. The wonderful New Year's Kiss.

"Happy New Year!" cheers sounded and I closed my eyes, hearing Jasper's soft greeting to me which I returned with much gratefulness.

"I'll see you when you get back," he assured and I hummed in confirmation, feeling sleep marching up to my body.

We said our goodbyes before finally hanging up, just as when I placed my phone down on the bedside table, the door clicked open and came in Celeste, beaming up at me as she rubbed her growing belly.

"Mind if I stay the night with my favorite sister-in-law?" she laughed, sitting on the bed next to me.

"I'm your only sister-in-law," I pointed out, shaking my head as I scooted so she could have enough space.

"Exactly," she winked as I shifted around to put the lower half of my body under the blankets, "Was that Jasper on the phone?"

"Yeah," I confirmed, "He's at a New Year's party."

She blinked at me for a moment, before tilting her head to the side in question, a bit of concern shining in her eyes, "And you're not worried?"

"About what?" I inquired, pulling my knees up to my chest.

After a short while, her lips twitched to a comforting smile as she stood up, "Nothing," she shook her head, "You must trust him a lot."

"Because he has given me no reason not to," I explained, "There's no need to think of it any other way."

She clasped her hands together and let out a small laugh, "Young love, so innocent and sweet."

"You were once young and in love too," I muttered, laying down on the bed, "And news flash, I'm not in love with Jasper."

"But it brought me so much confusion and hurt," she said, it was as if she was warning me, "Though, after everything, I thought it was worth."

Her gaze was looking down on me, but I saw right through her. Instead of threatening me about how this will end, she was sharing her experience. She was preparing me for what was to come, letting me brace myself for the hardship I may go through.

Some of which, she felt with her own heart. As she stood in front of me with a child growing inside her body, it was true when she said it was worth it for her. I have never seen a woman so happy and contented in all my life.

I then thought of Drew, he proud of his wife, it was no secret. I could remember the times he would go zombie-mode whenever he and Celeste have a fight, but here is, living the life he has always wanted. I wonder what he was thinking during his teenage years.

Did these two have the same doubts as Jasper and I were having?

"Have some rest," she told me, walking to the door, "We have a long ride home tomorrow."

When she went out, I stared at the ceiling, thinking of it as my company. The light that suddenly illuminated from my phone distracted me from my thoughts and I short message flashed on-screen was enough to put on a smile on my face as I closed my eyes to sleep.

Happy New Year, I miss you.

"Alright, we're back," my dad announced, pulling up in front of our house.

The minute I stepped outside the car, the house next door's front door opened and immediately came out Jasper.

I haven't seen him for about a week, and with the way he was looking at me, I felt like I had to stop my feet from running up to him.

"Hello there, Jasper," my mom called to him, waving to his direction.

He managed to nod in acknowledgement to her, before he slowly walked up to us, gathering the attention of my other family members.

"It was starting to be boring without you guys," he joked lightly, causing mom to laugh at this.

As they were started to become busy with unloading our belongings from the trunk of the car, Jasper turned to me with a soft smile gracing his face, "Hi."

You know those stories where girls melt with just one word? Well, thankfully, I haven't become one of those girls, maybe I've become immune or I'm used to Jasper's charm, but as protocol, I grinned at him, "Hello."

"You two are adorable, but help us here," Celeste cut us off, Jasper snapped out of it just in time to catch the duffel bag Drew threw towards our direction.

"Can I borrow you from your family today?" he asked, walking with me as we brought a few luggage into the house.

I looked over my shoulder towards the group, before switching back to Jasper, "Sure."

It was easy getting my confirmation, it was probably more difficult for Jasper to get pass through my brother and dad, and they fired a thousand questions before mom slapped both of them upside the head before we were able to walk away.

"So where are we going?" I asked when we walked by his house, instead of maneuvering me towards the direction of his car, he continued his descent.

He gulped audibly before I felt the ghost of his touch on my hand. I looked down and I could tell that he was shaking, as if hesitating to hold my hand.

Carefully, I reached out, but I didn't make a move yet. With a deep breath, he wrapped his around mine, providing it warmth from the cold air.

Great, we held hands, was that the main goal of this?

"Where are we going?" I repeated my question from earlier, but once again, he didn't reply. He stared forward and kept on going, it was as if he was blocking my question from his hearing.

So when I realized he wouldn't be answering me any time soon, I kept my mouth shut as I allowed him to pull me with him to wherever our destination is.

It was a little early in the morning, but it was late enough to have the sun shining down on us. The silence was oddly comforting, and when I closed my eyes, I felt like I was floating with peace this time was emitting.

Jasper was my guide, nstead of thinking where we're going, I trusted him and allowed me to drag me along, following his steps through every twist and turn we go through.

Our surroundings was lovely as it was coated with a thin layer of snow, showing us a white blanket that has been proven to be a sweet sight. When Jasper stopped in front of the entrance of the park, I barely noticed that he halted in his steps and I came crashing onto his back.

"Ouch," I groaned, holding my forehead that took the harshest blow.

"Sorry," he mumbled, before he gestured to the scene in front of me, "We're here!"

"At the park?" I scrunched my eyebrows in confusion.

"At the park," he nodded, pulling me along with him to the inside.

"And what are we do ng here?" I inquired, carefully stepping around the puddles, "Especially in the cold?"

"Because it's January first," he explained, finding a tree and he leaned against the tree, possibly dampening his thick coat, "And since we didn't see each other when it stroke midnight, I thought we could have fun right now."

Alright, I'm slightly curious where this is going.

"So as you know, New Year is a time for celebration," he said, pushing himself off the trunk and taking a step towards me, "And what do you do when you celebrate?"

Now I'm really curious where this is going.

Another thing, does he need to remind me how miserable I felt to be away from him for five days. It was drastic, especially with the expectation the both of us were having. We never admitted straight up what we were feeling, but in an indirect way, we had this mutual understanding.

I wanted to kiss when it hit twelve in the morning, I wanted to spend time with him. When Celeste asked me if I was worried, I told her no, but the more she showed me her emotions, I became a bit troubled. You couldn't blame me, he was at a party filled with jocks and cheerleaders, he could have anybody, and I wasn't even there to even observe him.

I was miles away, praying all day that my phone rings with him calling me. If only you knew how quick I was when he finally did, I practically sprinted to the room given to me, just to make sure it was like Jasper and I were the only people that was present at the moment.

Fuck the party from both sides, we were sharing something special.

"Make some noise, jump around," I tried to list off, before ultimately going for the end route, "I don't know."

"Well, when I want to celebrate, I usually like to put off some fireworks," he chuckled, trying to give me a hint.

But we all know I'm an idiot when it comes to Jasper.

"We're not putting off fireworks at the middle of the park this early in the morning!" I screeched, chastising him for even thinking of the idea.

He bit his lip, stopping himself from saying something, and as he took a deep breath, he reached out and took my hand in his once again, "I should have known that you'll react like that."

"Then how would you want me to react?" I questioned, trying to step away, my voice starting to show signs of annoyance.

"I didn't mean those kind of fireworks," he told me, licking his lips, making my eyes zone right at them.

Don't tell me...

He pulled me right to him, wrapping an arm right around my waist and that's when I finally got it.

He's going to kiss me, somebody tell me what to do!

He lifted a hand to slowly caress my cheek, and before I could even react to this, I felt his lips slowly press against mine, testing the waters to see if I would run away any minute.

But I completely surrendered, though I did not create those romantic scenes in movies where I'll slowly wrap my arms around his body and slowly feel him – I just stood there frozen.

My eyes closed and it felt magical, complete with the fireworks he was talking about. It made my brain into a jumbled mess.

He likes me, we got passed that, but to what point? Are we together? What about our friendship? Everything's suddenly on the line, and at the same time, it was like pieces were falling apart and new ones are replacing them.

It was happening all too fast.

So when he pulled back and stared into my eyes, I opened my mouth to say something, anything, but it closed shut.

I could see sadness starting to show in his eyes, I knew he was feeling rejected, but my throat suddenly became dry, rendering me speechless.

Before he could even ask me a single inquiry, I gave him an apologizing look, before I turned around and sprinted as fast as I can without slipping or tripping.

I should have listened to Celeste, she was right when she told me this is going to be full of confusion and hurt. Confusion on my part, and I think I just hurt Jasper when I came running out. This is literally one of the best and worst way to start the year.

Chapter 20

Pushing on the doorbell multiple times, I kept on praying that Kyla finally lets her butt get out of bed and answer the door.

I'm on the brink of hysterics and I need my best friend right now. I just want to cry and leap out of joy at the same time. I don't want to hurt Jasper, I really don't, but if this continues, how am I sure that we'll be both okay at the end?

The front door finally swung open to reveal Kyla in her fluffy robe and a bad case of bed hair as she had a hand cradling her head, "Do you have any idea what time it is?"

She yawned, rubbing her eyes before she fully examined my face. Her annoyed expression quickly turned into a one of concern as she reached out and dragged me inside her house, "What the hell happened to you."

"Jasper kissed me," I squeaked out, trying to stop a sob from escaping my lips.

She looked at me quizzically, her mouth hanging open, "And the problem here is?"

"I ran away," I frowned, covering my face with my hands, "I'm so stupid."

She shook her head as she grabbed my arm and took me to her room where she practically tossed me to her bed as she crossed her arms over her chest, "I think we've established your lack of common sense."

Groaning, I crashed into her pillows, "Not helping!"

"We're not going to have those emotional scenarios where you explain everything, I become sympathetic, you complain about everything else while you have a monologue inside your head, and I just stand here thinking you've gone nuts – which you already are – and with some hugs and saying you're the best friend ever, you're going to go on your merry way and have a relationship with Jasper!"

I sat up and stared at her for a good moment, opening my mouth for a quick remark, before closing it again. My eyebrows scrunched up in confusion, "How much beer did you drink last night?"

"Enough to know that this will end up in bullshit," she responded, going to her closet so she could get out of her pajamas, "Look, you know that I love you, but you left the poor boy hanging."

Slightly tugging at my hair, I bit my lip as I had the monologue that Kyla said that I was going to have inside my head.

What was I even thinking when I was on my way here? I have this odd personality to come crying out to whoever friend that I have, seeking for their advice and have a moment of contemplation inside my brain. In fact, now that I think of it, it's just to buy me enough time to think about the situation.

"How about we just skip to the part where I give you wisdom filled advice," she suggested, her voice turning into a fake dreamy one.

I'm going to wave off her sarcastic attitude right now, because I basically interrupted her, before she even got used to the mild hangover she was experiencing.

"Jasper has gone through hell and back, just so he could proudly call you his friend," she pointed out, pacing around the room, "And I know you have been too, and if I've been observant enough, you two are not doing this for the sake of your friendship."

"Then what else is this for?!" I yelled in exasperation and she showed me glare, silently warning me that if I interrupt her one more time, she' l personally kill me in my sleep.

She placed her hands on her hips and looked down at me, "You like him, he likes you, and you two are the only people making this complicated."

Since I still value my dear life, I kept my mouth shut as I nodded, I knew she was just as sick and tired of this drama as I am.

"The opportunity to get into a relationship with a guy you've liked for a long time has finally present itself to you," she said, waving her arms in the air, "And you just blew it away."

"Alright, so where's the wisdom filled advice?" I question when I felt that she was starting to insult me, once this girl starts, you'll be asleep before she even finishes.

She walked up to me and poked my forehead with her two fingers, "Go back to him and tell him what you feel, stop overthinking everything, you've done enough of that, it's time to finally savor the moment."

Seeing her frustrated expression, a small smile crept its way up to my face as I laughed at her, "And if it doesn't go along the way you want it to?"

"I'll go to Jasper and chop his balls off," she shrugged nonchalantly, "I've had enough of giving him advice on how to get you."

"What?" I questioned, and she snapped out of her trance after she realized what she had said.

Jasper was consulting Kyla about me? They were doing the same thing Tristan and I had been doing when he needed help with my best friend.

"Apparently he has zero knowledge on getting a girl like you," she explain sheepishly, "In my defense, I was starting to get annoyed how you two haven't been moving at all with this."

I couldn't be mad at her, which would be just plain old hypocritical. In fact, it just made me like Jasper ten times more.

Savannah Everett, you have one good looking guy fishing for you, all you have to do is get the bait. We've blown enough chances to let this one pass up.

"You know what, I'm going to Jasper," I told her, pulling myself up from her bed, "Right now, it's time to stop running away."

"Good," she nodded, pushing me out of the door, "You do that I'll go back to sleeping."

I rolled my eyes at her, but before I was fully out, I turned around and hugged her, just like what she said, I grinned as I spoke, "You're the best friend ever."

I heard her finally laugh as I pulled away, "I know."

Shaking my head at her, I put my coat back on as I went out of her house, running back to mine, knowing Jasper has already gone back home.

When I got inside, I ignored my family's question as I raced upstairs to my room. As I predicted, Jasper's window was closed, with the light escaping from the small gap between his curtains, it was indication that he was in his room.

I've collected some knickknacks that was laying around my room to gain some confidence that I will get his attention. Aiming right towards his window, I threw the first object, as predicted, it made no effect.

It took me quite a few sacrifices, before I stomped out in frustration at my failed attempts. Well, if he's deliberately ignoring me, I knew that I deserve it.

"Jasper!" I yelled towards his closed window, praying that he could hear me, "I'm sorry, okay? Come on, please talk to me."

I stood there in silence, staring at his blue curtains before I saw it shuffling. If he could only feel my relief when I saw him open his window, his expression stoic as he stared at me.

"I'm a complete coward," I confessed, hitting my windowsill, "Trust me, I want to be with you, but..."

"You don't want to ruin our friendship?" he guessed, and I nodded, "That's the most cliché thinking that I have ever heard."

Honey, life is a walking cliché.

"Here me out," he said, crossing his arms, "You've broke off our friendship, I tried to mend it, but nope, you just love torturing me, I ask you if it's possible for us to have a relationship, you said yes, then the moment I kiss you, you run away like you're being chased by a wild kangaroo."

"Well, kangaroos do pack a good punch," I mumbled, trying to lighten up the situation, but he shook his head, finding it less than amusing.

"Tell me, Savannah," he paused for a moment, giving me enough time to catch my breath and collect my thoughts as I waited for his next words, "Can we be a couple or not."

As I opened my mouth, I could practically hear Kyla nagging me inside my head if I even think about saying no.

We've been friends for who knows how long, it took us three years to realize that we can't live a life without each other, in a relationship or not, and just three months to find out that the both of us are thinking of risking this broken, but amazing friendship for something that might turn into so much better.

What an adventure this has been.

"You know, sometimes I wish that life has a control system," I muttered, "There's a pause button when everything going too fast, a thousand wires that can be rearranged when one desires it, an instructional manual to know how to work around it."

I looked back at him and showed him a soft smile, "But you know what I really wish life has?"

"What?" he asked, leaning forward as he took interest at what I was talking about.

"A reset button," I replied, "To erase every mistake and every horrible memory, to start again like nothing wrong has happened."

"But it happened," he shrugged, "And if that reset button means that we'll forget everything that occurred between us, even the past few hours of momentary heart break, I'd rather not press."

That was when the both of took different paths. I'm willing to search for that button that doesn't exist, and if the situation that it does present itself to him, he's going to turn away from it instead of pressing the thing that might resolve everything.

"Because that's what made us stand here, talking about it in the first place," he pointed out, "And just like when we were younger when I kept that flower bracelet you made me, I'll treasure every stupid thing that we have done."

"And you said that I was the cliché thinker," I managed to laugh out, "And that bracelet was not stupid."

He shook his head, thinking that I have completely missed the point. The thing was, I didn't. Hey, this wasn't really smooth sailing, but I'll still lift the anchors and continue on with this voyage.

"Hey, I'm Jasper," he gave me a toothy grin, "I like your eye color, it's different."

It was the same words he told me when we met. He claimed that the only reason he approached me was because I was the only person I our small class that had green eyes.

"I'm Savannah," I introduced myself once again, "And thank you, I got them from my dad."

If my memory serves me correctly, what came next is he asked me to become his best friend. That was how simple childhood friendship was made. Now, to become friends, you need to have those emotional moments when one cries their heart out and then after an emotional display, a silent bond will create between them. Unlike how we became friends, it was just a question.

What came next was something I wasn't expecting. Instead of asking me to become best friends, he gulped nervously as he stared intently into my eyes, "Will you be my girlfriend?"

My mouth hung open as I tried to relax myself, processing his words as I gripped the wood of my windowsill, damaging my nails in the process.

In some books, there's this grand and amazing gesture from the guy before they finally get together, but here, it's just a simple question. Did we have a romantic dinner with a movie? Nope.

And that was enough for me.

"See you downstairs," I told him, closing my window as I rushed downstairs. Mom tried to stop me as I ran to the door, knowing Jasper will be twice as fast as I am.

When I got outside, I ignored the raging cold as I walked to Jasper who used his long legs to transport him quickly through the fence separating our houses.

"Gosh, yes," I squealed, wrapping my arms around him, "Though, I would still want a proper date."

"Anything my girl wants," he grinned, gripping my waist, "She gets it."

"We're so cheesy," I laughed, "But I kind of like it."

He smiled as he slowly bent down, pressing his lips onto mine. This time, there weren't a thousand thoughts running along inside my head. There was only one – it Jasper.

Slinging my around his neck, I kissed him back fervently. For once, everything is going right.

Plus, I've learned today that we never needed a reset button in the first place. Being Jasper and Savannah was already enough.

Chapter 21

When I stepped inside the school for the first time since winter break, I almost dropped my book in shock at the amount of girls who greeted me and Kyla, looping themselves to our side as they giddily asked about anything under the sun.

"You two should go shopping with us later," one of them grinned with her brown eyes shining with excitement.

It took us a few moments to realize who they are. From the long years of observation, they were Jasper's lackeys, ranging from the cheerleaders to the girls volleyball team.

Now, since I've became a lot tamer since Jasper and I regained our friendship, I didn't catch too much attention when walking around the school, but now since I have a huge group of popular ladies latching on me and my best friend, we were kind of hard to miss as we tried to maneuver through the halls.

Kyla and I shared a look, a mix of curiosity and shock. When the bell rang, they momentarily stopped from their babbling, and I grabbed my best friend's hand as I pulled her away from the huge crowd.

"What the hell?" she practically yelled when we were in the safe confines of the classroom that was slowly being filled with students.

I would like to know what the hell happened out there.

"See, they're in our class," came in two cheerleaders who was elated when they saw the both of us seated on our desks. They practically shooed away the people who claimed the chairs next to us and sat down, turning to us for another chat.

Somebody please explain what's happening.

You could only guess that they followed us everywhere. Even during the classes Kyla and I didn't have together, they were still there to stalk each of us. It's like they suddenly became interested in our lives, squeezing any personal information they can.

When we exited our last class before lunch, I was relieved to finally see Jasper leaning against the locker, possibly waiting.

"Finally," he grinned, taking my bag from me, "I haven't seen you all day."

Just like every single moment we spent together, I started blushing madly at the simple yet sweet gesture.

Of course, my best friend squeezed herself in-between us, "Now aren't you two adorable together?"

"Kyla!" I complained and she gave me a sheepish smile as she whispered, "Don't leave me behind with them."

I subtly looked behind us, and I slightly jumped to see they were like a brigade marching behind their captain. Turning to Jasper, I nudged my head towards their direction, "Explain that."

He turned to them and gave them a slight smile, gaining a few giggles, "I kind of told them about us."

"What?" I gasped, "Haven't you read any romance novels out there? When slightly average girl gets together with popular boy, she's going to get tortured by the popular ones."

He scrunched up his eyebrows in confusion, before laughing loudly at what I said, "Alright, lay off on those books for a while."

"It's slightly true," Kyla agreed as she was still wedged in between us, "It's a cliché."

"Well, they might be as perky as cliché describes them to be," Jasper pointed out, "But they're nice ones, almost all of them are in their own relationship, they're just plain interested in you two."

"Because you and Tristan," I concluded in which he nodded in confirmation.

"Speaking of Tristan," Kyla jumped in, trying not to sound too eager, "Where is he?"

Jasper opened the cafeteria door, which made the girls behind us coo and Kyla stand mortified on the spot at the scene in front of us.

You know those corny and cheesy proposal? Well, this was like one of them.

Tristan stood on one of the tables, holding a huge bouquet of flowers in his hand and a few of the basketball team held a huge speaker playing some romantic song of some sort. A whole line of varsity were even holding up their shirts, spelling the word 'GIRLFRIEND?'

Like a dutiful best friend, Jasper lead Kyla to the center of everything, right in front of Tristan.

When he called me up a week ago, asking what's was the perfect way to ask Kyla to be his girlfriend, I jokingly told him about this book that did this exact same scene. I never expected that he would actually do it.

Kyla's cheeks heated up at the attention and the sweet gesture. I, on the other hand, created a diversion by cackling out loudly at what was happening, clutching my stomach as I doubled in laughter.

This is cliché it almost hurts.

Jasper blinked at me, before smiling amusedly at his best friend, finding situation as hilarious as I was thinking. Boy, he's definitely whipped.

"Ignoring Savannah in the background," Kyla coughed out as I saw her give me a glare from my peripheral vision, "I'll answer yes."

Pushing away the people who started to congratulate the new couple, I reached Kyla and gave her a smile, "Thought it would never happen."

"That's what I felt when you were being so stubborn with Jasper," she retorted, until she finally realized the amount of attention she was getting. Tristan finally stepped down from the table and endured the painful friendly slaps from his teammates until he reached where we were standing. He handed her the bouquet and she grinned, pressing a kiss onto his cheek.

At first, I thought it was torture to have Jasper and Tristan be our bodyguards earlier in the school year, but I've learned it was partially more horrible to have these sparkly eyes chicks follow you everywhere. I mean, I think I've learned every single shade of MAC lipstick from them, and it had only been a day.

When they were briefly distracted by a story that one of them was telling, we sprinted out of the place. We had to get to work some way or another.

Jasper and Tristan warned us that they would be busy, considering the championships were approaching. Just like that, their first day of school after break, they were dragged away by their coach for practice.

What we didn't knew was that they were preparing us to have a long time without them.

We both started relationships, and yet we've been seeing less and less of them, the cheerleaders were a bunch of girls that are trying to make up for the time without them.

Last time I checked, I signed up for a boyfriend, not a group of babbling girls. But hey, they're not all that bad, at least I got tips on how to make a homemade moisturizing facial scrub.

"Two weeks," Kyla sighed as she plopped down on the stool in front of me as I munched on the bagel I managed to sneak out, "Two weeks since Tristan asked me to be his girlfriend, and the maximum time I get to spend time with him is twenty minutes, not counting our lunch hour."

"They're busy," I chewed, though my tone wasn't as understanding as I wanted it to be. In my defense, I thoroughly miss Jasper, it was like walk to class, eat together, then say a goodbye before we part ways. That was it.

And up until now, he hasn't given me that date he promised.

She looked at the history book I whipped out so I could get some studying done while I was on my break. Kyla blinked at the textbook, before turning to me, "Have you told Jasper about the potential freshman program yet?"

Shaking my head, I ducked my head down and continued to write on my notebook, "It's not a big deal right now."

"Not a big deal?" she slammed her palms onto the counter, "That program isn't simply given to any ordinary student, and the fact you're being considered as a candidate is an incredible big deal."

"I just don't think it's not worth troubling about if it isn't official yet," I muttered in defense.

"And if he finds out during the last minute?"

My mouth pressed into a thin line as I closed my eyes and rubbed my temples. She was right, but we both knew it wasn't the time to say it. I was just a candidate, I have received no letter to confirm that I may part of the university freshman program. It will give me a big advantage, but still, I'm not willing to juggle everything if the time comes.

A part of me was screaming that I should grab the opportunity, but another was telling me that I only get to experience my high school senior year once in my life.

Kyla took my silence as a bad sign and she opened her mouth to speak, "I think I've grown attached those girls," she laughed, trying to make the conversation more lighthearted, "But please slap me when I start reciting the whole Chanel line."

"By the time that happen, I would already have handed you a gun," I joked.

The backdoor of the kitchen opened and everybody turned to its direction. We all stood up, looking at the figure that just stepped inside the workplace. Her pink lips curved into a smile as she dropped her sunglasses from covering her eyes, "Nice to see you all again."

Rebecca Williams, an old friend of Drew and Celeste's, she's currently the manager of all restaurants, café and any other catering service their company owns.

You could say she barely drops by, coming only a few times a year to check personally if everything is still in tip top shape, "Savannah, you're looking extremely well."

"Hey," I greeted her with a smile as she gave me a small hug, giving Kyla a nod of acknowledgement as she settled her purse on the counter, removing her jacket and sitting on one of the stools, "Have you visited the two yet?"

"Of course," she grinned, lacing her fingers together, "Though I could see why Drew looks so stressed, he's dealing with two of his angels."

I have never heard of an elaboration how they all became friends, Drew refused to talk about it, Celeste laughs it off, while Rebecca always shift the topic whenever I ask.

She examines my face for a brief moment, before she slightly frowned, "Is there anything wrong?"

I lifted a hand to check if I had anything stuck on my face, but nope, I was still good. I gave her a quizzical look, and she was still expecting for an answer. When I remained silent, she released a sigh before continuing, "That face only means you have boy trouble."

Well, she saw right through me, "What advice do you have to give for a girl who can barely talk to her boyfriend because they're both so busy?"

I'm a guilty party too when it comes to why Jasper and I conversations are turning less frequent. I did get a huge congratulations from the principal on a job well done with the formal, but my job doesn't stop there. As my vice-president, Kyla also has to tag around on whatever work I have to do. Plus, we still have a job to do. Tristan, on the other hand, requested through a formal letter that he would not be able to take the shifts his position required, cutting down his hours so he could balance with practice.

"Let's see," she tapped her chin thoughtfully, "Why don't you just simply talk to him?"

"If it was that easy, wouldn't be hanging here with a half-eaten bagel," I snorted, and Rebecca cracked a smile at my attitude.

"Just go and approach him. Corner him up if you have to, you just got to clear things up."

"But will that just make me look desperate?" Kyla suddenly joined in, leaning against the table, "Cornering a guy up?"

"It's not always the guy who should be doing all the chasing," she replied, letting Kyla's words die down, "A girl also got to work when she truly likes a person."

One look in her eyes and I knew what she saying, "You're telling this from experience."

She turned to me and gave me a small wink, "Correct, though I must say the results are not always as what you expect."

Since the moment I broke my friendship, Jasper had been the one who was always looking for me, but Rebecca was right, it was time that I do the work and let Jasper rest on this one. He's far too stressed to be the one planning everything.

"Now, it's a Friday night, what are you two doing here on the job?" she questioned, gesturing to the café that was almost approaching its peak hour, "You should be enjoying your youth."

"You speak like you're so old," I teasingly cringed and she laughed, shaking her head.

"Go ahead and have fun," she said, standing up, "Just see it as a day off."

"We actually have nothing better to do," Kyla admitted, taking the bagel that I was no longer interested in. It was quite true, instead of going out and about, we're here because we had no plans. You could say this café has become our comfort.

Other than that, the boys said they had this team meeting, which I presume is just them and the other boys hanging around with boxes of pizza and a few beers. We didn't bother in whining to them, we knew that they deserve the break so we allowed them to go.

Speaking of which, the swinging doors opened to reveal Tristan, and from the way Kyla instantly perked up, she was feeling sudden surge of emotion.

"I told you they'll be here," he yelled over his shoulder, and my eyes softened when I saw Jasper slowly come into view.

And just like that, it was as if all our mopping around minute earlier didn't happen. The worries we were feeling just suddenly disappeared, and as I stared at Jasper, a small smile was making my lips twitch upwards.

Rebecca whistled lowly, "Whipped."

I ignored her statement and jumped off of my stool, instantly lunging for Jasper as if I haven't seen him in days.

"Now you girls go have fun," we heard the woman say from behind us, "I'm sure these two gentlemen didn't go through the trouble of searching for you just for the hell of it."

Tristan recognized who she was and gave her a respectable nod, he whispered something into Kyla's ear, and the girl instantly nodded, rushing to the locker room.

Giving Jasper a look, asking him to be patient, I followed Kyla to the room where the girl was already dressed up and ready to go, "He's talking me out for a dinner date," she squealed.

Taking off my work clothes and changing into my jeans and blouse, I pulled on my jacket before releasing my hair from the ponytail it was in. Placing everything inside my locker, I took out my bag and slammed the metal door shut.

"What's your plan with Jasper?" she asked curiously, "If it isn't too personal."

Giving her a light shrug, I went back out to the kitchen. Honestly, I didn't care where he's taking me, at least I get to spend more than twenty minutes with him then it's absolutely perfect.

The four of us divided into two, while Tristan drove away with Kyla, Jasper offered me a hand for me to take and gave me those boyish smiles, "Shall we take a walk, milady?"

"Last time we took a walk, I ended up deserting you," I reminded him, yet I still took his hand, lacing my fingers through his.

"True," he replied, "But what happened later that day was one of the best things in my life."

My mouth clamped shut and I blushed at the memory. It kept replaying in my mind, and every time it did, it became more and more unbelievable. I'm so scared that I would just suddenly wake up and realize that this was all a dream.

Hugging my jacket tighter to my body, I tried to stir up a conversation, "So is the team shaping up good for the championships?"

"I hope so," he sighed wistfully, "Last year was the first time our school took home the trophy after five years, it's going to be horrible if we lose now."

And the pressure as team captain was now resting on his shoulders. No wonder he's always gone, I could imagine him barking up pep talks left and right.

He suddenly jolted up as if he remembered something. He turned to me, his eyes shining with excitement, "I have yet to take you out on a real date."

Tightening my hold of him, I stopped him from any potential rambling that may happen, "I think this is already the perfect kind of date."

"You're right," he agreed, pulling me along with him, "Once we're in college, we wouldn't be able to have moments like these as often as we do now."

And just like that, the thought of the freshman program entered my mind once again, and my steps slowly became heavier which each one I took. Jasper noticed this and he paused for a moment, looking down at me with concern, "Anything wrong?"

My mouth opened, before it closed again as my brain tried to process what to say. Then, Rebecca's words echoed inside my head.

Why don't I just simply tell him?

"Nothing," I shook my head as I continued on walking.

Because moments like these are too precious to break.

Chapter 22

I've become accustomed to sitting with the cheerleaders to the point they don't phase me anymore. Jasper was right, they may be quirky and a bit crazy, but they were genuine for the most parts. They were friendly with us and even invited us to the outings they usually do.

One of the girls raced from the outside and quickly sat down on the table, grinning towards everybody, "Barbeque at my place tomorrow."

I saw Jasper and Tristan slowly approached our table, both of them holding two trays each. Smiling in appreciation as he set down my meal on the table, the girl once again told them about her plans.

"Let me guess," Jasper said, leaning against the chair that was next to mine, "The parents are out of the house?"

She nodded as she turned to some of the varsity, requesting for help in getting the food drinks for the said party.

"Are we going?" I asked Jasper, turning to him as I munched on the sandwich he bought for me.

Smiling down towards me, he slung an arm around my shoulder, "Only if you want to."

When my eyes lifted up towards Kyla, she was giving me a pointed look, before turning back to her boyfriend. My best friend was partially pressuring me to tell Jasper about the freshman program, but I kept insisting that it was nothing of importance.

Alright, so maybe I should tell him, but she should just let me do it when I know that we're both ready.

Since it was finally Friday, the boys were freed from their training and they were allowed to go on their merry way. Jasper decided that it would be the perfect opportunity to have a fancy date, but , on the other hand decided to just hang out in a chill environment.

So that's how we ended up inside his room with him sprawled out on the floor as I used one of his pillows as a chair while I continuously flipped through my notebooks so I could get my homework done.

Jasper suddenly popped his head over the book I was currently holding and he reached out a hand to snatch it away from me, "Would you please stop working for a second?"

Blinking towards him, I dropped my pen to the floor of his room and leaned towards him, "Alright then."

"I want to catch up," he mumbled, rolling to his stomach, "It feels like I haven't seen you in a week."

"You have," I pointed out, "But not as much as you used to."

"I missed you then," he muttered, even though it's light-hearted, there was still a meaning in there.

I wonder how much we'll miss each other if we have to move miles away from each other after we graduate. That's if we still stay together after high school.

And here's the disadvantages of being a pessimist.

Jasper noticed my silence and he reached out to take my hand in his, "Please stop worrying about it, I'll make time for us."

He's gotten the wrong idea. He thought that I was depressed because I've seen less and less of him, it may be a contributing factor to my dampened mood, but the thought of the freshman program was running inside my head, making it impossible to concentrate on anything else when I'm with him.

"We survived three years without talking each other," he tried to give me an encouraging smile, "This is nothing compared to it."

With my eyes focusing to his features, I tried to commit it to my memory. How his lips will press into a slight frown when he's upset or how his eyebrows will scrunch up in a funny way when he's thinking too hard.

"I have an idea," he brightened up, "Let's go on a vacation this summer, just you and me or we could invite Tristan and Kyla," he grinned, "Just to get some time together before college."

If I were to ever be accepted to that freshman program, I wouldn't have time to experience a summer vacation like what he's planning. I would be traveling away before we could even hop on a car to whatever spectacular thing he had planned out.

I wouldn't be experiencing those cliché last summer trips with my boyfriend.

But with the smile he was giving me, I thought that maybe I could push the idea of telling him to the back of my head, "I'd like that."

You could say that I was slowly being warmed up to Jasper's crowd. At least I no longer felt like an awkward mess while standing beside him as he interacted with his other friends.

Jasper then thrusts a cup of beer into my hand, giving me something to occupy myself with as we strolled along the house. Getting greeted by a few people along the way.

"Just a normal day for the both of us," he muttered, guiding me through the huge amount of people, "Are you enjoying yourself?"

"Yeah," I nodded as I subtly pointed to the table where all the foods are located. He laughed and maneuvered us to it, falling in line as grabbed our plates.

Just then, somebody climbed up to the stacked coolers, yelling at everybody to shut up. We turned to him and he raised his cup, starting to propose a toast.

"This is for Jasper," he grinned. Turning to my boyfriend, his eyes widened in shock as he started to sprint his way to him, shoving and pushing the people that's in his way, an act of desperation to make the boy stop talking.

"You're really great, man, who else could have…" before he could even finish his sentence. Jasper tackled him to the ground, pulling him off of the coolers. Both were unharmed, but when I slowly approached the mini pile they made, I stared at Jasper, waiting for an explanation.

Kyla cautiously made her way towards my side as Tristan helped his best friend up along with the other guy. He reprimanded Jasper, but the latter only huffed in annoyance as he helped the poor boy he attacked.

"You alright?" Kyla questioned and I gave her a numb confirmation that I was. What was running inside my mind was what made Jasper panic like that.

"Don't do that again," Tristan warned under his breath, "You both could have gotten hurt."

"Yeah," Jasper murmured as he gave the guy a pat on the shoulder, "Sorry about that."

"It's alright," he waved off, dusting himself off, "Next time, don't man handle me."

With no hard feelings between them, they quickly forgave each other. I, on the other hand, still stared at him with outmost curiosity and worry.

"Jasper," I finally called out, making people's attention turn to me, "What was he saying?"

All color drained from his face as he opened his mouth to explain, but he quickly closed when he couldn't find the words. I couldn't get mad at him if he's trying to hide a secret, since I am too, but I don't think I would go to an extent where I might physically injure my friend just to keep it hidden.

"Boy's in trouble," somebody hollered from the crowd, easing the tension a bit. People gradually came back to what they were doing before the sudden scene caused by Jasper.

But my body couldn't move, it was like waiting for a word from him to assure myself that it was nothing.

He looked like a deer caught in the headlights and I was a car speeding towards him. This time, I turned on my heel, giving him a look that clearly showed that he should follow me so we could talk in privacy. Kyla tried to reach out to me, but Tristan quickly pulled her back.

This time, I was thankful for Tristan's intervention, he knew that this was a matter that should be discussed with just the two of us.

Who knew that the least crowded place was the girl's front yard?

"So…" I trailed off, kicking a pebble that was sitting on the green grass, "Are you going to explain?"

"It's nothing," he mumbled, trying to wave off the topic, "It's has no importance."

Those were my exact same words when Kyla pressured me into telling Jasper. Somehow, it scared me to be the receiving end of that statement. He could be in the same position as me, but I didn't want to jump into conclusions.

If I was stubborn of keeping my own secret from him, then I shouldn't be such a hypocrite, but the cat is already out of the bag, I just have to chase it, it's practically impossible for him to shove it back in.

"Got it," I smiled rather bitterly as I started to stomp away from him.

"Where are you going?" he called out after me.

"Home," I yelled out as my reply, not even pausing to see if he was running after me. I already know Jasper enough to figure out that he's already sprinting the small distance I placed between us.

He yelled out my name, but instead of turning back, I kept on going. Never mind the fact that he could easily go into his car and catch up.

Because of how fast he is, he managed to find his spot next to me, now walking to match my pace, "Savannah, come on."

Nope, I was holding my ground on this.

The place wasn't actually far away from our houses, but it still took a bit of time to get there on foot. You could only imagine how irritating it was for me to listen Jasper's attempts to snap me out of this mood. I was near seconds away from banging my head on the stop sign.

I felt so relieved when I finally saw my house come into view. Unfortunately, even on my way to the front door, Jasper followed me.

Just when I was about to enter, Jasper said something that made me chest drop.

"It's as if you weren't hiding anything," he said, making me turn to him with shock. I'm pretty sure he was smirking victoriously inside his head because he accomplished his mission to make me notice him again, but he masked it with a hard look, "I know about the freshman program thing."

My body felt numb and all color drained from my face as I released the doorknob I was clutching. I blinked several times at him, trying to wrack my brain for something to say.

How did he find out? What should I do?

"You must have a good reason to hide it," he continued, "Then you need to understand that I do too."

"I'm sorry," was the only thing I managed to say. Looking down towards me, he shook his head and reached out take my hand into his.

"Let's go back," he suggested, running smooth circles on my skin, "And forget this ever happened."

"That's kind of impossible," I muttered, but to compensate, I leaned up and pressed a kiss on his cheek, "I'll see you tomorrow?"

"Savannah, don't be like this," he mumbled under his breath, obviously frustrated how this is turning out.

Trust me, I was getting annoyed as well.

The both of us needs to cool down and have a nice and peaceful conversation tomorrow. He needs to tell me about whatever secret he's keeping and I need to explain why I even hid my own secret from him.

He ran a hand through his and sighed loudly, "I don't want to tell you yet because I feel like you're going to act different-ly."

Whatever it is, it mustn't be as bad as mine, or am I just denying myself?

"Now come on," he tugged on my hand lightly, a signal that he thinks that this was over, but before he could even take a step forward, I closed my eyes and pulled back.

"I didn't tell you because I was scared that the end was finally coming," I almost yelled, "It's very far away, Jasper, almost across the country, and I didn't want to be separated from you."

That line was exclusive for a girl who was so desperate for her boyfriend and thinks that she can't live without him. It wasn't fit for me, yet here I was, blurting out those words to him.

"The freshman program requires me to be there earlier than the start of the school year," I explained, my voice becoming weaker with every word, "And that means that I wouldn't get to spend the summer with you, I was scared that I would be crushing whatever you were hoping for."

"Then you should know that I'm extremely proud of you," he expressed out sincerely, effectively shutting me up, "I mean, my girlfriend was amazing enough to do that."

I forced a small smile so he would stop his little speech that I'm sure would break me down. I allowed him to drag me back to the barbeque where we were greeted with a bunch of questions, I allowed him to introduce him to his lackeys that I know ran away from me months ago, I allowed him to see me happy.

Knowing him, he's going to be so disappointed if I tell him that I got accepted to the program and I'm considering on going. He's only trying to be positive because his knowledge is only limited to the fact that I might not want to go.

Chapter 23

My finger was hovering over the enter button of my laptop as my brain tried to reason itself out with me. Just one press of the button will send my confirmation letter out and that means I've officially accepted the freshman program.

It also meant that I said no to whatever summer Jasper was planning.

"Savannah, could you please help me with my packing?" Celeste knocked on my door, gently cracking it open, "We have to get everything ready for our flight tomorrow."

She took one look at my face for her to realize there was something wrong. Clicking her tongue, she shook her head and completely entered my room, "Let me guess this one, boy trouble?"

"Kind of," I sighed, turning my laptop so the screen was shown to her. She squinted a bit as she read the words and a small smile was creeping onto her face. She was proud of what she had seen, but she was still aware that this was upsetting me.

"Grab your jacket, we'll go for a walk," she said, heading to the door, "My sister-in-law is much more important than packing."

Closing my laptop, I quickly stood up and took my knitted cardigan from the back of my desk chair as I followed her out. Drew popped his head from his room and caught the sight of the two of us going down the stairs, "Where are you two going?"

Celeste reached out her hand towards her husband and beckoned for him to come near. He looked back inside the room, probably contemplating if he should leave whatever mess that exploded inside there, but of course, he went with his wife.

"Now where are we going?" he repeated as he held Celeste's hand in his. I can never ignore how in love these two are, it was sickening yet sweet at the same time.

"We're going to tell Savannah a little thing we learned while we were in high school," she replied as the two of them led the way while I obediently trailed along. She took a quick detour to the living room first, grabbing her bag before continuing on the journey.

We passed by Jasper's house and I frowned, the reminder of my decision lugging with me as I continued to follow these two. They were chatting to themselves, often shooting a quick look towards me, making sure I was still there.

The streets got busier as we walked on and the rising skyscrapers were coming into view. They entered one of the buildings and I gulped as I follow, knowing this all too well. Celeste shot a smile towards the guard who bowed his head respectfully towards her.

"What are we doing at your old place, Celeste?" I questioned, looking around the fancy lobby. She winked at me as she asked for a piece of paper from the reception desk. She handed it to me and I examined it, "It's blank."

"Pretend that's an acceptance letter from the university," she told me, "Now what would have you felt?"

"Pretty excited," I shrugged, completely lost in this situation.

She shook her head and plucked the paper from my hands, "When I got mine, I was scared."

"Are we going to relive your life or something?"

"She's got it!" she clapped, removing her hand from Drew's arm to grab mine, "I believe teaching in actions is much better than words."

We then got dragged out and continued our quick descent to wherever else Celeste decided to take us.

I don't know how long our adventure was, but I was soon becoming familiar to the surroundings. They halted right in front of a medium sized house with a white picket fence protecting it from the world. It had a rusting bench on the front porch and the grass grew tall with the years it must have been deserted from.

"Welcome home, Savannah," Celeste smiled, opening the gate which made a loud creaking noise. I cringed at the sound but I observed the couple as they walked to the porch,

"I then visited your house and told Drew what was happening."

"You should have seen the look on her face," my brother cracked a grin, "She was terrified and in such a panic, I had to pull her out of the house before she started to have a meltdown."

I cautiously walked in, my feet trying to make sure I only stepped on the rocky path that lead to the front door. The plants surrounding the place had withered and died, it was always a mystery why they refused to sell this place, I mean, we already have a better house.

Drew opened the door, indicating that it was never locked all these years. We stepped inside and I examined the dust filled walls and corners of the house. From the foyer you can see the doorway leading up to the living room and kitchen and at the side, there leans the small staircase leading to the upstairs.

"You know, if you never left this house, you might have never been best friends with Jasper," Celeste pointed out, casually circling around the room , "I mean, maybe you could have bumped into each other, but you've grown so close because the fact you two are neighbors."

"Then nothing would be bugging your head right now," Drew added, "You could have sent that confirmation letter days ago with no hesitation."

Biting my lip, I agreed with their words and it was slowly breaking down my insides. If I haven't been best friends with Jasper, then I wouldn't have fallen for him, get into a huge mess called a broken friendship, and then at some point, get myself in a relationship with him.

Then I could get myself shipped off to university without batting an eye.

"Picture yourself four years from now," Celeste spoke which made me close my eyes, "What do you see?"

A very stressed college chick who's about to graduate.

"Me trying to finish up everything so I could leave college with flying colors?" I answered and I saw Celeste blew out a breath of frustration.

"What's the point of this?" I asked, my patience running thin. How could this be possibly related to my problem?

"Alright then, let's go straight to the park," she announced, "Forward, my mates."

I dragged myself behind them, mumbling incoherent words under my breath, finding this less than enjoyable. We entered the park where the trees were just beginning to grow back the leaves that old man winter stole away.

They took a step to the side, no longer hindering my view. My eyes widened as I saw Jasper sitting on one of the benches, nervously twiddling with the falling button on his jacket.

"Called him here when we were walking," Drew said as he turned to Celeste who took out an envelope from her bag. She waved it to me, telling me to get it.

When I cautiously slipped out the paper from it, I gazed over the paper that indicated the offer to the early freshman program. It was a letter that came in the mail weeks ago, something I never took out of the house before.

"I snatched it before we left," Celeste explained, "Now how about you talk the guy you used to hide that thing from?"

Jasper lifted his gaze and it landed towards where we were standing. He lifted up a hand as a wave of hello and I returned it with a soft smile. I took a step forwards, but before I could continue on, I turned back to the happy couple who claimed something important happened here, "What did you two do after Celeste walked to our house?"

"We talked about prom," Celeste informed, exchanging a look with Drew. From the glint in their eyes, I knew it was something more than that.

"And?" I urged and they shook their heads, refusing to say more. Letting out a sigh, I lifted my brows, "Then why did you take me on this grand escapade?"

"To buy Jasper time to get here," Drew answered smoothly, "Plus, it was a good trip down memory lane."

"You two are ridiculous!" I groaned, tugging on my hair in frustration.

"Are we the ones who are ridiculous right now?" they fired back, "It's a simple yes or no question on whether you'll go to that freshman program or not."

My lips slowly turned down into a frown and Drew gave me a slight push towards Jasper's direction, giving me an encouraging nod. Stiffly letting my feet walk forward, I forced a smile when I finally got to him.

Jasper lifted his phone and then nudged his head to subtly point towards my brother, "Any reason why they called me up here?"

My hand that was gripping the envelope lifted up so I could hand it to him. He understood the message and took it, reading the words printed on paper, "I already know about this, Savannah."

"And I'm going," I muttered softly, partially hoping that he didn't hear it. Unfortunately, he did, and his head snapped up with his mouth hanging wide in shock.

Oh come on, he should have known that I was seriously considering it.

He handed me back the envelope and sunk back down on the bench. I blinked down at him, my hands fidgeting as I tried to collect the right words, "I'm still considering, I mean, one word from you and I won't go."

For heaven's sake, Savannah, stop being one of those girls who will change her whole life around because of one stupid boy.

But the thing is, this boy isn't stupid and I'm starting to be one of those girls.

"Do you seriously think that I'm going to be that jerk who stops his girlfriend from having this great opportunity just because he doesn't want her to go?"

I don't know what I'm thinking. It's like a part of me is silently hoping that he'll beg me to stay, to say that he needed me, like he was going to miss in our time apart. Then there's this other part that is asking him to let me go, because I this will look amazing for my grades. This really confusing, but hey, I'm a woman.

Sitting on the bench beside him, I sighed, recalling the words Celeste said to me earlier, "Picture yourself four years from now," I finally got what she was trying to imply, "What do you see?"

I missed the point earlier, but it was like a test, if I saw Jasper there, then that means that I really want to be with him, if I didn't, then it's a blurry future.

"I hate doing that," he mumbled, my idea going down the drain. I stared at him dumbly for his refusal of the action as he opened his mouth to explain, "I'm not good at keeping promises, Savannah, that's why I rarely make them."

"How's that related to this?" I asked, my brain getting jumbled, trying to grasp what was happening.

"Because if I close my eyes and picture myself, it's like I'm promising myself to an image that my present self is conjuring up," he said, "And I know for one thing is that I want you to be there."

Oh gosh, that was enough for my whole mind to be cleared and allow a rushing sense of adoration directed to the boy in front of me.

He took my hand and pressed a soft kiss to it, "I'm not going to promise you anything, because it might just hurt us both."

There goes the relief and comes in a new set of doubts.

It's like he indirectly told me that our relationship wouldn't last. He implied that he had no confidence that we could make this work. The insecurities and fears came into my mind, and I had to fight the quick urge to slap my hand onto his mouth, just for him to stop adding more to this horrible ordeal.

"But I promised to be with you, didn't I?" he told me, attempting to soothe me, "Please, let that be enough."

"Can you at least promise me one other thing?" I requested, staring up at him, "Promise you'll try to make this work."

I expected this to turn just like any other puppy love romance where he'll blindly say yes. Heck, even I know it's difficult, but I was hanging by a thread right here.

When he shook his head, my hand dropped from his grasp, "It's like I promise to stab as both. We're not Romeo and Juliet."

My mouth refused to say any more words, for one thing, I couldn't handle it. Was there a future beyond college for this relationship or is this just some high school romance that I'll be able to tell my children in the future and warn them to never go through it?

Due to Celeste and Drew, I had a bit of hope that we will last. I was silently praying that I ended up like my brother, that even when Celeste came anxious about everything, as she had told me, all Drew did was assure her that they'll stay together.

But apparently, I don't have a Drew, I have a Jasper.

"If that's the way you think..." I trailed off, looking down to my shoes, "How about a trial period?"

This was more of a way to clear my mind. He was silent and I still refused to meet his eyes, fearing what I would feel when I do, "Let's pretend we're not together for a while."

It was a training ground, since if he's not willing to fight, then I have to shine my armor myself.

"Are we breaking up?"

Shaking my head, I denied whatever he was thinking, "Just to see what it feels like. I mean, we're still going to be friend, but we're just going to act like we're not boyfriend and girl-friend."

And we're back to square one.

He seemed to understand what I was trying to say and he nodded. Sucking in a deep breath, he jammed his hands into his pockets, "Alright."

"Alright," I forced a smile, that word just reminds me of so many things, "Shall we head home?"

What I'm doing is to make sure the blow wouldn't be too hard. Because as I understand it, we're going downhill.

No holding hands, no kisses, not even a single touch as we walked back to our houses. A simple wave was all our goodbye.

I walked past Celeste who came back with Drew while Jasper and I were talking. Before she could even ask how it went, I ran upstairs and locked myself inside my bedroom. I closed my curtains and I laid on my bed, biting my lip as I was internally cursing myself inside my head.

"Stupid Savannah," I whispered to myself, "Why did you have to let yourself fall for Jasper?"

Perhaps that was the only time I came close to crying my eyes out for a boy.

Chapter 24

"Do you think that I did the right thing?" I asked Kyla over the phone as my eyes fell upon the clock hanging on my wall. It was already half past midnight, but I was lucky that she was willing to talk to me right now.

She was silent for a while, probably thinking of the right answer, but as she clicked her tongue, she spoke, "I'm not really sure, I think you were just talking out of fear."

Well, I am scared. College is not as simple as high school, where if you live in the same city, you're probably going to see each other again. It's much more complicated to the point it's unsure if you're even going to stay in touch.

"Kyla!" I whined, even I'm sick of hearing myself think this over.

"How about you go get some sleep, the boys have their championships tomorrow and we have to be there to support them," she muttered before I heard her yawn.

A small frown overcame my face, but I agreed with her, I felt kind of guilty for making her stay up with me, but like

I said, I'm extremely lucky to have her as my best friend, "Alright, good night."

"Night," she mumbled before she hung up. I threw my phone on the bed beside me and I looked up at the ceiling, trying to get myself some sleep, it was nearly impossible though.

Pushing myself up, I walked to my window and opened the curtain. My eyes were expecting Jasper's curtains, but to my surprise, his window was open. It was kind of weird considering he usually kept it close during the night.

I squinted a little bit and saw the moving light from his phone, indicating that he was still awake. I watch him glance up to his window, giving him a good view of myself. My eyes widened and I ducked down so he wouldn't see me.

Not yet, I wasn't ready.

"Savannah?" I heard his voice, and I clamped a hand over my mouth to prevent myself from saying anything. Once again, I heard him call out my name, "Savannah?!"

Thankfully, he gave up only after two tries. I peeked a bit and saw his retreating figure, probably going back to bed. I bit my lip and shook my head, slowly closing my windows and curtains, making sure they didn't make a sound.

If you think that I got sleep after that escapade, then you're wrong – completely and absolutely wrong.

When it was nearing six in the morning, I finally gave up and I kicked my blankets off after a night of tossing and turning on my bed. I was frightened by what I saw in the mirror, especially my eyes, they were nearing the color red.

I tip toed around the house, making sure I woke nobody up. The first thing I did when I got in the kitchen, I prepared myself a huge cup of coffee, I'm going to need it if I want to survive the day with a functioning system.

Opening the cupboards and fridge, I gathered enough ingredients to make everybody in house' favorite – chocolate pancakes.

My mom was the first person to go down, she saw that I was already preparing breakfast and she gave me smile as she poured herself some orange juice, "I rarely see you up so early."

"I figured it's useless to push myself into something that's impossible," I replied tc her statement, sipping on my mug of coffee, before I flipping the pancake on the pan. Whether if I was talking about my situation about Jasper or I was just being melodramatic about sleep, I may never know.

I finished up the last pancake and placed the big plate on the dining table as my mother prepared the rest of the breakfast as we waited for the other members of the family.

Dad was the next one to go down and he licked his lips at the delicious sight of the pancakes, "Good morning, girls."

It took some time before Celeste and Drew come, probably because as they went down the stairs, they were already dragging their luggage with them. When they caught sight of me, Drew scrunched up his eyebrows as he stared at my face.

"What happened to you?" he questioned, sitting down on the chair next to his wife, "You look like you didn't get a blink of sleep."

"I didn't," I stated, trying to be nonchalant, but in fact, I was holding back a yawn so they wouldn't press on more.

He shook his head as he settled a hand on top of my head, "You need to rest, don't get so worried about one guy."

Celeste laughed next to him and shook her head, "If a girl really likes that one guy, she'll always worry," she said, forking in some pancakes into her mouth, "And sometimes, that includes losing sleep."

"Amen," mom nodded from the other side of her table. My dad turned to her and she gave him a sheepish smile.

"I'm just worried about my little sister," Drew protested, crossing his arms like a child, making the others laugh.

Celeste looked up at me and offered an encouraging smile, "It's part of the learning experience."

If I wasn't upset enough, I stood there in front of the van that will drive my brother and my sister-in-law to the airport. They're going to be gone again for a very long time, which is a bigger bad news than everything.

Drew packed the bags at the trunk while Celeste approached me and pulled me into a tight hug, "I'll miss you."

"What am I going to do?"

She laughed at this, probably finding this amusing, but for me, it was absolute torture, "Just so you know, everything will fall into place, just trust yourself and Jasper."

I looked at her skeptically and she turned to back at Drew, before speaking, "I'm married to your brother, he's my complete opposite and if we were able to stay together after all the crap we've been through, then I have confidence you and Jasper will too."

I still question how Drew managed to get her. She's prim and proper, on the other hand, my brother is the idiot who accidentally opened one of the bags while loading it, causing most of its contents to fall to the pavement.

Rolling my eyes, I walked over to him and helped him pick up the stray clothes. He stuffed them all back into the bag and closed the trunk, wiping the beads of sweat that was forming on his forehead.

"You're leaving me again?" I asked, my voice small like a little child getting abandoned by her parents.

Drew laughed and shook his head, "I'll be back, who else is going to pull you out of trouble?"

"I think I'm old enough to do that myself," I retorted.

"To me, you're still that annoying kid who jumps on my bed to wake me up every damn morning."

For the first time all day, I smiled. He lifted a hand and I have him a high five, before I jumped into his arms, surprising him. His shoulders shook to indicate he was laughing once again, before returning the hug, "Finish your story with a good ending, baby sister."

"Of course," I fist bumped him, "We siblings need to have our happy ending."

It was far from a tearful goodbye, mostly because I knew that I would be seeing them again. I waved at them as their van slowly drove away.

My eyes looked up to the house next door and they instantly connected to Jasper's. He nodded a hello to me, and I gave him a soft smile back. He gestured for me to wait for him to go outside, but I shook my head, pointing back to my house to indicate that I needed to go back inside.

I opened my laptop and once again, went to the page where my application was ready to be sent. It just takes on press of the button and everything's done.

This simple thing is the reason why I can't go on peacefully.

So I did the mature thing I could do, I lifted my middle finger at the screen as if it would make a difference.

I fell down on the couch and blew a sigh, my eyes were still glued to my laptop, it was freaking taunting me, and the deadline was coming up soon, if I don't make a decision, I wouldn't have any choice at all. It may be a good excuse, but I feel like I'm going to regret it for the rest of my life.

Somehow, I fell asleep while having my dramatic contemplation. When I woke up, my eyes bugged out when I saw the time and when I scrambled around to look for my phone, I almost fainted at the amount of missed calls coming from Kyla.

Panicking, I grabbed a jacket and my car keys, rushing out of the house, dialing Kyla's number as I sprinted to my vehicle that was parked in front of the driveway.

"Where the hell are you?" she growled as I heard the loud noises coming from the background.

"I fell asleep," I answered, my voice frustrated as I tried to maneuver to the street, "I'm so sorry."

"I thought you got into an accident or something," I heard her voice filled with relief, "Just come here, the game's starting to get intense."

"Got it," I said, hanging up on my phone, concentrating on the road as I tried not to go over the speed limit. When I reached the school, the parking lot was already packed. Cursing under my breath, I just decided to double park, I'm going to get into a lot of trouble because of this, but I'm already screwed anyways.

I rushed into the school and I could already hear the loud screams from the gym. puffed out as I entered, feeling like I just got slapped by the face with the huge commotion. I looked up at the scoreboard and felt disappointed to see that we were lugging behind.

Scanning the bleachers, I walked over to where Kyla was standing, right at the near bottom where she was already leaning to the railings, I was quite afraid she was going to fall.

"Oh finally," Kyla mumbled when she saw me, "You should have seen how badly it's been."

The cheerleaders who was standing in front of us from the other side of the concrete separating the bleachers from the main court turned to us when they noticed my arrival. They nodded in agreement to Kyla statement and approached us, "This has probably been the worst game Jasper has ever played," one of them frowned, "And he's been doing this for a long time."

Kyla looped her arm around mine to get my attention, "Look at him," she whispered and my gaze placed itself on Jasper, "He looks tired and upset."

She was right, he looked horrible. His eyes were puffed out and red, maybe a mirror of what I looked like before my nap, and his steps were slow, a huge change from his usual swift movements. That used to be his biggest advantage – his speed.

When the opponent shot another basket, our coach looked like he was ready to throw away the clipboard he was holding. Jasper scratched the back of his head, looking completely angry with himself and Tristan approached him to pat his back.

The referee blew his whistle and the boys went to him where the ball was once again passed to initiate the game.

"Excuse us, we have to do our job," the cheerleaders smiled to us, setting into position as they faced court, executing their routine as they encouraged the crowd to yell whatever cheer they were calling out.

It looked pointless though, the boys were still doing a lousy job, that's when I felt that they were really a team. If one of them were down, they all were. It wasn't just ordinary teammate that was off his game, it was their captain.

Stupid Savannah, you just had to do it right before the game.

"Let's go, Tigers!" the girls screamed at the top of their lungs, doing different tricks and flips.

I watched as Tristan snatch the ball from one of the players from the other team and he did a three-pointer. Our school hollered their joy that we finally got a shot in, Kyla squealed proudly next to me, her eyes set on her boyfriend.

"Go Tristan!" Kyla cheered, with her loud yell, Tristan was able to recognize her distinct voice from the crowd and his eyes fell on us. He grinned and waved to her, at the same time, Jasper turned to where he was looking and saw me there.

Last night, it was dark so it's possible that I didn't see it, earlier, I didn't look at him long enough to notice it, but now, as we stared at each other, I felt like somebody punched me a thousand times.

His eyes showed distraught and every kind of sadness I could think of. His mouth was set on a perpetual frown and he was pale, an indication that he wasn't in the best condition.

Oh fuck, I did this.

"Good luck," I mouthed, forcing myself to show him a small smile. He needs this, I need to hide how depress I am for him. We're going to fall apart more if we go on like this.

He nodded as he went back to the court. Kyla tapped my shoulder before telling me, "About your question earlier, you did the right thing."

"What do you mean?" I questioned, thoroughly confused.

"You'll know sooner or later," was her simple answer before turning her attention back to the game.

Jasper finally shot a basket and I unintentionally allowed a yell escape my mouth, jumping up and down in excitement. Kyla laughed beside me, finding my sudden outburst amusing. He turned to me and grinned when he saw me with my hands up in the air, cheering for him.

That was all it took for Jasper to get his head back into the game, and our school quickly caught up with the score. With the consistency of our points, the supporters were getting wilder and wilder.

There were only a few seconds until the game ended, but we were still behind by two points. My eyes were glued to Jasper who was dribbling the ball in front of an opponent, trying to find a way to circle around him.

Tristan rounded up behind him and he quickly passed it. The gym fell silent, finally feeling the tension as the timer kept counting down.

Since he was finally free, he ran to the other side of the court and got the ball from Tristan. We all held our breath when he tried to run to their basket, but a bastard ran against him and he hit him. He started to fall backwards and everything went in slow motion inside my head.

I don't know why or how, but I cupped my mouth and screamed his name, "Jasper!"

He snapped out of it and praying that the odds were with him, he threw the ball just before he hit the floor. The crowd gasped as all of us watched the ball zoom pass across the court. It spun around the rim of the basket a few times before it finally fell in.

Our side of the gym started going into a frenzy, finding the outmost happiness in our team's victory. The boys of the basketball team shook hands with the other school before going to Jasper who refused to move from his lying position on the floor.

More and more people came to him, causing me to worry. Kyla and I exchanged a look before we pushed past the people to get down the bleachers and to where he was.

"Move!" I demanded, shoving the people who circled themselves around him. I found him at the center, clutching his right shoulder as he winced in pain. Tristan was kneeling beside him, patting his best friend, saying a couple of encouraging words to him.

I fell down on the floor and I grabbed his face, rubbing comforting circles on his cheeks. His eyes opened to reveal that I was glistening with unshed tears as he groaned, trying to even out his breathing.

"You alright?" I asked a very stupid question, but to my complete surprise, he closed his eyes shut and nodded.

"Alright."

The team all worked together in order to carry him to the clinic while inflicting the least pain possible on him. Of course, I followed obediently behind them with Kyla who looked at me with worry, as if I was the one who came crashing down earlier.

We were all kindly asked by the school nurse to wait out as he looked over his injuries. I think I was about to waste my nails for I was so near to going back to my bad habit of biting them caused by the anxiousness.

Tristan wrapped one arm around Kyla's shoulder and the other one on mine, "He'll be fine, we're talking about Jasper here."

I nodded numbly as I stared at the clinic door, waiting for it to open so I could see him again. There were still a lot of people in the hallway, which isn't a big surprise since the star player is in there getting treated.

"Poor Jasper," one of the cheerleaders who was passing by said.

"But I think it improved his chances, the agent seemed really impressed with his last minute move," her friend piped in.

My attention snapped to their direction and I felt Tristan stiffen, making me suspicious.

"So, do you girls want some ice cream while we wait?" he tried to divert my focus, but nope, I had to hear this.

"Just imagine," the girl giggled, "A scholarship to Europe."

What did the pompom waving love child of a rainbow and a drop of sunshine just say?!

Chapter 25

Should I be furious? Angry? Saddened? Depressed? Confused?

All I knew was one thing, I was out of here.

Pushing myself off against the wall, I started to march down the hallway. I heard Kyla call out for me, but I kept on walking, there's no freaking way that I would be staying there.

I heard footsteps behind me, and I knew Kyla and Tristan are following me but are keeping a safe distance just in case I decided to explode in front of everybody in the hallway.

How dare Jasper Dean makes me feel all guilty when he was the one moving away?! I'm just going away for an early summer, he's moving to another fucking continent here!

When I stepped out of the school, I cursed everything in the world to see that somebody has parked in front of my car, making me stranded in this stupid place. Turning around, I reached out my palm to Kyla, requesting her to give me her keys.

She frowned, but she seemed to understand as she took it out from her pocket. Just as she was about to give it to me, Tristan snatched it from her hand and quickly pocketed it, "You're not going anywhere until you hear his side."

"He's going to study in Europe!" I screeched, my voice much higher than I expected, "Europe, Tristan, and he can't even find a single second to tell me about it."

Using his hand, he covered my mouth to stop me from rambling on any further. He gave me a stern look, telling me not to argue with him, "I don't know how the hell those girls got the conclusion that he was running for a scholarship in Europe, but calm yourself because he isn't."

Huh?

When I fell silent, he took away his hand and allowed it to run along his hair, "Please think for a moment, Europe's not that interested in basketball, well, to the level of Americans that is."

Say what?

He snapped his fingers in front of me, trying to make me respond to his words, "Are you even getting any of this?"

No Europe?

"She has officially lost it," Kyla threw her hands up in the air in exasperation, "Maybe we should get her inside?"

She tugged on my arm and I blinked multiple times before my gaze focused on her face. She was still lightly pulling me, trying to make me move. I was squished between Tristan and Kyla as if I was a small child, getting assisted as I did my first steps.

There were still some people loitering along the hallway, some even got their snacks and were now contentedly sitting on the floor like they were all having a large picnic.

When the nurse got outside the school clinic, he jumped up in surprise at the amount of students just casually waiting outside the room. He tried to make his way to the center, doing his best to make sure he didn't step on anything or anyone.

"Alright, I want everybody to leave now," he announced, clapping his hands so he would be able to catch the attention of everybody. They stared at him for a quick moment before they completely ignored him, returning to their individual businesses.

His look settled upon me, clearly asking for help to herd everyone out. The thing is, even I don't want to go.

I shifted my gaze so I didn't have to force myself to do something I'm not willing to do. Months ago, I would have yelled at these people in a heartbeat for even ignoring somebody in authority, but right now, my only concern is Jasper.

Get a grip of yourself, Savannah, you still have a job to fulfill.

I'm defeated — completely and utterly defeated.

Tristan placed a hand on my shoulder and gave me an encouraging pat, "I'll stay here with him, you should all go, I think he'll be angrier with himself if he finds out you're acting like this because of him."

I pursed my lips into a straight line as I saw Kyla nod her head in agreement, "Come on, I kind of miss the old terror that is our student body president."

She gave off a light laugh to lift up my mood. The nurse were still cupping his hands around his mouth, yelling at people to leave, even going as far tapping the students out.

Taking a deep breath, I crossed my arms over my chest and screamed at the top of my lungs, "Everybody out!"

Silence.

They were all shocked, most of the paused at whatever they were doing. The nurse blinked up at me, silently thanking me.

Tristan took an instinctive step backward as his girlfriend did the complete opposite, just like what our tag team used to be, she was the pretty face that got everybody calmed and assured that I wouldn't be murdering anybody while I was the one throwing commands that everybody needs to follow.

"Do I have to repeat myself?" I questioned, lifting a brow. My voice getting colder and more threatening, they shook their heads and little by little, the full hallways were starting to become empty.

When the last student came running out, I dropped my arms to my side and I let out a sigh, "They hate me again."

"No they don't," Kyla quickly shot down my assumption, "They were surprised more than anything, we haven't seen that side of you since, you know..."

"Jasper meddled?" I finished for her.

"Since he made you happy," she corrected. She turned to Tristan and gave him a smile, "You got this?"

He nodded as he walked back towards us, "You girls go home, I'll keep an eye on Jasper."

"I want to stay too," I blurted out. They looked at me and simultaneously shook their heads, turning me down.

Kyla pressed a kiss or Tristan's cheek before she walked towards me and took my hand, "Let's go."

She ignored my protests as she continued to tug me with her. I looked back to where Tristan was standing, waving as goodbye until he completely disappeared from our view. Even though I was half expecting it, I was shocked to see the crowded parking lot almost empty.

My car was now happily able to smoothly drive out of this place. I could just wait until Kyla goes away and then I can sneak back in there. Unfortunately, my best friend was a little bit smarter than that and she was basically glaring holes at the back of my head until I was inside my car. Even when she was inside her vehicle, she was still staring at me until I went off.

I seriously have no escape around this.

So with a pout of defeat, I drove back home and Kyla acted like a police escort who followed me around until I reached my house. She grinned triumphantly as she watched me enter, giving her a dirty look.

The only thing I could do was pull my curtains back and pray that when I wake up, Jasper would be safely back inside his room.

When the annoying birds started chirping in the morning, my eyes shot open and I got out of bed, immediately looking at my window, sadly, Jasper's curtains were covering whatever view I can get.

So I did the next good thing, I grabbed my jacket and I headed down. Mom called me up for breakfast, but before she could even finish her sentence, I was already out of the door.

I waked to the neighboring house and rang their doorbell. Not too long, Jasper's stunning mother opened the door and gave me a welcoming smile, "Savannah, it's rare to see you here quite early in the morning."

Looping my arms behind my back, I forced myself to reach her joyous mood, "I'm just kind of worried about Jasper."

I wonder if her grin could get any bigger. She stepped to the side and opened the door wider, "Well, we're just having breakfast, why don't you join us?"

"I don't want to be a bother, I'll just come back later."

Of course, she was having none of my excuses. She pulled me in and ushered me to the dining room, "I can't have my future daughter-in-law starve."

I froze to my spot at what she just said. When she turned to me, she started laughing at my mortified expression as she turned back and continued on walking.

Going too fast there, lady.

When I finally got to my senses, I rushed to follow her into the room. Jasper's father was seated on the table next to him who had his shoulder wrapped in a white bandage.

"Savannah's here," his mother announced as she headed to the kitchen, probably to prepare me my own plate of whatever breakfast they were having.

Jasper's head shot up to look at me and I waved awkwardly to them. His dad looks up from his phone and smiled towards me, "Good morning, you came to visit Jasper?"

"Oh why else would she be here?" his mom piped up, walking in with a bowl of cereal, "Young love is so precious."

At times like these, it's no wonder how my parents and his parents got along so easily.

Jasper stood up from the table and walked up to me before turning to his parents, "Savannah and I are just going to talk."

"Don't forget your cereal," she beamed, approaching me before thrusting the bowl into my hands, "Most important meal of the day."

"Thank you," I nodded with a small smile as Jasper escorted me out.

I was one step behind him as he went up the stairs and into his room. He closed his door and I gulped audibly, fearing the worst.

Wait, I'm not ready for this!

When a guy usually gets a girl in his room, doesn't he mean that he wants do something with her? But Jasper's a gentleman, he's not like that. Plus, it's broad daylight and his parents are just downstairs, thinking that we're having a friendly chat over this bowl of cereal.

"Savannah..." Jasper trailed off, approaching me.

Fuck.

I looked around frantically for something to distract myself. I grabbed the spoon and I started to stuff my mouth with this cereal, the milk spilling to the sides of my mouth.

He was looking at me as if lost my head, but you're not getting a piece of this glorious creation until I finish this cereal.

It's quite good if you ask me, I better ask her what cereal this is.

He grabbed my shoulders and my mouth fell open; I probably look the most unattractive codfish in the world. He slowly took the bowl from my hand, but I refused to let go of it. I knew he was forcing to keep that smile as he struggled to take it from grasp.

No, this cereal is my only salvation!

"When the hell is a bowl of processed wheat and corn your saving grace?!" he questioned the most ridiculous thing.

Did I just say that out loud?

Letting out an impatient sigh, he finally took the bowl from me and carefully placed it on his desk, "Calm down and forget the cereal for a moment."

When he took another step forward, I was ready to propel myself to that bowl, praying that the amazing milk-cereal ratio would somehow create another diversion of my attention.

"I heard from Tristan," he started off.

Oh great, why in the world is he and Tristan talking about cereal? Wait, I thought it was about doing it.

"Savannah," he snapped his fingers in front of me, "Please stay with me on this one, I'll get you another bowl of cereal after."

Do they usually eat breakfast both before and after the activity?

He slid his hands down his face, trying to calm himself. Well I'm sorry if my mind is trying to find a good debate when breakfast should be eaten.

Probably giving up, he went to his bedside table and pulled out the desk. Oh no, is he getting the contraceptive?!

Where the fuck is my cereal?!

I stared dumbly at him when he showed me an envelope. He placed it inside my hands, nodding for me to open it.

Then I'm reminded why I came here in the first place. I scanned the outside, and I was confused when it didn't show any school seal on the corner like most schools.

I looked back at him, before I gingerly opened it. I took out the multiple pieces of paper inside, my eyes scanning the words printed on it, before examining the other content.

Let's just say that my heart fell to the floor at this news.

"I was saving it after you decided whether you'll go to the freshman program," he scratched the back of his head, "I planned that before I found out, I don't want to be the reason why you would not go."

With my gaze switching from him back to the paper, I tried to make a formidable sentence, but nothing, I was complete-ly speechless.

"The thing about the scholarship, I didn't want to tell you until I was sure that I got it," he explained, "I was offered this basketball thing and the agent was at the game last night."

I don't even know what I'm more concerned about.

"Look, you should know that whatever your decision is, I'll accept it," he reassured, gesturing to the paper in my hand, "But I don't think you should bend your idea about the freshman program because of this."

My hand went into the air and I sent it rapidly towards his cheek, but just a centimeter away, I carefully touched his face, my heart swelling with this new piece of information.

"How can I say no to you?" I held back a sob at how overwhelmed I was, "This is just..."

He kissed the top of my head, running soothing a hand through my hair, "Is that a yes or no to the freshman program, I just want to know."

I then glanced at the paper I was clutching. The itinerary, the plane tickets, even a map, my head and heart was screaming for him.

I mean, Jasper just basically told me that he was planning to take me to Europe for the summer this whole time.

Chapter 26

With my laptop under my arm, I took a deep breath and rang the doorbell to Jasper's house.

This is it. I can do this. I've faced much harder things in life than this.

When the front door swung open, I almost fell to my knees due to how nervous I was, "I can't do this!"

Jasper blinked at my sudden outburst, looking at me as if I lost my mind. Tell me boy, how in the world did you decide to get into a relationship with this mad woman? If I were you, I would have ran away the minute I saw myself.

Darling, I think I just lost my sanity.

I showed him the device and he nodded in understanding, letting me inside his house. We climbed up the stairs and went to his room, and this time, I'm not panicking over the same thing all over again.

"Help me," I practically begged him, sitting down on his bed, opening my laptop and browsing back to the application screen. Once again, the form was filled up with the necessary information, all I need was to press the button.

There was also the option of ticking the box that said that I will not be going to the early freshman program but I'm still admitted to the university.

He gave me a comforting smile as he positioned himself next to me, craning his neck to get a good look of the screen. He showed me his hand and ignoring the idiotic thing on my lap, I rested my hand on his and he intertwined our fingers together.

"I already told you," he said, "I'll go with whatever decision you'll make."

The fact he's so supporting makes me cry and I'm here having a bitch fight with my brain over this thing.

Being indecisive really have its down sides.

"I want to go to Europe," I admitted, "I want it more than this stupid program."

"But?" he questioned, placing his chin on top of my shoulder.

Sighing, I looked back down on the screen, "But I know this is something that's going to be so good for my college life."

"If you have an answer for that, then let me ask you something," he started, "Why do you want to go to Europe?"

Cheesy as it may sound, it's because I want some time with Jasper. I neglected him for three damn years, I let him go through circles before we got together, I was slightly the reason why his shoulder is currently in pain, and because I love him too much that I allowed myself to actually reject this.

May that love be the one I'm feeling because of how deep our friendship is or the love that a couple feels, I may never know, but what I do know is, I want to have those moments with him.

The moments where we'll take cliché tourist pictures with the landmarks or get lost in an unknown country and wander around endlessly, having fun along the way as we pray that we get back home.

For once, I want to have that dangerous and crazy kind of fun.

Can I please make a reckless decision?

"We still have prom, graduation" he listed off, "And I'll always visit you."

"Are you telling me to go to this program?" my eyes widened, turning my head to look at him.

He placed a kiss on my cheek as he reached out for my other hand, "Together?"

Biting my lip, I let my finger hover over the enter button. With the aid of Jasper's hand, I finally pressed it down. The screen started loading until we were presented the 'Thank you for applying' page with the instructions on what to do next.

What just happened?

"Now how about I get us some ice cream," Jasper said, taking the device and placing it on top of his covers, "Then let's watch any movie of your choice."

How the hell can he stay nonchalant after what he just did?!

Here I was, having an inner monologue about enjoying my youth and doing something irresponsible and here he goes doing something mature.

Gosh, I sound like I've completely lost my head already.

"Jasper!" I exclaimed, shooting up from my spot. His eyes focused on me, telling me to continue with whatever I was going to say, but I can't think of any way to put it into words. I balled up my fist and screamed a long, "Aaaah!"

He leaned back a little in shock, but then he spoke, "Or pizza could work too."

He's missing the point.

"Do you have any idea on what did you do?" I started flailing my arms, "You can't just do that out of the blue and expect me to be alright with it."

He also pushed himself up off of his bed and grabbed my shoulders to make me look directly up to him, "If I didn't do it, this would have dragged on for a few more chapters."

"Chapters?" I questioned, tilting my head to the side, "What are you talking about?"

"I meant days," he corrected himself, "It may even go on for weeks."

I was being dramatic, I knew it, but this had been puzzling me for a long time and out of the moment, he decided to just do it.

"I wanted to see the sights with you," I mumbled, defeat finally leaking into my voice, "I want to taste the exotic treats," I continued on, "Heck, I want to get lost."

"You really are one of a kind, Savannah Everett," he chuckled, "Calm down, this isn't the end of everything."

"What if I do something out of the blue with you?" I muttered grumpily like a child, "What if I suddenly decided that I want to break up with you?"

Without even a second to think about it, he answered my question with no hesitation, "Then I'll try every single day to win you back."

Perhaps I was getting soft, because with that simple statement, it was enough to melt all of my annoyance away. I finally relaxed from my rigid stance, and slightly look down on the ground in shame, I apologized under my breath, "I'm sorry."

He wrapped an arm around my shoulder and offered me one of his boyish smiles that I couldn't help but ravel in, "It's alright, I understand where you're coming from."

God, tell me what incredible thing that I did to deserve this man?

"Now how about that movie?" he reminded once again, guiding me to the door, "So are we going for ice cream or pizza?"

Trying to push away the negativity, I faked a smile towards him, "Both."

He shrugged, "Anything you want."

"Savannah!" Jasper called out, running to catch up with me as I was already on my way to the small room for the student body officers.

I halted in my steps and waited for him to reach me. With his speed, it wasn't really that hard, "Let's go home together, we can stop anywhere you want."

I was still slightly bummed out about the whole ordeal, but I was trying to hide it from Jasper. I was hoping that he was buying the act, but for the fact that I noticed his sudden increase of affection, I'm sure that wasn't the case.

Sure, he's always sweet, but if he stuffs your locker with flowers every single day, you know that it isn't normal anymore.

He was trying to cheer me up, and as much as I appreciated the efforts, the thought of going to the freshman program just pops back into my head every time I tried to push it away.

"I have to go to a meeting," I muttered, shooting him an apologizing look.

He frowned slightly, but he quickly perked himself up, "Then I'll wait for you to finish."

"I don't know how long it's going to take," I tried to reason, "You could go ahead without me, I don't want you waiting for too long."

"Savannah..." he trailed off, finally losing his cheery act.

Come on, Savannah, liven him up.

"Let's go out tomorrow after school," I told him, leaning up to kiss him on the cheek, hoping it would lift up his mood.

His face did lit up the moment I did the gesture and that was already a success for me.

"I know you're still upset," he mumbled under his breath, praying that I didn't hear it.

Sorry, buddy, but I heard it.

"I'm not," I said. Lies, all you spout are lies!

Of course, this boyfriend of mine could just see right through me.

"If I could just cheer you up," he sighed.

Honestly, I just want to get out of this funk already.

"I'll see you tomorrow." I bid him goodbye.

When I walked into the room, everybody was already there and it looked like there were in the middle of the meeting that wasn't supposed to start yet.

Kyla was at the head of the table and when the door swung open, everybody looked up to see me, "What's going on here?"

"I thought we should start the meeting earlier," our beloved student body vice-president shrugged, "So I texted everybody."

Scrunching my eyebrows in confusion, I set down my bag and joined her at the very end of the table, "It would have been better if you informed me."

"Oops," she gasped. Like I said before, she's the worst actor.

"Whatever," I sighed, deciding that there's no point if I kept on pushing in with the subject, "I hope you did something productive."

She grinned, before subtly glancing at the rest of the people in the room, "Oh we did."

Alright, I feel like this sn't going to be pleasing for me.

I called up a meeting to discuss what we're going to do with prom. This was the day we were supposed to determine the theme and start with the planning, I was silently praying that they were able to do something with the so-called 'early start'.

Kyla pointed to the small whiteboard standing behind here and I instantly paled at what they have decided.

"Around the World," she read the words that was neatly written with a black marker, "I could almost picture it, we could recreate the landmarks, have boarding passes as tickets, and we could even decorate the hallways instead of just the gym."

Oh she's clearly doing this on purpose.

She was the first person I told about what happened with me and Jasper, and she knows how much I wanted to go to that trip with him. If this was her idea to make me feel like I still went to Europe with Jasper, then she could just bury this idea six feet under.

"And you all just agreed with this?" I groaned, turning to the other students. To my surprise, they all agreed, nodding their heads towards my direction.

"Is there any problem, pres?" Kyla batted her lashes innocently as I sent her a sharp glare.

As much as I want to turn this down, it was the voice of the majority, and who am I to become a dictator and just act on my own?

"Fine," I finally sighed, giving up.

With that grin of success that I really wanted to wipe away, Kyla turned back to the other people in the room and started to say her ideas and plans for the event.

I had no other choice other than to sit down and look like a child not-so-subtly hiding a tantrum. I just responded at the short questions thrown to me, but other than that, I was just being a silent moody bitch at the side.

"Alright," Kyla breathed out, looking at the whiteboard that was now filled with notes, "I guess we can stop for today."

She looked expectantly with me and with the most bored expression I can muster, I announced, "Meeting adjourned."

People started filing out of the room and when the door shut close after the last person left, I shot my best friend a dry look, "Kyla!"

"What?" she asked, looking amused.

Girl, you know what's what. Wait, did that even make sense?

"You know I'm still a bit chuffed up about the Europe thing," I grumbled, resting my chin on top of my palm.

She reached out and placed a hand on top of my head, "Would you please stop doing that?"

"Doing what?" I questioned dumbly.

"Stop us from cheering you up," she replied, sitting on the table, "You know Jasper's also worried about you."

"I know..." I trailed off.

"Now trust me on this," she smiled comfortingly.

And that was the day I entrusted Kyla Bailey to handle everything about prom. This may lead up to the worst or best night of my whole high school life.

Chapter 27

"Do you think she suspects a thing?" Tristan asked as he taped up the string on one of the beams.

I'm hope not or else everything will be a goddamn waste of everybody's time and precious money. But hey, this could be somewhat of a good publicity for the café.

When Tristan called me and asked me to help him with his promposal to Kyla, he started listing off ridiculous ideas, some of which includes him bungee jumping - I then quickly turned it down by saying how the cord might break and he may pummel to his death.

Sometimes, you have to scare the boy in order to get him to give up.

So I pitched in and told him to just put on a simple sign in the café. The minute she walks in, she will see the huge four-letter word that will inevitably make her Tristan's date to the dance.

"Thank for always helping me," he said, jumping off of the chair he was standing on, "Without you, I would have never gotten the permission to do this."

Shrugging, I reached for the next letter that he has to tie up and gave it to him, "It's nothing, we just have to focus on finishing this before Kyla arrives for her shift."

I lied to Kyla saying that one of our co-workers asked me to cover for her so I was going ahead an hour early and she easily bought the excuse. We all knew Tristan was supposed to be working today so he has no reason to lie to his girlfriend about anything.

But to tell you the truth, it was a little bit awkward standing here as we arranged the surprise as the customers continued to file in and out of the café.

Just because we were doing this, doesn't mean we were closing the place.

It did grab some attention, some are here since the time we started hanging up the letters, and they continued ordering treats and coffees, probably curious on what will happen.

The bell by the door chimed, indicating a new customer came in and Jasper went marching up to us, carrying a plastic bag from the store, "Got the poppers you wanted."

He reached into the bag and threw the party poppers to his best friend. Tristan caught it with no problem and said his thanks before going back to hang the letters.

"He's incredibly whipped by Kyla," Jasper chuckled, standing next to me, "I've never seen him this anxious."

"Yeah," I agreed unconsciously, he's the reason why I don't worry about Kyla as much as I used to. Back before we got close to these boys, we'll be at each other's side since it's us against the world. I might say, I do miss our private girl days, but we already have Jasper and Tristan to keep us occupied.

As much as I trust her, I'm still worrying about the prom preparations. Yes, I still overlook everything and she does deliver to me the necessary information for approval sake, but other than that, she's insistent that I'm kept in the dark.

I'm praying nothing too extreme happens.

"There we go," Tristan grinned, hopping off of the chair and looking proudly at his handy work.

"I hope she'll be happy," I muttered, staring up at the job Tristan did. I saw Jasper turn to me from the corner of my eye and I glanced at him, giving him a questioning look.

"Why do I have to be here?" Jasper grumbled under his breath, his tone slightly grumpy. He puffed up his cheeks and crossed his arms over his chest, "It's not like I work here or anything."

Cracking up a smile, I poked him at his side, "Oh be a little supportive, will you?"

He wounded up an arm around my shoulder and pulled me closer to him, "You need to smile more, you know."

I've always knew that Jasper would keep finding ways to cheer me up, even if it's just a small gesture. I nodded in response to his statement as we watched Tristan look at his phone and his eyes started to gleam with panic, "She's on her way!"

My gaze set out beyond the glass walls of the café, showing the parking lot. I saw Kyla's familiar silver car pull up into her usual space and I gestured to Jasper to look at where she was, "Should we tell him?"

We turned back to his best friend who was now running around, holding up a flimsy party popper as he started to ask a few of our co-workers to clear the way. Jasper smirked and he shook his head, "It would be a lot more entertaining if we didn't."

Tristan turned to us and when he noticed that we were just standing there, he started to yell, "Stop flirting, and help me, grab some party poppers, we need to surprise her."

He handed us each a popper and I gave him a tight lipped smile as I watched Kyla exit her car and started to make her way to the back door, probably to change into her uniform.

"She's here," a chef popper his head from the kitchen to inform Tristan, who in return, started to become a lot more frantic.

He accidentally bumped on the string that was holding up the letter P and it came falling down, and since there were all tied together, the other letters started to get dragged down with it.

He stared down in horror at the sudden mess, before he turned to the chef who was now giving him a pitiful look, "Stall her!"

As the chef went back into the kitchen, Tristan attempted to do the repair work on the mess. He once again, started to command us, "Don't just stand there, help me!"

I bit my lip as I tried to hide my laughter. As much as it was painful to watch a friend like him suffer, the situation was hilarious. Here he was, spending all morning trying to put up the letters to spell out prom and everything went coming down just because he was so nervous.

Maybe the bungee jump wasn't a bad idea now.

"Why are you guys-" the kitchen door swung open to see the girl we all wanted to stay on the other side of the door. When she saw the scene that was happening, she mumbled the end of her sentence, "-stopping me?"

"What's going on?" she questioned, scanning around the room. The costumers who witnessed the event stopped whatever they were doing and was now watching this. Actually, the whole café fell silent and the staff that was inside the kitchen, slightly opened the swinging doors to take a peek.

Just for comedy purposes, Jasper walked up to Kyla and pulled on the string off the party popper, sending a wimpy amount of confetti and string to fall on her hair, "Surprise!"

That was it, I held back too long and I started to burst into a fit of giggles, covering my mouth to prevent myself from making too huge of a scene. It was too late though, their attention was now on the crazy lady laughing her ass off at the corner.

Oh this is just horribly hilarious.

Jasper placed an arm on Tristan's shoulder and gave him an encouraging pat on the back, "Just ask her."

Kyla still had her eyebrows scrunched up in confusion, though I could almost see the gears in her brain working as she kept processing the scene. It would be a lot easier if the letters fell into a recognizable way, but nope, you can't identify a single letter since they're all piled in one big mess.

Tristan took a deep breath and approached Kyla, taking her hand, he spoke, "Will you go to prom with me?"

Without even missing a beat, she smiled and nodded, wrapping her arms around her boyfriend. The café that was once completely quiet, clapped at the spectacular show, before going back to their business.

"Now that's done, we have to get back to work," I reminded them, snatching my apron which I placed down on one of the spare tables and tied it on me, "But congratulations."

I then saw a grinning Kyla snatch me by the arm as we marched back into the kitchen, leaving the two boys outside to clean up after the fai attempt.

"Did you see that?" she scuealed, taking a seat on one of the stools and cupping her blushing cheeks, "I can't believe that just happened."

Trust me, neither can I.

"Thanks Savannah," she stared up at me, "And also say thank you to Jasper for me as well."

"What for?"

"I sincerely believe that even as amazing Tristan is, he couldn't have thought and done that on his own," she explained, standing up before giving me a hug, "I'm so lucky."

Alright, maybe I'll reserve the story about the almost bungee jumping promposal for my speech at their wedding.

What? Going ahead to fast?

She then released, but still keeping her hands on my shoulder, "I just can't wait to see what Jasper will do."

"Will do what?" I questioned.

"His own extravagant way of asking you to prom," she gave me a small wink, "Knowing him, it's going to be nothing but special."

I wasn't even thinking of it until she mentioned it, and thanks to her, I started to become restless, expecting that he would just pop out the question any time.

During school, the hallways started to become filled with couples, asking each other out. From roses to huge cards, they were putting out all the stops.

My eyes were gazing at everything, scanning all the happenings. Of course, this didn't go unnoticed by Jasper who cleared his throat and made me look at him, "You seem a little distracted today."

Gulping audibly, I took a deep breath to ease myself, before replying, "Not really, I'm just thinking about prom preparations."

"You need a break," he stated, stopping right in front of my locker, handing me my books that he volunteered to carry as I stuffed them in there, "You want to go somewhere?"

Giving him a side eye, an idea popped into my head as I showed him a smirk, "We can go dress shopping," I joked, preparing for him to back out.

Surprisingly, he shrugged, "If that's what you want."

"Hey there lovebirds!" Kyla greeted, walking up to us, "Ready to start working on the decorations?"

"Um..." I trailed off.

"Actually," Jasper piped in, wrapping an arm around my waist to pull me closer to him, "We made some plans for today."

My cheeks started to heat up and when those words escaped his lips, Kyla perked up with a new kind of enthusiasm, her eyes gleaming with excitement, "Of course, we could survive a day without her."

I can't even find a way to respond to that, because I was using all my concentration to make sure my blush wasn't obvious.

Kyla then waved us goodbye as Jasper whisked me away to the school exit. He escorted me to his car and once we started driving away, he said, "So where do you want to go first?"

"Well, the mall is always a good place to start," I told him, leaning back against the seat.

"We're not going to the mall," he chuckled, "Girls flock to that place that there's a high chance that you will have the same dress as another person."

"Then where else are we going to shop for dresses?" I inquired with a teasing tone.

He smirked as he kept his eyes on the road, "I know a place."

I was a bit curious to where we were heading but I placed my trust on him. I kept my eyes trained to the outside, watching as zoom past the buildings until we were no longer at the main part of the city.

Alright, now I'm getting really curious.

The area outside became a lot more spacious, when I saw the sign that said that we were leaving the city, that was when I repeated the question to Jasper, "Where are we going?"

Then, several boutiques came into view, they were all lined up, circling a small lot that I soon identified as the parking lot due to the small amount of cars there.

Jasper pulled up in one of the spaces and got out, walking around to open the door for me. I looked around the place and eyes the stores, looking at their displays which showed unrealistic beautiful designs, "Where are we?"

"Having Macy as a sister really got me to know this place," he explained, closing my door and locking the vehicle, "As a wedding planner, she used to take some nearby clients here, this place is pretty great if you're looking for dresses and gowns."

We entered one of the stores - the woman who was lazily drawing on her desk looked up when the chimes that was on the door sounded. When she caught sight of Jasper, she broke into a huge grin, running up to us, "Jasper, dear, it's so nice to see you again."

She gave both of his cheeks a kiss and I just started fidgeting there awkwardly, "How's Macy? I haven't seen her in so long, just because the lady got transferred to the big apple, doesn't mean she should just forget about me."

"I'll tell her to give you a call then," he said, instantly charming the older woman. She smiled before her gaze finally fell upon me.

She stood up straighter in her high heels as she scanned from head to toe, "And who is this lovely girl?"

I was about awkwardly introduce myself, but before I had a chance, Jasper beat me to it, "She's Savannah Everett."

"Everett?" she tilted her head to the side as she tapped her chin, recalling my last name, "I've heard that our boss is a close friend of theirs, such a good looking couple."

"And she's the extremely good looking sister," Jasper winked, "We're here to shop for prom!" he informed, being all giddy. I couldn't help but smile at his antics and the woman hurriedly went to the back, coming back with hangers and hangers of dresses and gowns.

"You're in luck, the boss dropped in this morning," she told us, hanging each article of clothing at the metal rack that was displayed in front of us, "These are all the new designs, never before seen by anybody."

I marveled at the dresses, they all ranged from sequined masterpieces to simple elegance. Even as their own, they looked amazing just hanging up there, how much more if they're being worn by somebody who's gone all out with the makeup and accessories.

She reached for one of the cream dresses and showed it to me, "How about this one?"

"I'll leave it to you two girls," Jasper said, "I'll just grab a coffee from the coffeehouse out there."

As he left, I turned to the woman and gave her my most serious face. She saw how determined I was and smiled grabbing one dress, she shoved it in my arms, "Shall we start?"

I stayed inside the small dressing room, stepping out to see myself in the mirror before rushing back inside, waiting for the woman to hand me the next dress in line.

When she handed me one dress, I stared at it while it was still in the hanger. Marveling at the sight of it, I knew that I wanted it. The color and design wasn't too overwhelming, but it was perfect.

Stripping off the previous gown, I pulled this one on and twirled around in it, making sure that I could still move even though the fabric was hugging my body. Swiping away the curtain, I showed the lady and she commented, "I think I like this one the best."

"Do you think it's too much?" I questioned, turning to my side and saw the cuts that was along the torso.

"Well, you have the figure for it," she pointed out, bending down to fix the flowing bottom, "If you were to ask me, I think you should go for this one."

Taking one look at myself, I turned to her to ask the one question I knew would cause a problem since I entered this place, "How much does these stuffs go?"

"Depends on the design," she muttered, placing back the dress that I tried on earlier back on the rack, "The Jessica Smith brand is not cheap though."

And that was what I was afraid of.

I'm pretty sure even with One-Eighty Degrees backing me up, I certainly don't have enough money to spend on such an expensive dress.

The woman saw my worry and leaned against her desk, "Want me to reserve the dress for you, just in case?"

Nodding, I thanked her as I went back inside the dressing room to change back into the clothes I came in. I handed it back to her and she placed it inside the plastic it was in. Just in time, Jasper came in, holding two cups of coffee, being as happy-go-lucky as always.

"So how's the shopping?" he asked.

Masking my disappointment, I plastered a big smile on my face, "Great, but maybe this isn't the store for me."

"Oh," he breathed out, "Don't worry, there's a lot more stores out there."

He said goodbye to the woman before he made his way to the exit. I continued to stare at the dress that I was in love with, yearning for it. I wanted it, maybe I could ask my parents to loan me some money for this one.

"Savannah?" he called after. I snapped out of my trance and quickly followed him, waving goodbye to the woman.

Once we were outside, he handed me the hot beverage, "Drink up, there's still a whole line of shops here."

Sighing, I took a sip from the drink he bought me, "This is actually good," I told him, looking at the cup to see what brand this was. I froze at what I saw, I looked up at him and he was showing me that toothy grin, scratching the back of his neck.

Right there, written on the cup was the word that had been troubling me since that unfortunate day in the café.

Prom?

It was written with a black marker and it was a bit smudged, but it was comprehensible and it was enough for me to smile up at him, nodding my head.

"Are you okay with it, even if it isn't as grand as what Tristan attempted to do?"

He was simple, this was simple, and honestly, that was all that I needed. Who needs a grand gesture like hanging up letters or lighting up a whole field? What's important is that he did something to ask me and it was enough - more than enough.

"Yeah," I muttered, leaning up to press my lips to his cheek, "Thank you."

He kissed the top of my head, taking my hand in his, "Now tell me the real deal with that dress in there."

Forget the dress, I could walk in there with my pajamas and I won't mind at all as long as Jasper was there.

Chapter 28

"**A**re you going to tell me anything at all?" I questioned as I stood next to Kyla who was barking commands at the people who was helping us to fix up the gym for the prom.

My best friend turned to me with a tight lipped smile, giving me a happy yet annoying reply, "Nope."

When she saw my pouting expression, she grinned before wrapping an arm around my shoulder, giving me tight squeeze, "Oh come on, don't give me that look."

"Fine," sighed, "I trust you."

"There we go," she cheered before releasing me from her grasp, "Now after this, come with me to look for my prom dress."

Don't even remind me of that stinking prom dress. In the end, I left empty handed in that chain of stores that Jasper brought me, it wasn't because they were all horrendous, but it was because nothing was better than the dress I saw in the first shop.

God damn it, I wanted that dress!

She noticed the frown and her face also fell. I told her about it, and even though she was sweet enough to tell me that she would loan me the money so I could buy it, I quickly reminded her that she needed her own money for her dress.

And that placed us back to square one.

"I'm pretty sure the mall is a cheaper place," she said, walking to the bleachers where she left her bag.

Nodding I adjusted the strap of my own bag on my shoulder before turning to the students who were just finishing up with the cleaning for the day, "Good work, everybody, we'll see you again tomorrow."

We received their collective goodbyes before the both of us started to walk out. The two of us paused in our steps when we were in the parking lot as we saw Jasper and Tristan, leisurely leaned against my car as they chatted without a care in the world.

When they noticed us standing like idiots right there, they gave us each a smile, "Took you girls long enough."

We exchanged looks before giving them a questioning look, "What are you guys doing here?"

"Overheard that you two were going to the mall," Tristan replied, scratching the back of his head, "We were wondering if we could go along since we also have to buy our tuxes."

Kyla lifted a hand and allowed it to zoom really close to her boyfriend's face before giving him a flat, "No."

Certainly, Tristan was not expecting that rejection from her as his jaw slowly dropped open, "What?"

"Our prom dress is a surprise from you boys so there's no way you're coming along with us," she explained, crossing her arms over her chest.

Tristan groaned in exasperation before gesturing to Jasper and I, "But Savannah allowed Jasper to come with her when she was scouting for dresses."

"And that's why she didn't buy anything that day," she pointed out before shooing them, "It's a girls' shopping spree."

I held back a laugh as I saw Tristan's face turn into a childish pout, before sullenly turning around and slowly walking back to wherever his car was. Jasper chuckled openly at his best friend, shaking his head before approaching me, "I'll see you when you get home?"

Nodding, I showed him a small smile, "You better go and cheer him up."

"Got it," he grinned, leaning down to give my cheek a kiss - evidently making me blush - before he started to follow Tristan who was already halfway down the parking lot.

Turning to Kyla who was now staring at her boyfriend with amusement, I gave her a look. She noticed and shrugged, "I want to surprise him."

"Poor boy," I muttered, walking around to reach the driver's side as I unlocked the vehicle, "I'm pretty sure he's currently troubling about which colored tie he would get for you."

From her cheerful disposition, it's obvious that she was touched with his gesture even after she gave him the cold shoulder. It doesn't matter if they're already an official couple or not, both of them act like before they were dating. With Tristan acting all chill in front of her but a complete wreck when she's not looking, while her on the other hand, still acts like a fangirl behind his back.

As a normal person, I envy their relation but why would I when I have my Jasper?

When we reached the mall, I felt like we suddenly entered a marathon. It was definite that it was prom season and even though it was a school day, that didn't stop the many seniors from going into the mall to shop for their outfits for the dance.

If this was the situation on a weekday, just imagine it while it was on a weekend.

But of course, the amount of people and competition only fueled my best friend's fighting spirit as she cracked her knuckles and smirked, "You ready, Savannah?"

"I think," I mumbled, unsure if I was going to make it alive or not.

She was ready to barge in and when I meant barge in, she was pushing and shoving people to get to shops. But this was Kyla we were talking about, I'm betting that she already knew where to go.

She grabbed my wrist and didn't even bother with the escalator, she went straight ahead to the stairs. Well, looks like I'll be getting my cardio done for the day.

We reached a particular shop on the third floor and it was fairly packed, but you could still walk around and pick out the dresses and gown you would like to try on.

She certainly had her target locked on as she didn't even bother to say an apology to the few people she bumped into as she walked up to the employee. Even though the woman's patience was already running thin with the costumers, she still mustered a smile, "May I help you?"

"May I know if I could try on the dress that was on that mannequin?" Kyla questioned, pointing to the dress that was being presented on the shop window.

The employee frowned and shook her head, "I'm sorry ma'am that design is sold out, and we only have that display piece left."

Darling, you don't say that to Kyla Bailey.

"Then I'll buy that display piece," she said, her eyes reflecting desperation. From the sigh the woman released, it was obvious that she was told the same words a lot of time, and as always, she rejected it.

"I'm sorry, ma'am."

"But..." she trailed off, staring back at the dress like the same way I looked at the dress back in the shop Jasper took me into.

"We'll pay extra if you allow us to get it," I jumped into the conversation, giving Ky a a supportive smile. There's no way am I allowing my best friend to be as disappointed as I was.

Still, she shook her head, "I really am sorry, ma'am."

I don't really like using my brother and his wife's influence, but if it's for Kyla, I can bear the guilt for one day, "I'm Savannah Everett, Celeste Graham-Everett's sister-in-law."

The store manager that was passing by stopped when I said her name, she instantly knew the name, and how could she not? Half of this mall belongs to Celeste's family, but as I always say, I never like using their power.

"Excuse me," she said, slightly pushing the saleslady to the side, "How may I help you?"

I almost snorted at the sudden change of attitude. These people who treat people with power with an extra service should just go down, because just like the other people shopping in this store, we're just costumers.

"We would like that dress," I informed, pointing back to the same mannequin that Kyla was practically worshipping.

Who knew that in just a few breezy minutes, we would be walking out of the store with the dress inside a box that was now wrapped in Kyla's arms? The smile that was gracing her face was really something else, she was practically glowing with happiness.

"How about you?" she asked as we were waiting for the elevator, "What store shall we scout first?"

"I'll pass for today," I told her, "I can just ask my parents for some money so I could buy what I wanted."

I guess she noticed that I wasn't in the mood so she nodded and followed me to the car. Surprisingly, it was already dark when we got out. Maybe the dress buying was fast but from the line to the crowd, it did took us some time to get in and out of the mall.

The drive to her house was filled with nonsense chit chats and before she got down when we stopped in front of her house, she released her seatbelt and leaned forward to hug me, "You're the best."

Returning the hug for a brief moment, she smiled at me as she pulled back ad opened the door, "Pick you up tomorrow morning."

Waving goodbye to her, I started to drive back to my house. The second I parked the vehicle in my driveway, Jasper emerged from the house next door.

"Finally!" he yelled into nothingness, he reached out a hand for me to take, "Come on."

"Why?" I questioned, giving him a skeptical look.

"I want to show you my tux," he replied, taking my hand and pulling me along with him inside the house.

If we reach his room again, I'm hoping he has prepared me that cereal bowl he promised the last time. Thankfully, we just stopped in the living room and he walked out to get his suit.

Looking down on the coffee table, there was huge white box and even though it was wrong to snoop, I was tempted to look inside. Because hey, if you see a huge box that was occupying the whole surface area of the coffee table, of course you would get curious.

I plopped down on their couch, still staring at the box. That was until Jasper emerged, even though he only had his t-shirt on, the suit jacket and pants combo rocketed his hotness ten times more.

Did I really just say the word hotness? Oh god, Savannah, we should stop.

When he did that spin, I allowed a small giggle to escape my lips. He slid through the slippery floor of his living room, before digging into the inside the pocket, "The best has yet to come."

He then pulled out the tie he was going to wear, and my eyes widened at the color. It was the same lavander color of the dress that I was eyeing. Of course, I didn't want to put my hopes up so I took a deep breath before raising an eyebrow, "So I have to match your tie now?"

"Well, originally I planned a nice dinner to cheer you up because Kyla told me about the dress," he said. That girl is dead to me for telling Jasper about it, "But I thought that this could be better."

"What?" I asked, and that was when he put down the tie to lift up the cover of the box. I gaped as I was now staring at the same gown that I saw last week on the shop Jasper took me. My first instinct was to jump into his arms and give him the biggest bear hug for how much I appreciated it, but I balled my hands into fists to control myself, "How?"

"I called up Macy to see if she can do something about it," he started to say, "Then I learned a valuable piece of information," he told me, taking my hand and placed it gently on top of the fabric, "Your brother and Celeste is a good friend of Jessica Smith, the designer of that dress."

Look at that, I also got my own prom dress from her influence. Oh great, my pride is getting stabbed right now.

"Jessica Smith actually gave this as a gift to you," he informed, "I was surprised she was willing to give up an expensive piece for free."

"Jasper, I can't accept this," I gasped, quickly scrambling around to find the box cover. I need to shield my eyes from this beauty, before I start regretting it, "You've done too many good things to me and I can't even spend the summer with you."

To my shock, I felt his hand on my head and stopped all of my movements, making me look up at him, "Calm yourself please."

I clamped my mouth shut as he released me, sitting down on the sofa next to me, he gave me a gentle smile, "First of all, I've always said that I don't give a damn if you spend the summer with me or not, because I know what you're doing is something very important to you."

Doesn't he know that he much more important to me?

"Second, I enjoy treating you right," he stated, making my heart melt with his words.

Dear heavens, what did I do right that made me deserve this amazing human being?

"And third, I also have that nice dinner on its way here."

What?

As if on cue, the doorbell rang and Jasper quickly ran to the door. When he came back, he had a large pizza box in his hand, lifting his other one to give it that exaggerated gesture, taking a whiff of its delicious scent.

It's because this girl has no time to go on diet before prom. There's a Jasper with pizza currently standing in front of me.

"I'll go get the drinks," I muttered, standing up as I walked into their kitchen. The fact that I've practically grew up with jasper makes me feel like this like an extension to my house. When I opened the fricge to see what they have in stock, I reached in to grab the large bottle of Coke.

I filled up two glasses with the soda before walking back to the living room. Unfortunately, that was the same time Jasper was on his way to the kitchen to grab some plates, and well, you could imagine what happened next.

We ended up crashing into each other, causing the coke to splash everywhere. The only good thing was the glass came in contact with the carpet so even though they slipped from my hands, they didn't shatter, they only showed some cracks from the impact.

I cringed at how sticky I've become because of the Coke that spilled all over me. Well, looks like I'll need a shower as soon as I get back home.

Looking up at Jasper, I gasped at his white shirt. He looks like he took more of the damage than I did, "I'm so sorry!" I started apologizing, crawling up to him as I tugged on his shirt, "You need to take this off, it would be horrible if it stains."

"Are you trying to get me naked?" he managed to joke. And even with the blush coming up, I gave him a dirty look, before telling him in a commanding tone, to once again, take off his shirt.

Thankfully, he listened to me and pulled up his shirt to remove it. You can say that the only thing I was able to do was stared at his shirtless figure.

Damn, those muscles look fine.

"But now I'm a bit cold," he started once again to tease me, "How about you come here to give me a hug?"

"Jasper Dean," I growled under my breath, showing him a fist to make him stop.

But we all know that I'll be oh-so-willingly to throw myself to a shirtless Jasper any day.

If your tiny little girlfriend decided to give you a threat, of course you wouldn't take it seriously even if this said petite girlfriend used to be the terror of the school.

He reached out and wrapped his arms around me, pulling me to him, "Nice and warm."

"Release me!" I demanded, trying to break free from his grasp.

What came next made me stop in my movements, rendering me frozen in spot in his arms, "I love you, Savannah."

Darling, you cannot say that out of the blue!

Chapter 29

Savannah's prom dress is the picture up there!

"It's prom, it's prom, it's prom," Kyla sang when I opened the front door after she massacred my doorbell.

Under her arm was a huge paper bag that contained her dress and shoes. She was grinning from ear to ear as she grabbed my hand and pulled me inside, dragging me up the stairs.

"It's too early to get ready!" I complained, but my I allowed my feet to follow her.

She dropped off her bags on the floor of my bedroom, before quickly shuffling into the bathroom, "Now how about we start this beauty montage?"

I lifted an eyebrow at her as she showed me the grin of hers, "A beauty montage?"

She shrugged before grabbing most of the beauty products I stored in there before laying them all on my dresser. She went for her huge bag and took out her makeup bag along with a scary amount of hair products, "Between painting our nails, doing our hair, plus our makeup, trust me, there's no such thing as too early."

She pushed me down on the chair and instantly grabbed a comb. Even though I thought that she was acting ridiculous, I smiled as I allowed her to make me into her own doll, knowing she's delighted with all of this.

Plus, I don't have to do too much work in preparing.

I reached out and took the bottle of nail polish that I've selected for the event. Grabbing the other necessary stuff, I started to do my nails as I listened to Kyla's words.

"Congratulations, by the way," she said to me, as I watch her reflection in the mirror pin around my hair.

"I should be the congratulating you," I told her, twisting off the cap of the nail polish and taking out the brush, "I was worried at first, but from the progress I've seen, I think you've done a really good job with the dance."

"Not that," she rolled her eyes, but she still concentrated with what she was doing, "I mean Jasper getting the scholar-ship."

The brush I was holding slipped out of my hand and fell into the floor. I cringed at the sight of the stain it would probably leave, but I couldn't help but gape at the sudden piece of information.

When Kyla noticed my reaction, she gasped and slapped a hand over her mouth, "Oops."

I wanted to burst into happiness because of how proud I am of him. I suddenly jolted up from my seat and I started to walk to my door, "I have to congratulate him."

"Hold it right there, missy," Kyla commanded, grabbing the back of my shirt to pull me back, "You're not seeing him like that."

I glanced at the mirror and I almost laughed at the sight of my half-done hairstyle that still had a lot of unnecessary pins scattered along the top of my head.

"You'll still see him tonight, go congratulate him later," she said, before pushing me back down on the chair, "I did not waste two hours of watching tutorial videos on youtube for you to run away when I'm not even done yet."

If I value my life, I would just stay still as she dolled me up, because a very determined Kyla Bailey is a very dangerous Kyla Bailey.

I managed to survive through the so-called 'beauty montage' and now I was just waiting anxiously in my dress as I clenched my fist to my side so I wouldn't go biting my nails because of how nervous I was.

Kyla entered the room, twirling in her pretty red dress. She smile up to me, before walking up to the full-length mirror, "This is perfect."

A hand unconsciously went up to feel the stiff curls going down up to my back Kyla approached me and swatted my hand away, "Don't touch my masterpiece."

I laughed at this, before the two of us froze when we heard the doorbell. Even though she was pretty enthusiastic seconds ago, her face slowly broke down into panic. She hurriedly ran to the chair where she left her clutch, but she tripped on the hem of her dress and slowly toppled over, grabbing the edge of my desk to keep herself up.

"Are you okay?" I quickly scrambled up my feet to go after her. She slowly started to stand upright, but I was too focus on making sure I didn't do the same mistake that as she lifted up her head, she hit me right in the chin.

I jerked back quickly, which wasn't really a good idea, before I lost my balance on these stupid high heels that I started falling backwards. She quickly reached out for my hand pulled me with her, but in the end, I dragged her with me to the floor.

"The boys are here," mom suddenly informed, opening the door to my room and finding the both of us crouched down on the floor.

She blinked at us, before casually yelling over to the boys, "They'll be right down."

Releasing a small sigh, she grabbed each of our arms and pulled us up, and helped with the small mess that we made with ourselves after the mishap, "Relax, will you. I bet you girls are more nervous compared to the winter formal."

"In my defense, I never knew Tristan would ask me out," my best friend grumbled, pertaining to the fact that Tristan appeared at her house just minutes before the winter formal to ask her out.

"And the only question I got from Jasper back then was his excuse about saving gas," I spoke.

"Don't be nervous and the boys look spiff, if I might say," she winked, before nudging us to the door, "Now go, my camera's ready."

Oh I would love to skip the picture taking part.

When we got down the stairs, we searched around for them, before mom guided us to the living room where the two of them were occupied in a basketball match with my father.

"If he gets that in within the next minute, they might have a chance," dad observed as the two boys nodded in agreement.

Dad, you're stealing our dates!

Kyla cleared her throat, before announcing, "We're ready!"

"Yeah, three minutes, babe," Tristan waved off, his eyes glued to the tv screen.

We shared a look, before returning our attention to them. Oh seriously?

As if a sudden realization hit them, Tristan and Jasper suddenly jolted up and turned to us, "We're so sorry."

Why can't we have those normal romantic scenes where we come down the stairs and they'll stand in awe? Instead, we have them totally distracted by a basketball game from the television screen.

"We thought you girls were still going to take long so I invited them to watch with me," dad chuckled, turning off the tv, "They looked as every bit of anxious as you were, I couldn't just leave them fidgeting at the front door."

"Sir, please don't tell them that," Jasper suddenly blurted out, before I saw his ears turning red - which, I might add, is completely adorable.

"Now four of your gather by the fireplace," mom commanded, "Your mothers requested that I take enough picture of all four of you."

Just imagine this, all four mothers want to have a picture. Not just any picture, a different set of photos for each of them, so basically, there's no such thing as 'enough'.

Just saying, my mother with a camera is a very deadly thing.

At first, we were alright with the flash turning on every freaking second as we showed them those nice smiles, but soon, our cheeks started to hurt and we were slowly getting blind.

Sending a plea to my dad - who was always the one to stop my mom whenever she goes too far - he dropped a hand on her shoulder, "That's enough, Ariel."

"Alright, you can go ahead," she permitted, before escorting all of us out the door.

A limo was parked right outside my house, though we already knew that these two rented one. It was one of the main reasons why I suggested that Kyla could just stay over at my house so it would be less of a hassle.

Kyla and Tristan went on ahead, but before he could follow them, I reached out and grabbed his wrist. Slowly turning around, he gave me a puzzling look but presented me with a wonderful smile when I showed him the boutonnière that I snatched before we went out the door.

I pinned it on his lapel and when he took out a hand for me to take, I graciously placed mine on top of his and we went to the vehicle hand in hand.

Once we were inside he took the corsage that he left on top of one of the seats and tied it around my wrist, "Perfect."

We caught Tristan and Kyla grinning at from the other side I gave them a questioning stare, "What?"

"Even though it's special for all of us," she muttered, "I think you both know already that I had this prom organized especially because of what happened to you two."

I was lucky to have her. She's a whole package, a quirky and temperamental girl but she is filled with this loyalty and kindness that would take me years to repay.

"Thank you," I said to her, my gratitude and sincerity flowing out from those two words.

When we arrived into the school, we weren't surprised at the amount of people just standing outside, conversing with each other. That, and there was an excessive amount of rented fancy vehicles for the occasion.

"How about you to go on first, we'll be right behind you," Tristan aid, giving us encouraging nod once the four of us were all out of the limo.

"We can't deny them of their request," Jasper gave a light-hearted shrug as he offered his arm, "Are you ready for our trip, my lady?"

Looping my arm around his, we slowly walked towards the school steps. A few students greeted us along the way, but we never actually stopped for a chit chat. We were both thrilled to see what the inside looks like.

It didn't disappoint.

The first thing you'll notice was the huge cardboard pyramids that decorated the entrance of the school. As soon as you stepped in, it was like you were taken into a magic carpet ride by Aladdin.

Different monuments from all over the world lined up the hallway and you can see a whole string of Chinese lanterns on the ceiling.

The only thing I could do was follow Jasper's guide as my eyes were trailing all over the place, trying to sink in every single thing that I saw.

When we entered the gym, my eyes bulged out at the large Eiffel tower replica. It almost reached the ceiling of the gym and speaking of the ceiling, it was a good mixture of white thin cloth and fairy lights.

"So what do you two think?" Kyla suddenly asked, getting in between the two of us, "Better than a trip to Europe?"

I completely surprised her when I released Jasper and threw my arms around her, giving her the hug she deserves.

A sudden flash made us pull apart to see Tristan with his phone, grinning at the picture that he shot, "Got to record these memories."

"Now enough about that, let's dance," Kyla squealed, grabbing her boyfriend's hand and pulling him to the dance floor.

The gym was filled with an upbeat tune since Kyla mentioned that the DJ will be playing the slow songs later on. It was really a good feeling to be jumping around in your heels without feeling the pain because of exhilarating it was.

The first slow song started to play, and of course, everybody scampered around to find their dates. I looked around the dance floor, since I was just dancing along, Jasper and I got separated and my eyes desperately scanned the huge amount of students for him.

Suddenly, somebody grabbed my arm and pulled me to him. Looking up at the culprit, Jasper winked at me, before spinning me around into the usual couple position.

"Kyla did a good job," I said, my gaze couldn't help but glance around the decorations once more.

"We should really thank her," he whispered into my ear so I could hear him through the music, "This is the best."

Somebody tapped my shoulder, making the both of us turn to the person. Tristan was there dancing with Kyla, and he gave us a crooked grin, "Want to switch?"

Once we changed partners, just one look at each other, Tristan and I shared a small laugh, "This is rather nice."

"By the way, I have yet to pay you," he suddenly perked up.

"For what?" I inquired.

"For helping me with Kyla," he answered immediately.

I lifted my hand from his shoulder and slightly gave him a small pat, "Hey, it was a fair trade for that cake you helped me with."

"I'm pretty sure that it wasn't equal at all," he chuckled, "That was just a small moment, what I acquired was something really amazing."

Staring up at him, I gave him a smile. It was true that what Tristan helped me only lasted for a few minutes, considering that after the whole apology scene months ago, we shared the cake with a few others. You would think that he got the bigger end of the stick, but I beg to differ.

"As corny as it sounds, every small moment with Jasper is something really amazing," I explained, "Plus, you made my best friend happy, that tself is a good enough payment for me."

"I'm sorry for hiding my job and our friendship from everyone else before," he apologized, "It was a coward move and I knew how much it will bother Jasper."

"Well, it bothered him a lot," I reminisced. During those times, you would think that the boy was in his man-period.

"I wonder what would have happened if you never became a chef at One-Eighty Degrees," I spoke, "You wouldn't have met Kyla, I wouldn't be friends with you, and I would still be avoiding Jasper like a plague."

"I didn't do much to for your romantic escapade with him, you know," he chuckled.

"I believe that you were," I retorted, "You have as much importance in this love story as anyone is."

"Thanks Savannah," he smiled.

Jasper appeared with Kyla and he turned to Tristan, "Mind if I steal my girlfriend again?"

Tristan released me and went right ahead to Kyla's side. Jasper took my hand and waved them goodbye as he escorted me out of the doors. Looking back, I gave him a questioning look, "Where are we going?"

"We're going to have our summer trip a little bit earlier than planned," he responded with a slight chuckle.

I stared at his back, before letting out a sigh of defeat as I allowed him to drag me alone. If I was given a choice, I would stay like this with him forever.

But we all know that it's impossible for that to happen.

Chapter 30

I laughed along as I allowed Jasper to pull me all the way out of the gym and into the empty hallways. Well, almost empty aside from the few couples who also wanted their privacy.

"Kyla gave us only twenty minutes before she smacks us because we've been gone too long," he informed as his grip on my hand tightened.

Talk about going around the world in eighty days – we're doing it in twenty minutes.

"First stop, Italy," he grinned, rushing to the other end of the hallway where a puny cardboard replica of the Leaning Tower of Pisa. He gave me that adorable smile of his as he reached behind it and produced a huge bottle that looked like wine, "It's just grape juice, before you think of anything."

Scrunching my eyebrows together, I craned my neck to look at the back and saw that there were also two wine glasses behind it with the top being covered by a plastic circle to prevent the dust from going in.

Don't tell me that every European destination in this place right now has that.

He poured it into the two glasses and handed one to me, "A toast to the start of this great journey."

"Why do I get the feeling that this journey is more than just this impromptu trip around the school," I voiced my thoughts out loud. Instead of replying, he clinked our glass together and took a sip of his juice.

He didn't even bother waiting for us to finish the two glasses as he took my hand and led me to a long cardboard cutout of what appeared like the skyline of Barcelona.

Reaching out to the back, he took out a plate that was currently being protected by cling film, "Everywhere I read, one must surely try some tapas when visiting the amazing country of Spain," he said, peeling of the plastic cover and offered the various amounts of snacks that were stuck to a bunch of toothpicks.

"Alright, how long did it take you to do this?" I questioned with a slight laugh, taking a toothpick and examining the food that was on the other end, before placing it in my mouth, nodding in satisfaction with the savory taste.

Picking out his own sample, he ate his first before giving me a quick wink, "That's something only I can know."

"That's no fair," I pouted, though I continued with the snacks and finishing up my drink.

"If you're frowning about this, then I don't think you would enjoy getting your feet a bit dirty with the next destination," he chuckled, placing the plate back down behind the cutout.

Looking down on my high heel clad feet, I was both excited and fearing whatever destination we were going to. I gulped down my drink before setting down beside the plate and grabbing Jasper's hand as we breezed through the hallway.

"Greece," he grinned, presenting the single country that Kyla gave the most attention to. The backdrop was an amazing beach with the bluest sky I have seen and right at the bottom was a box that occupied half of the width of the hall. It was filled hallway through with a good amount of sand that was obviously been played around by a few people before us.

I grinned as Jasper bent down to help me release a foot from my shoe. He gestured to the sand and I stepped my foot on the sand, feeling the small and fine grains on my soles.

This is perhaps the nearest thing to a beach that I will experience for now. Oh the joys of living a full-on city life where there is not a single beach in sight, unless you were willing to drive for half a day for it.

Bending down carefully, I extended my arm and picked up the sand, letting it slowly drain through the gaps between my fingertips. As all of it fell out, the space it was once occupying was then engulfed by my boyfriend's strong hand.

Looking up at him, I gave him a small smile, "You know, if I weren't so stubborn in the first place, we wouldn't have waited until this year to start dating."

"That, and also if you weren't so stubborn, I wouldn't realize how horrible it is to not spend every day by your side," he countered, "So don't regret that."

He first helped put back my shoe on – and may I add, it was an impossible task to keep whatever poise I had in my body to do it – before helping me up.

He led me to the next place, a wonderful tea party set-up, complete with the fancy pastry stand that was filled with tiny cakes and scones. I couldn't help but release a giggle at the large 'DO NOT EAT' sign hanged on the table.

"That's just for the others," Jasper told me, pulling out a chair for me, "Though this is just going to be a quick cup of tea, because our clock is ticking."

He picked up the fancy teapot and filled the two teacups, placing one of them in front of me. When my fingers wrapped around it, the hot temperature had already dropped and it now felt like a lukewarm "drink more than the normal hot tea.

But hey, you can't expect the temperature to last that long.

So far, I've noticed that this trip was in fact a food fest more than anything.

And I'm not complaining.

Looking out to the dark night through one of the windows of the school that was left bare, I marveled at the sight of the thousands of stars sprinkled around the sky with the crescent moon resting n their midst.

"I promise that one day we'll be drinking actual wine in Italy, we'll be tasting tapas in Spain, we'll visit the beautiful beaches of Greece, and we'll be having a real afternoon tea in England," I swore to him, keeping my gaze on the sky.

The same sky that we would look at wherever we may go. We'll be seeing the same moon, illuminating the world with the company of the stars and constellations.

Finally peeling my attention away from it, I looked to the boy in front of me who was staring at me, giving me his undivided attention, "Will you promise me that as well?"

Now I just sound plain stupid, who was the person that made this trip impossible for this summer in the first place?

But without a second to contemplate about it, he nodded, "I promise."

Setting my cup back on the saucer, I was ready for the next place. He stood up, and offered and arm for me to take, guiding me to the next hallway.

"I had a feeling that Kyla is in love with Amsterdam," he said to me as we turned, showing a whole hall dedicated to the said city, complete with the walls to the floor, imitating the roads of it. Jasper opened the janitor closet and took out two small bikes, "Not much of a trip, but this might get us around just in time for your best friend's deadline."

I gestured to my dress, showing him that I wasn't really in the right attire to be cycling around the first floor of a high school. Instead of tucking away the idea, he shrugged me off, "You don't actually go to a beach in Greece wearing a long gown, so who says you can't ride a bike with the same thing?"

Looking back at the bike and the up at him, I realized that he was completely serious.

Oh well, being a tourist is all about the experience.

Bunching up my dress, and getting up on the bike, I was quite nervous to actually move. I'm just thinking in my head that the school hasn't been destroyed yet under my reign as president, then I can ride this in ensemble.

Jasper was obviously ahead of me, but he was slowing down his pace for me, since it wasn't the easiest to pedal around while wearing heels. It wasn't really such a long ride since the moment we reached the hall, we were done. We leaned the bikes onto the wall and went on our merry way.

"One last place," Jasper informed, taking out a hand, "And I saved the best one for last."

I was expecting to meet another cardboard cutout or something, but imagine my confusion when we came back to the doors leading back to the gym. Before we got in, Jasper glanced down on his wristwatch and grinned, "Twenty minutes on the dot."

He pushed the doors open and we stepped back into the venue. Kyla was on the mic, requesting everybody to take their seats as the dinner was about to start, and as she was about to go down, she saw and gave an excited wave.

It took her sometime to reach us with Tristan trailing along behind, but once she did, she clasped her hands around my wrists and practically bounced with enthusiasm, "Finally, we could have a nice double date."

She walked up the round table that was situated right in front of the Eiffel Tower replica. It was clearly meant to be special as it was elevated just a few inches above the ground by a platform, but it was low enough so that it did not grab too much unwanted attention, and it also blended with the other table around it.

"The last destination is a dinner on the Eiffel Tower, over-looking the city of Paris," Jasper explained as we got ourselves seated.

"Or in this case, overlooking the school gym," Tristan commented.

We clinked our glasses of iced tea and ate our dinner, meaningless chatter filling the air.

"When we're all rich and successful, let's have another double on the real deal," Kyla smiled.

And that's what I would like to hear in the middle of the whirlwind topic known as the future. It's an implication that in years' time, nothing will change expect that we would all be holding a title under our belt.

The present is heavenly, and the future would be just fine if you keep it that way.

"High school is about to end," I mentioned, "And for once, I'm not worried."

"Who knew a trip through the first floor of the school could be the cause of that," Tristan joked.

"Though I'm a bit guilty about the money," I said, turning to Jasper who didn't seemed to be a bit fazed by this.

"It was refundable, so don't worry about it," he told me, but I also didn't miss the slight look he shared with Tristan.

Kyla and I also sent our own silent conversation with each other, what are these two up to now?

"Should we tell them?" Tristan asked, gesturing to us girls.

"I was saving it for graduation," Jasper chuckled, being lighthearted with whatever secret they were hiding.

Alright mister, I may be completely relaxed with graduating, but I still had some aftershocks from every surprised that I've managed to get for the past months, so if I hear another one, I might strangle somebody if it isn't anything near good.

Jasper cleared his throat before he started to speak, "So after a quick assessment of everybody's schedule for the summer break..."

He paused for dramatic effects while Kyla and I were about to lie on the table from leaning too much, waiting anxiously for the news.

"We pulled out our resources and checked everything..." Tristan added, piling up the suspense.

After what felt like forever, they gestured to the Eiffel Tower, their grins practically ripping out their faces, "What Kyla suggested might come earlier than planned."

"We're going to France?" I gasped, getting what they were trying to let on.

"Just for an overnight stay, but yes, all four of us are going to Paris," they said.

Oh god, this night is perfect, they're perfect.

And it's not over yet. Kyla placed down her napkin and pushed herself up, "Come on, Savannah, we need to announce the royalties."

Nodding, I followed her and carried the pillow that had the plastic crown and tiara before climbing up the stage.

"Attention, everyone," she said through the mike to get the people's attention, "It's time to announce this night's king and queen."

She waved the small envelope in front of everybody's eyes, before slowly opening and reading the text. Smiling, she said to the mic, "And your king is," she paused for a second for dramatics, "Jasper Dean!"

As if there was ever a doubt.

I watched as my boyfriend stand up from the table we were occupying as he made his way to the front, nodding politely at the people who threw their congratulations to him on the way.

I placed the crown on top of his head, letting out a small clap, resisting the urge to embrace him in front of the huge crowd.

"And for the queen," Kyla announced, opening the other envelope, and releasing a loud gasp as she read out loud, "Kyla Bailey."

Honestly, I'm more shocked on the fact that she was surprised by this outcome. She tends to overlook the fact that she was the vice-president that everybody adored. And those boys she used to tell me stories of how friendly they were? I always knew they had a thing for her, and not to mention that the girls held a certain admiration for her.

And as her best friend, I couldn't get any prouder.

I took the plastic tiara and propped it on her head, giving her a hug before I let her step in front next to Jasper. Since she was now out of duty, I took over the microphone and requested everyone to make space for the king and queen's dance.

Some of them glanced towards my direction, and a few to Tristan's. I knew what they were thinking – they were wondering if we were jealous of the outcome.

Something with our group is that it went through a series of misunderstanding. For the longest time I thought that Jasper was in love with Kyla and for a brief moment Jasper thought that Tristan was interested in me.

After everything that has happened, it's hard to doubt our relationships right now.

They swayed to the beat of the music, and I saw their mouths moving, having their own conversation. Smiling, I went down the stage and placed the pillow on one of the empty tables beside the sound booth.

I watched as Tristan tapped Jasper's shoulder, asking for Kyla's hand. He nodded and stepped back, allowing the couple to start their own special dance.

A pair of arms snaked around my waist and I leaned back, knowing just from the build of the body behind me that it Jasper, "How's my king?"

I felt the weight on top of my head and I lifted a hand to see what was place there, aughing when I felt the fake crown that Jasper was previously wearing.

"You know, you never gave me a reply to my confession back in the house," he reminded, resting his chin on top of my shoulder.

I froze at the memory, it wasn't really the perfect way to say those three words. We were both on the floor with our sticky bodies due to the coke residue, and he chose that of all times.

But now that I think about it, none of the developments in this relationship was ever the right timing.

I never gave him an answer, as I just sat shell shocked that day. When he realized how much of a surprise it was to me, he dropped the subject completely.

Only to be brought up today.

Loving can hurt, love can hurt sometimes.

The sudden song change made me smile, thinking that this somehow fits the soon-to-be long distance relationship.

Yes, my dear Ed Sheeran, love can hurt sometimes, but in your own words, it is the only thing that makes us feel alive.

And in every sense of that statement, it was true. Without love, you wouldn't feel the fast heartbeat whenever you see the one you like, you wouldn't find the motivation to wake up every day, and you wouldn't have the strength to battle everything.

It makes us feel alive.

Turning my head, I placed a kiss on his cheek, "Jasper Dean, since the moment I fell for you, there was not a single day when I thought that I didn't love you."

We keep this love in a photograph, we made these memories for ourselves.

I felt him grin, returning the small peck as he started to slowly sway us to the music.

So you can keep me inside the pocket of your ripped jeans.

"We only have more or less than a month, Savannah," he mentioned and I nodded softly.

"We still have more or less than a month, Jasper," I corrected.

Holdin' me closer 'til our eyes meet and you won't ever be alone.

Thank you Kyla for always being there for me when everything was going down, thank you Tristan for being a great support system, thank you to that freshman program for triggering the series of events that lead to this moment.

And thank you Jasper, just for simply being you.

"I love you," I whispered, this time directly to the point.

When I'm away, I will remember how you kissed me under the lamppost back on 6th street, hearing you whisper through the phone, "Wait for me to come home."

Distance? Pfft... you're talking to Jasper and Savannah here, we'll take you on.

Chapter 31

I lifted a pair of shoes and Kyla shook her head, rejecting them. I huffed before throwing in them in the box that was supposed to be sent to charity. I showed her the next pair and she nodded, gesturing to the box that I will bring with me to college.

"Why are you packing so early, we still have finals to worry about," Kyla asked from her position on my bed.

"Because I only have about a week after graduation before I leave," I explained, sealing the box with packaging tape, "I don't want to spend the whole time doing this."

She hummed at my answer before going to the stack of books on top of my shelf. She carefully slid out one thin book and showed it to me, "Middle school yearbook?"

My eyes widened at the sight of the yearbook that had been piling dust since I got it. I rushed to her and grabbed it from her hands, "I can't believe I forgot about this."

I flipped through the pages until I landed on Jasper's picture, smiling at the awkward boy staring at the camera. I lifted a hand and allowed my fingers to trace the text below the image, my skin going over his name.

His hair flopped down, covering most of his forehead that I knew he used to be so insecure about. He had this crooked smirk that he did instead of a smile because he thought that he looked cooler than that, and judging from the multi-colored shirt, his fashion sense wasn't the best as well.

But either way, he was still the Jasper I loved.

He wasn't even in the basketball team in middle school, it wasn't because he didn't make it, but because he didn't have the courage to go to the try outs. If I wasn't there in freshman year to push him to the gym on that faithful day, he would have never earned his scholarship today.

I looked through the pages once again until I saw my picture. Kyla craned her neck to look at the picture before glancing towards me, "You haven't changed that much."

She was correct, I might have lost some weight and my hair was definitely longer, but I didn't change as drastically as Jasper did.

"Well Jasper did work hard during that summer before high school," I grinned at the memory, turning to the page where the different group shots were printed on.

I wanted to laugh at the sight of Jasper and I standing side by side. There was only about half an inch difference between us, but now, puberty hit him like a speeding bus as he now is a good six inches taller than me.

"Is that Tristan?" Kyla gasped at her boyfriend who stood at the back in one of the pictures. I squinted my eyes to confirm that it was indeed him.

I never knew we went to the same middle school.

"What are you girls doing?" somebody knocked on my door.

"Going down memory lane," Kyla replied, "Weren't you a little cutie."

Jasper visibly blush in embarrassment when Kyla lifted up the yearbook to show him his old picture. He scrambled around to snatch the book from her, slamming it shut and gripping it tightly by his side.

"Don't you dare," he said.

Too late for that, babe.

Kyla laughed and she bent down to get her jacket, "Well, it looks like I'm no longer needed here."

I frowned as I shook my head, "Stay, we can all go out to eat or something."

Her gaze switched from me to Jasper, her eyebrows rose as she showed her signature smirk, "You two enjoy, besides, I still have to get ready, I'm having dinner with Tristan and his parents."

Even with that excuse, I could practically see through that mischievous twinkle in her eyes.

"Fine," I mumbled and she smiled, approaching me to give me a small hug, "Thanks for helping me."

"Besides," I heard her whisper into my ear, "I don't want to be the one who cock blocks dear Jasper."

I pulled away and gave her a light slap on the shoulder, shoot her a dry look. That smile from earlier turned into a full grin before she started laughing once again, "See you two!"

Jasper looked confusedly at my best friend's retreating before turning back to me, "What was that all about?"

"Please ignore her," I picked up the box that we last sorted out and put it on top of the growing pile at the corner of my room. The huge amount of belongings were slowly disappearing, only leaving a few furniture for me to get back to whenever I come home.

He set down the year book onto the shelf and took a good look at my packed stuff. "When are you leaving?"

"A week after graduation," I informed, turning to him and I saw his distraught face. I froze on the spot as I slowly felt my heart breaking just from seeing that expression on him. He doesn't want to admit it, but I knew that deep down inside, he didn't want me to go.

Yet he kept his mouth sealed, but that doesn't mean I didn't catch the small glimpse of sadness that will sometimes overcome his features.

When a guy puts your happiness before his, you should never let him go. Just don't.

"I'll be back some time in between, we'll be going to France with Kyla and Tristan, remember?" I reminded in an attempt to reassure him.

He seemed to be brought back to reality by my words and he quickly shook off that expression before giving me a relaxed smile, "Right.'

When I pretended to busy myself by tidying up some parts of my room, I watched him open the yearbook he confiscated earlier from Kyla and flip through the pages.

His eye wishful and longing, probably reminiscing those days before the great fall of our friendship. If we didn't end it because of some stupid jealousy, we could've gotten more time to be like this. For all I know, we could have been dating since sophomore year and we wouldn't have to worry how short the days have become.

As much as it pains me to see him like this, I was glad it happened. It gave us time for ourselves. If I were to blindly continue on with our lives, I would have lived the life thinking that he actually liked Kyla. In fact, Kyla and I wouldn't be this close and the same goes for Tristan and Jasper. He wouldn't have branched out and dedicated his time to basketball, and I wouldn't be able to rethink my actions that would lead me to becoming the president.

And perhaps that one moment was what triggered our relationship. From a series of nostalgic feels to the ache of longing.

If we were always together, we wouldn't have experienced the pain of getting separated.

But, to be on the sensitive side, my boyfriend is still staring at a picture that was obviously in the past already. He shouldn't be doing that when we're currently in the same room.

They do say some distance is healthy for a relationship.

I grabbed a crumpled piece of paper and chucked it towards him. He lifted his gaze from the yearbook and turned to me, giving me a questioning look.

"You want to talk about something?" I asked, praying that he'll open up.

I understand that he's doing this for my sake, but I would explode if I learn that he's just bottling everything up.

As I predicted, he shook his head and closed the book. He forced a small smile and I responded by giving him a dry look. When he saw that I wasn't buying it, his lips fell into a frown and walked towards me, tucking a stray strand of hair behind my ear, "Don't worry, I'm fine."

I grasped his sleeve and my steel gaze didn't falter as he tried to reassure. You're quite forgetting who I am, I can see through that façade as quickly as you can see through mine.

"Jasper," I muttered, "Tell me the truth."

I won't be angry if he was to tell me that he was only pretending when he said that it was alright for me to go to that scholarship. With a sigh, I retreated his arm and it went limp to his side, "I don't want you to go."

Ah, there it was.

I took a step forward and wrapped my arms around his waist, burying my face into his chest as I felt his body become stiff for a second before he responded by embracing me in his arms.

If only there was a third option where I could go to that university on a scholarship yet still be able to enjoy a summer vacation with Jasper.

But in the end, I still have to do the responsible thing.

I reached down and took his hand in mine, watching as our hands intertwined, fitting perfectly with each other, "Just four years, please endure it."

"I will," he stated with the most determination he can muster.

It might be ridiculous to think that we can say the word 'only' to define four years. Trust me, half of that is the amount of time that we used up ignoring each other and if you multiply it by another four years, it would be equal to length of our friendship.

Four years is nothing to us.

We released each other and he pressed a small kiss on my forehead, "I'll wait for you if you're willing to wait for me."

No matter how long, I'll wait for him.

"Can't Celeste or Drew do something?" I grumbled under my breath from the kitchen island as I helped my mother in preparing for our dinner by cutting the vegetables.

She looked over her shoulder and clicked her tongue, "Sa vannah..."

"I didn't mean it seriously," I muttered, my eyes focused on the task at hand, "I was just thinking."

Even if she was carefree most of the time, she was strict with the life lessons. She taught me to never just live off of the wealth that my brother suddenly became part of when he married my sister-in-law. That was the main reason why I was working in that café.

But in times like these, I just want to use whatever power to my advantage.

"I though you and Jasper talked it out," she said, "What's with the worry again?"

"Well, I've learned that he straight up doesn't want me to go," I grumbled, finishing up with the slicing, "And I want to seriously go mad."

With a strong finger, she poked the back of my head, causing me to slightly tilt forward. Holding the spot, I turned around scrunched up my eyebrows in confusion to her sudden attack. Let me tell you, she was less than amused and with the knife she was holding, she looked like she was ready to murder.

Do not cross my mother, that's my warning for you.

"I've been watching in frustration as you two go through your different loops," she told, her tone getting lower, "Time to stop acting like children in the playground and start thinking like adults."

"What?" I gaped and she grabbed my wrist, turning off the stove behind her and pulling me with her to the door. She took my jacket from the coat closet next to our front door and shoved it into my arms before pushing me outside.

Again... what?

She pushed back her hair and gave me a stern look, "Fix everything now because I don't want to see my daughter moping around anymore."

She closed door in front of my face and I was left there staring wide-eyed at it.

Well, that was an interesting development.

I looked to the house next door and let out an extremely loud sigh, putting on my jacket before taking the short trudge.

Ringing their doorbell, I was less than surprised to see that it was Jasper who answered it, "Hey?"

Don't worry, I question my reason of being here as well.

"So my mother kind of kicked me out," I explained, making him more confused than before, "And I guess I have no choice right now but to talk to you."

"I don't really get it..." he trailed off before opening the door wider, "But come on in."

"Are your parents there?" I asked, trying to peek past his figure. He nodded and I blew out a breath as I nudged to my end, "How about outside instead?"

He quickly agree, yelling to his parents that he was going out before he quietly closed the door behind him. We slowly started to walk leisurely to the sidewalk right into the familiar neighborhood that we've grown in.

The people in the houses that was passed in had come and go, only a few families actually stayed. We've come accustomed to it though, from dressing up in order for a friendly dinner to simply delivering some gift to show hospitality.

The ones who were here since the day we moved knows Jasper and I well enough to give a small wave when we pass by their dwelling.

"Savannah, Jasper!" we heard the lady living in the quirky blue house call out. We offered her a polite smile and nod, but before we could continue on, she waved for us to come over.

"You two have grown," she grinned, "Last time I've talked to you two, you weren't even in high school."

We laughed at her words, trying to find our way around the conversation so we could go on our way, but nope, she kept going, "Come by more often or else the next time I see either of you, you're already married."

She let out a hearty chuckle and we only managed to let out that forced amusement before our eagerness started to shine through, "We should really be going."

"But then again, you two still have college to worry about," she reminded the one topic we were both sensitive about.

Please ma'am, if you want any of us to preserve our sanity, please let us go.

"Well, I don't think you two went out to talk to me," she finally said, "I'll see you two soon, alright?"

We offered her another forced smile as we walked as quickly as possible away from her. Now I remember why we purposely avoided her house.

That lady kept yapping and yapping away.

"Now that I think about it, I should really go back and help my mom with dinner," I remembered, looking back at the direction we just walked through.

He let out a chuckle at my statement as he maneuvered us back, "You cooking? Don't make me laugh, Savannah."

I gave him a playful g are, "I would have you know that I'm starting to get good at the culinary arts."

"Getting ready for marriage like that lady said?" he joked.

"Who am I getting married to?" I shot at him.

He paused in his steps and gave me a surprised look, "Who else but me?"

Did he just indirectly blurted out a proposal?

I also halted with my movement as I stared at him. Realizing what he just did, he started mumbling under his breath, "Never mind."

My shoulder slumped but as he walked pass me, he took my hand and held it in his as we continued with our walk, "Someday, I'll do it more properly."

Suddenly, I felt like my insides were lit up as I started practically skipping beside him.

Yup, four years is nothing if the end game is that.

Chapter 32

You would think that after a full year as serving as the student body president, I would be ready for this moment. Strangely enough, I wasn't.

Jasper tugged my hand gently as he led me into the school building with our families following right behind us. My feet were shaking in my high heels and I would have probably fallen down onto the ground if Jasper wasn't holding onto me.

I mean, I may not be the valedictorian so I had no right to have a speech, but I would still be the first one to get my certificate as the last duty of this position. All I'm praying for is that I don't trip right in front of everybody.

I bit my lip, cringing at the taste of my red lipstick. This is the one day that I wished would never come.

After this, it's goodbye high school and hello college.

"Savannah," Kyla suddenly appeared, latching onto my arm, making me release Jasper. Tristan came around and placed a hand on Jasper's shoulder, pointing towards their teammates who were gathering for a group picture.

Jasper turned around to me and I nodded, gesturing for him to go. Turning to Kyla, she was smiling softly and slowly released me, "You ready?"

"Not really," I sighed, walking next to her as we went ahead to the gym when we saw that the boys were still busy with their other friends. We're not the kind to monopolize them, this might be the last time they were going laugh around like this.

I greeted Kyla's parents and she did the same with mine. We took some pictures before we finally got seated, ready to start the ceremony.

We were kind of trained by the teachers to sit still and be on our best behavior during the ceremony, but it was kind of hard when you have to go through the principal's boring speech.

Bailey, Dean, Everett, Hansen. It was kind of impossible for any of us to be seated next to each other considering the first letters of our last names, nonetheless, we shared quick looks and glances.

I could feel my eyes slowly starting to close and my head bouncing, my body trying its best to fight off sleep.

After for who knows how long, the principal concluded his speech and announced, "And now, it is time for the handing of diplomas to the graduating seniors of..."

I basically blocked out the rest of chatter when I was suddenly snapped back into the waking world. I instantly stood up, completely forgetting about the cue the principal had told me.

All eyes were turned to me and I bit my lip harder, threatening to draw blood. The principal, on the other hand, remained composed as he continued on, "And we shall start the giving with this year's student body president – Savannah Everett."

The audience clapped and I pretended to straighten up my dress before walking to the front, my eyes focused on the ground as I prayed that I don't take a wrong step.

When I got to the stage, I took a shaky step up the stairs. Taking a deep breath, I started to ascend up, my eyes peeling themselves off of the floor until I was locked in by the principal.

He handed me the rolled up paper, being held close by a red ribbon. I transferred it to my other hand before I did a handshake with him. As I did so, he patted my arm, giving me a smile, "Thank you, Everett."

"Just doing my job, sir," I told him truthfully.

After I started my escapade with Jasper, I lost sight of my goal. I was determined to reform this school, bring it back to its former glory. Slowly, I became friendlier with the students and the fear subsided, but what I failed to notice was the fruit of my efforts stayed.

We were no longer a school that dwindling to the ground and the appreciation in the principal's eyes was the biggest sign that whatever I did, I did it right.

He released me and nodded, gesturing for me to continue on with the walk as the speaker called up the next name. I made my way to the center, ever so gently holding onto the tassel and transferring it to the other side before taking my bow.

That was it, I was finished with this place. The same place where I broke off with Jasper and found my place beside him again. The place where I met Kyla, the girl who would soon be my right hand man, and the place where I found out Tristan was that ever supporting guy.

I reveled the moment before I smiled at the crowd and finally went back down onto my seat. As I was about to return to my chair, I passed by the line that was waiting for their turn for their diploma and one of them wrapped an arm around my waist and pulled me to him.

I didn't have to ask to know who it was.

"Congrats," he whispered in my ear, kissing it before releasing me again. I was rendered speechless as a blush was slowly creeping onto my face. Jasper winked at me before moving forward with the line.

I swear, that guy would be the death of me.

Fixing myself, I glanced to the stage and saw that it was already Kyla's turn. She stepped to the center stage and grinned with that million dollar smile of hers as she transferred her tassel before doing the bow.

I dropped my diploma on my seat and started clapping loudly, when she lifted up her head, she saw me practically jumping on my spot and she laughed.

Out of all the people here, she's the one I'm most thankful for. She stayed by my side when practically everybody hated me and she might be the reason I broke Jasper and I's friend-ship, but she was also one the reasons why we're together.

We didn't even wait for the end of the ceremony when she came running to me after she stepped down the stage. She jumped into my arms and I was so shocked that I stumbled, making sure I sat down on the nearest chair.

"I'm going to miss this," she stated, pushing herself up.

I raised a hand and she gave me a high five, "Good job, president."

"Thank you, vice," I said. If anyone here underappreciates her, I'm going to strangle them.

She headed back to her seat as they were finishing off the last people in the line. The principal called up the class valedictorian and we all listened as she delivered her heart-warming speech.

Perhaps the remains of the ceremony was a blur. It was a series of getting pulled to different of groups of people for pictures, getting congratulatory hugs from my parents, and the final pose from Jasper, Tristan, Kyla, and I.

"Smile!" mom told us, looking through the lens of her cam-era. I kept myself still as I had one arm wrapped around Jasper and the other arm around Kyla. The four of us grinned at the amount of gadgets currently taking our pictures.

A few people approached us and started talking to the boys. Jasper took my hand, making me look up at him. He remained composed, still nodding to whatever one of his teammates was telling him about. Resting my head on his shoulder, I closed my eyes and engraved this moment into my memory.

"We'll miss you," mom said, holding my face in her hands before giving me another life-crushing squeeze. If ever my mom comes for a hug, avoid it at all costs.

I tried to hug her back, but her grip was too strong for me to even move. I gave my dad a pleading look and he chuckled, detaching my mother from me. He stepped forward and gave me a lighter hug, "Take care of yourself, Savannah."

I watched as Jasper loaded the last bag into the back of my car as I was squished in between my parents, "I think that's it."

"Thank you," I told him. We stared at each other in silence, trying to find the words around this, plus the fact that both of my parents are watching doesn't make this any less difficult.

Dad thankfully sensed the mood and he spoke up, "We'll give you two a moment."

"B-but," mom stuttered, obviously hesitant to leave. Dad wrapped an arm around mom and gave an encouraging smile, leading her back into the house.

I waved at them before turning back to my wonderful boyfriend, "Upset?"

"My girlfriend is leaving, how else do you want me to feel?" he quipped, even with those words, he delivered it light-heartedly.

Lifting a hand, I caressed his cheek, pressing a chaste kiss on his lips, "See you soon, Jasper?"

"Close your eyes," he whispered.

Quirking a brow, I questioned his motives, but when his expression continued to be completely serious, I complied with his wish.

I felt a cold sensation around my neck, making me instinctively open my eyes. I noticed that Jasper has moved closer to me and his hands were currently working behind my nape. Glancing down, I almost started bawling at the sight of the ring being held by the silver chain.

"Jasper..." I trailed off just as he finished clasping the necklace. He stepped back and gauged my reaction, waiting for a response.

I let my fingers touch the ring, feeling the smooth metal. Seriously? Is he stopping me from going? Because this is completely working.

"Not the real deal yet," he muttered, "But I promise, okay?"

This will be a silent reminder that I'm his. If anyone wants to even get near, all they have to do is take on look of this ring to know that I'm taken. No matter where, no matter when, we're together.

The promise has been done and sealed.

You might find it ridiculous that we're so young and doing this, but like he said, it wasn't the real deal yet. This was a trial, will we survive four years of separation? If we do, then a new ring will be given, if we don't, then this will be just a precious memory.

Though I'm praying to God that this ends up well.

"So about that reset button..." he pointed out, reminding me of that drama that we had back then.

I threw my head back as I laughed, slightly pushing him, "It kind of worked."

He leaned against my car, chuckling along, "Really? I don't remember pressing it."

Metaphorically, we kind of did, "How else did we become friends again?"

"An English project," he raised a brow.

I would love to go back to that English teacher and thank the hell out of her. Props to you Shakespeare, you brought me boyfriend.

He saw my expression and he laughed harder, "We never needed a reset button, Savannah."

If that was the case then this whole situation wouldn't be happening, "Then what did we need?"

"Just a good old wake up call," he answered simple, "Besides, if we did reset it, then that time of self-discovery wouldn't have happened."

"Self-discovery?" I questioned.

"You know what I mean," he scoffed, pushing himself off of the vehicle.

He held out a hand for me to take and offered me a courteous smile, "Shall we, m'lady?"

It was like we were transported to our Winter Formal. I placed my hand on top of his and he gently led me to the front, opening the door for me, "I love you, Savannah."

"And I love you," I responded, sliding into the car and waited for him to close the door. He popped his head through the window and allowed us to share one more kiss.

My hands found their way to his face, holding it gently as I closed my eyes. It was like our first kiss, it was like our first dance, and it was like our first moments of this relationship.

A relationship that bloomed from friendship, got broken and bent, but still found its way back together until we were in our current position.

Pulling away, he stepped back and gave the top of the car a good pat, "Goodbye."

"It's not goodbye unless we'll never see each other again," I stated, starting up the vehicle, "It's see you soon, Jasper."

He smiled and nodded, "See you soon, Savannah."

Facing forward, I flashed him one more grin before I drove forward. We still have a long road ahead of us, and by the looks of it, we don't mind the journey too much.

Chapter 33

I saw him round up the corner of our bedroom and I gave him a smile that he could see through the mirror as I was putting on the finishing touches on my makeup.

Jasper walked up to me and wrapped his arms around my waist, setting his head on my shoulder and giving my neck a little kiss, making me instinctively crane my neck to the other side to him more access.

He still have that same effect on me.

When I felt him smirk, I suddenly realized what was happening and I turned, giving him a dry look. He flashed me an innocent look with that playful grin, "What?"

Oh I'm not falling for that again.

"We're already running late as it is," I muttered, going around him to get my purse. He didn't seem to like my statement though with the reaction he gave. He placed on a childish pout, making me let out a slight giggle. I approached him and kissed his cheek, before giving his chest a little pat, "Now come on."

"They wouldn't notice a few minutes," he tried once again but I shook my head, nudging my head to the door.

I do feel sorry for the poor boy, but he already had his fair share of fun, and besides, we were going to be late if we even drag around for even a minute. You would think that it was only Thanksgiving, nothing too fret about.

But if you were to dine in a very fancy set up with your brother's classy in-laws, you wouldn't want to risk it. Besides, I'm already dying to see my family again and this time, even Jasper's side was invited to join us. Also, with a few coaxing, Tristan and Kyla were also invited so this meant that it was going to be a full house tonight.

Let's be honest though, their house is big enough to host a freaking carnival.

Begrudgingly, Jasper got the car keys and followed me outside into the cold autumnal temperature. Thankfully, we were at our main house instead of the apartment we got at the neighboring city.

Jasper was so kind enough to grant me that apartment, it cut my commute to work by an hour. After graduation, Drew took me under his wing and got me a job at one of Celeste's companies. It wasn't that far that I had to really move out, but the distance was already a hassle for me.

And so, after two months of seeing how difficult it was for me, he surprised me with an apartment. It was small, but it did its purpose. Jasper didn't really care that much since he was always off during the days with training with his team, and I always proudly state to everyone that my husband was a player in the major league.

At weekdays, we stay there and on the weekends, we come back here. We were thinking of really buying a bigger apartment, but I made him pause with that idea of reasons.

Reasons which I'm going to tell him pretty soon.

When were on the drive to the house, I felt his hand on my thigh, his palm facing up and I already knew what he wanted. Placing my hand in his, I watched him smile as his eyes were focused on road ahead.

In the end, we didn't grow past this part of our relationship and I'm perfectly fine with it.

The memory of our wedding was still engraved in my mind. On the day after my graduation, Jasper took me out to celebrate and at the very end of the evening, he got down on one in front of the whole restaurant we were eating at and popped the question.

Since his sister was a wedding planner, everything went without a hitch. It took us about six months to get everything down and on that special day, we kissed at the altar in front of all our friends and family.

So now I lovingly wear three rings on my finger. One is the promise ring he gave me just after we finished high school, the second is our engagement party, and the last one is the wedding ring. A simple gold band that was identical to Jasper's.

When we arrived at their home, it was no surprise that there was an abundance of cars in the lot. From the looks of it, it seemed like the guests were up to their standards.

The house was like an epitome of what a modern mansion was supposed to look. From the art displayed all around to the open concept of the interior designs, you could already tell the people living in here were well off.

Yet, it had that warm and welcoming feeling that you would like. When we stepped inside the foyer area, a maid approached us and offered to take out jackets and coats before she ushered us to the living room that was already packed with people.

There was a corner where my brother and his wife stood, surround by their friends as they laughed goodheartedly at whatever they were talking about, at another side were the two house owners, making up a conversations with some other guests, when you switch your view to the other end, we can see the Everett's making a happy conversation with the Dean's, and a few more groups just chatting away as we all waited for the food.

Please, even the children have their own circle, and including them are my eight years old nephew and my six years old niece.

"Look who finally decided to show up," we heard my best friend's familiar voice say as we saw her walk to us with Tristan following right behind her.

Nine years of dating, and the question has yet to pop between these two. Kyla is waiting, she had told me multiple times, but she's also trying to be patient with Tristan. Though, it's kind of hard to keep my mouth shut about Tristan's plans to propose on her birthday. You could imagine my glee when he called me up to help him with the plans and to distract her.

Even after years, the dynamics of our friendship never changed.

"Hey," Jasper perked up, giving Kyla a small squeeze before he did that guy-hug thing with Tristan, "It's been so long since we've seen you two."

"Everything has been so busy," they laughed and we nodded in agreement.

Kyla looped her arm around mine and gave me that all-knowing grin, making me laugh. She turned to our partners and excused us, "We're just going to have a little catch-up talk."

When they said they didn't mind, Kyla quickly pulled me away from their earshot, "Did you tell him yet?"

"No," I answered, "And what's with the rushing?"

"Please," she snorted, "Even his sister found out before he did."

My gaze then switched to Macy who had been part of the Everett-Dean circle with her fiancé completely all over her. Right after I called Kyla, I called up my mom and she, being very good friends with my mother-in-law told her straight and consequently, it led to her big mouth to spill the information right in front of Macy.

Thankfully, I was able to beg them to keep it a secret until I told Jasper.

"At least you're already married," I heard her mumble.

"Kyla..." I groaned, showing my disapproval.

I saw her face fell and she started to play with the ends of her curled hair, "I know that he doesn't need to give me a ring, but when you and Jasper got married, I thought that he would finally ask."

Giving her a hug, I did feel bad, but I also know the happiness that was about to come. She only has to be a little more patient and she'll her wish.

She's a simple girl and she rarely asks for anything.

"So how are you and Jasper?" she asked casually.

Just as I was about to answer her question, a maid approached us with a tray of champagne. Kyla gratefully took one and as I was about to reach for a glass, she swatted my hand away, "Thank you."

He curtly bowed before moving on to serve the other guests. I pouted at her direction and she wagged her finger, "I'm only looking out for you."

Well, I do thank her for being the voice of control when god knows that I'm lacking it.

"I think I need to buy him a leash," I joked, reminiscing the happenings before we left.

She laughed at this before commenting, "Come on, he loves you."

"I know," I smiled.

I'm not going to be one of those girls who even though the guy gives her the world, will show every bit of insecurity she can. I may have been like that when I was a teenager, but something I've realize battling out a long-distance relationship for four years is that if we were able to survive everything, we were for the long run.

He loves me and I love him, what else is there to it?

"Everyone," one of the servers announced, "Dinner is served."

We all piled up into the dining room. First, I thought that there's no way we could all fit in there, but boy was I wrong. I just saw the longest dining table that could possible fit in the room. The center was filled with the deliciousness of traditional Thanksgiving delights and each chair was perfectly set up for the guests.

You would think that you were dining in a fancy restaurant, but nope, you're just inside a home.

A maid was circling around, filling up the glasses of the adults with a delectable red wine. When she reached to me, I heard Kyla clear her throat loudly from her spot across from me and gave me a warning look.

With a sigh, I declined the wine and Jasper raised a brow, "What's wrong?"

"Why?" I questioned.

"My wife just turn down some wine?" he quipped, "Are you sick?"

"Very funny," I said sarcastically, "But I'm really not in the mood for it."

Lie.

Celeste's father tapped his glass with his knife to signal our attention and he started saying a very long speech about how he was glad that everybody was gathered today.

You know, the usual stuff.

I leaned my head on Jasper's shoulder, making me look down on me, "Alright?"

"Alright," I answered. My comfort word, something we haven't exchanged for quite some time now.

I felt him slip an arm around my waist and I felt myself relax. Even though it was still early, I found myself getting tired more easily.

When the man finished his speech, Celeste then stood, "Well, just like what my father said, I'm so glad that everyone is here."

My attention shift to her and I sat upright once again as she continued, "And since this event is all about giving thanks to the blessings we've acquired, I think my sister-in-law would want to announce this new blessing she has."

My eyes widened in realization of what she said. When I talked to her on the phone about jokingly announcing it during dinner, I never thought she would have taken it seriously.

"Savannah," she encouraged.

"What?" Jasper asked, turning to me.

All attention were on me and from the corner of my eyes, I could see Kyla smirking. Well, might as well get this over with.

"I'm pregnant," I finally said. It took a second for the news to settle in, but as soon as it did, the people started giving me their congratulations, they started squealing and bringing out their phones to capture the moment.

Jasper, on the other hand, looked like he was just robbed, "What?" he gaped.

Grinning up to him, I repeated, "I'm pregnant," I told him, "You're going to be a father."

There are many ways to react, like crying of happiness or smiling with the widest smile but the son of a gun took a different route and he actually fainted.

And not just the kidding ones, but he actually fainted.

Oops.

I gasped at the result, but his sister casually stood up and inspected him, "He'll be alright."

As I watched him get woken by others, I couldn't help but laugh and shake my head.

Looks like another amazing chapter is about to begin.

Epilogue

Her POV

I hummed a random tune as I held my pen in between my fingers, my eyes on the notebook on my lap, and yet, my attention was on the pressed against my ear, listening to my boyfriend's deep voice.

"And then when I passed the ball to him, he threw it to the basket," he told enthusiastically, "It got in and we won the practice match."

"Really?" I grinned, genuinely happy for him. I didn't really care that much about basketball, but Jasper loved it and whatever makes him happy is enough to make me smile. In the end, he snagged the scholarship and is currently the front man of his college's team, making me extremely proud of him.

Whether it was the championships or simply a game he and his friends played for fun, he would always report the results with so much enthusiasm that I couldn't help but laugh.

At least one of us is enjoying their time.

When your days are packed with classes and the few moments of break that you have is filled with revising, you can't really say you're having a blast. Don't get me wrong, I do have a social life here and I do get invited to those parties and such, but that excitement quickly died down when it started to become more and more frequent.

He probably thought that I was gone because I didn't speak for too long so he called out my name, "Savannah?"

"I'm sorry," I said back, "I'm glad you won, Jasper."

"Are you alright?" he questioned.

"Yeah," I replied softly, "Just a little tired."

I could practically see him frown at my statement, one of the few things that I love about Jasper is that he's extremely caring. Even if I told him that I got a papercut, he'll be the one doing the panicking for me while I calmly wrap a band aid around it.

Looking down on my wristwatch, my eyes bulged out of their sockets when I realized that I'm about to become late to my lecture, "I got to go, Jasper, I still have class."

"Oh," he muttered, disappointment rolling off of his voice, "I'll call you tonight, okay?"

"Like always," I said before hanging up.

It was a routine, a good night call from Jasper would be the only thing that can put me to sleep even in the most stressful times. We've been doing this ever since we got separated, and that was a good few years ago. If there was a time that we wouldn't be able to take the call, we'll just text that everything was alright.

Just the assurance of his voice was already a sweet lullaby.

Stuffing my belongings back into my bag, I swung it on my shoulder before running to the hall where my class was being held in.

When I snuck inside, I saw that the professor was just about to start since he was still setting up his presentation. Sliding myself into an available desk, I zipped open my bag to get my textbook. When I didn't notice it there, I started digging for it before I suddenly remembered that I left it on my desk back in my dorm.

Letting out a slightly audible groan, I dropped my bag on the floor with a huff after setting up my notebook and pen. Suddenly, I felt someone tap on my shoulder, making me look at my side.

The guy seated next to me placed his textbook on top of my desk, "I have a feeling you're going to need it more than I will."

"No need," I politely declined. I don't really have the heart to make him understand the lesson less just because of a careless mistake.

He shook his and insisted, "I already read the chapter so it's alright."

I was still hesitant but with his kind smile, I finally gave in and turned to the page that the professor was talking about, making sure I jotted down some notes.

An hour and a half passed by and the professor concluded the lecture, turning off his presentation and making a move to erase his writings on the board.

I closed the textbook and handed it back to its owner, "You're a big help, is there any way that I can repay you?"

"No problem," he muttered, "But how about getting coffee with me as a thank you."

Red alert.

Now, this can go two ways. One, he might end up thinking that it was going to be a date or he simply just wanted a coffee and a chat.

The amount of guys who approached me asking me to get coffee with them is too damn high, I'm about to graduate and I know from experience that most of them are expecting something more from that little coffee chat.

I used to work in a café, I watched first-hand people's tactics of getting a date over a caffeinated drink.

Though that could be just me being assuming. In my defense, I'm very guarded when it comes to these things.

"You did ask if you can repay me," he reminded and sighed.

Maybe it would have been better if I didn't accept that textbook.

Packing my belongings and stood up, giving him a nod of defeat and he grinned, gesturing to the door, "After you, m'lady."

"Please don't call me that," I told him, making sure I had this lighthearted tone.

Only Jasper can call me that without making pissed.

He shrugged and we went on our way to this coffee shop that was inside the university. Small, homely, and warm.

"Two regulars please," he ordered at the counter as I went on to find us a seat. Luckily, there was a group of students who were just about to leave so I easily claimed their table when they were gone.

My hand instinctively reached out and felt the ring currently being held up by a chain around my neck. There was not a day that I didn't wear this, no matter where I went, I held on to Jasper's promise. Just a few more months and the wait will be over.

The guy came back with a tray holding two white mugs of coffee. He set it down on the table before plopping down on the chair right across from mine, "I just realized I haven't caught your name."

"Savannah," I introduced myself, "And you are?"

"Chris," he answered, pushing my mug towards me.

"Money," I remembered, taking out my wallet to pay him back.

He shook his head, declining the cash, "My treat."

Yup, red alert indeed.

"This is supposed to be payback," I reminded him, slapping a five dollar bill on the table, sliding it to him, "You don't have to give me the change. '

Patience, Savannah, don't snap yet.

He slowly sipped his coffee before speaking, "Look, I don't want to beat around the bush so..."

Oh god, this is where I stop him.

"I have a boyfriend,' I declared and he paused, blinking towards me.

I know I shouldn't have made it last this long, but how else could I bring it up without sounding to assuming?

To my complete surprise, he said, "Okay, congrats."

Huh? He seems chill about this.

"I was about to ask Aaron, that guy you share marketing class with," he continued on, "Is he single?"

Excuse me?

When I remained unresponsive, trying to comprehend what he was saying, he cleared his throat before clarifying, "I'm gay."

I slammed my head on the table, taking him completely by surprise. I don't know whether to laugh or to scream, but all I can confirm is that I feel completely stupid.

"Is that a no?" I heard.

Lifting my gaze, I offered him a tight lipped smile, "How about I get myself a pastry first and then I'll help you."

I really need the damn sugar.

His POV

"Come on Jasper," one of the boys said as I threw the ping pong ball which landed straight into the opponent's cup. My side cheered, watching as the guy downed his beer before clumsily missing one of the red cups laid in front of me.

Another victory, another party.

He was almost done and I only managed to drink two cups. Smirking, I watched as he held up his hands in surrender, admitting defeat, making my teammates cheer. Taking one of the untouched cups, I walked away from the table, drinking it slowly.

I saw the group that usual hang out with lounging by pool and I sat at one of the available chairs. They also said their hellos and gave me those random high fives, "Heard you totally bagged beer pong."

I chuckled, lifting up my red cup with a nod, "Was there a doubt?"

I do admit that after entering college, the frat parties that I was invited to gradually increase. By my fourth year here, this was no longer an unfamiliar scene. The people here are strangely easy to get along with and even though we have a few stumbles here and there, everything is smooth sailing.

"We were just talking about going out during the break," one said, "Why don't you join us?"

Just when I was about to speak, a friend of mine swung an around my shoulder and laughed, "This fella is going home to his girlfriend."

"Oh, the sexy, mature, and older girlfriend," the girl huffed, leaning back against the lounge chair.

When I accidentally let it slip that I was already dating someone, they started joking that this girlfriend of mine was all those three.

Well, technically they weren't wrong. Savannah really is amazing looking, maybe mature when it comes to it, and she is older... by a month and a half.

But it's really amusing when they talk like that. Only I know what she's really like.

Temperamental, a little sensitive, and sometimes out of it. But she's also smart, caring, and an all-around kind of girl. Have I mentioned she's studying under a scholarship to one of the best universities out there?

Not to brag but, that's my girl.

"Are you sure she even loves you Jasper," the girl said, casually sipping her drink, "You two have been separated for years, how are you sure she's not cheating on you?"

I kept my mouth shut, not because I was doubtful but because I was using my self-control to make sure I didn't snap at her. I'd rather stay quiet than to suddenly yell at her or do something horrible just because of some mere words.

I trust Savannah, and I'm honored to have her trust.

"If she's really as pretty as you say, then she surely has this long line of men after her," she continued on, "You seem tired, Jasper, I think you're putting more than its worth."

Is she provoking me? If she is, then it's working.

My voice was low, probably because I was using my willpower to make sure it was still leveled, "If you say any more, I'll be mad."

My tone was more menacing than I expected and that quickly shut the group up. Realizing what I just did, I set down my red cup and stood up, "I'm going back to my room."

I all but slammed my door of my dorm room. It was so tiny, only fit for one, but I didn't have much of choice since is this is the kind of free room you would get if you were part of the team here. At least you didn't have to pay the overpriced dorms that most students were offered with.

Crashing down on my bed, I reached into my pocket and called up the one person who I know will be able to calm me down.

"Hello," I could hear her quiet and tired voice ring from the other line.

"Did I wake you up?" I questioned, afraid that she might have already been asleep. We already talked before I left for the party so unlike the other times, she wasn't just waiting for a call.

"No," she answered, "I was studying, but my roommate is asleep."

You know, I could just listen to her voice and I can already calm down. She can talk about anything and everything, and I wouldn't get tired. I feel relaxed just by knowing that she's still there. I wouldn't admit it, but there was always a part of me that was afraid.

I know she's loyal, but I don't the guys around her are willing to listen to her.

She quickly sensed my uneasiness just from my tone, "Are you alright Jasper?"

Turning to my side, I shook my head as if she could see, "I miss you."

I heard her shift and move, a few rustles came through and when she started peaking again, it was in a normal volume so I presume that she went outside of her dorm, "What happened?"

"Nothing," I sighed, "Tell me about your day."

Though she was hesitant, she started retelling the happenings she went through. About her class, her annoying professors, how her roommate was so loud even though she was studying, but the moment when she said another guy's name, I froze.

"Chris gave me his textbook and we went out for coffee," she laughed.

Who the hell is this Chris guy?

I shot up from my lying position as I tried to tell myself that this was nothing. She's loyal, she won't doing anything behind your back. Just take deep breaths, he's just a friend, there's nothing else there is to it.

"He even paid for my mug," she informed, her tone light and happy, "He was so sweet."

So hold up, someone's making a move on my Savannah?

Maybe that chuck was right, Savannah may be good, but I have no idea what can those boys do to her. I've always assured myself that no one can go near because she's quite a spitfire and will literally just turn her back on you if she wasn't interested, but how come this is happening.

Damn it, we survived more than three years like this and only when on the last year did we start having problems?!

I went and open the drawer beside my bed, opening the lamp so I could have a clear view. I pushed away some knickknacks and other pieces of paper so I could see the box that I've hidden in there to keep safe.

Reaching out for it, I flipped it open and examined the ring that I've bought for her. I plan to ask her the ultimate question on graduation, but now, I have this underlying fear that my plans wouldn't go through as I imagined.

I looked down, box still clutched in my hand. The jewel there shone when it reflected the light from the lamp, and the grip I had on it was slowly loosening.

I don't want to lose her.

"Jasper!" I heard her snap through the phone, "Are you even listening?!"

"Yeah, Chris is a great guy," I muttered bitterly.

With an audible sigh, she spoke, "Yeah, and I think he and Aaron will hit it off. They're both amazing guys."

Oh so now there's an Aaron. Any more to add to the list?

You know what? This is my fault for asking her to tell me about her day in the first place.

"I'm sure they'll keep you entertained while I'm gone," I spat.

Clever as always, she quickly got the hint and her story died. With a relaxed voice, she concluded, "Well, at least I know now that you weren't paying attention."

Huh?

"Chris is gay and I'm helping him get together with Aaron," she explained, "Did you seriously think I was going to cheat on you?"

Well, now I feel incredibly stupid.

"No, it's just that you... some guys... and this girl," I tried to say, fumbling around with my words. When I realized I was making no sense, I let out a groan of defeat before apologizing, "I'm sorry."

"You know I love you, Jasper," she stated without a hint of hesitation, "And you know I'm yours."

My gaze went back down on the ring and I felt myself getting emotional. The once loosening grip on the box tightened and I nodded, "Yeah, I love you too."

"Please endure a few more months," she pleaded, "I'll be waiting for you."

I don't what the hell I did right, but thank you god for rewarding me with this girl.

"Get some rest," she said, "I'll call you tomorrow."

And with that, she hung the phone up and I carefully placed mine on the bedside table. Examining the ring, I smiled. Just a few more months and we'll be back by each other's side, and in just a few more months, I hoped she'll be my fiancé.

The future has always been blurry for us, but we've managed to get through with it.

9 781930 112919